PRAISE FOR

M000033296

"Delightful and clever, th...
—Libr...

"Pleiter's inspirational debut...reflects the true meaning of faith and family. Characters learn to trust God's goodness and provision even when things appear hopeless."
—*Romantic Times BOOKclub*

"*Bad Heiress Day* is a heartwarming and soulful book for cold winter nights.... Darcy and the secondary characters are warm and real, and this book will not let you go. This is a top-notch story for all of us, and brings to light some of life's problems and the surprising answers God can guide us to."
—*Romance Reviews Today*

PRAISE FOR ALLIE PLEITER

"With humor, wisdom and lots of practical ideas, Allie encourages us to renew our commitment to the high and holy calling of motherhood."
—Cheri Keaggy, Christian recording artist, on *Becoming a Chief Home Officer*

"Whether you're desiring to learn how to apply your business skills to the business of parenting, or wondering why and how fancy underwear can help your mothering, Allie Pleiter draws you the perfect word pictures."
—Charlene Baumbich, bestselling author of the Dearest Dorothy series, on *Becoming a Chief Home Officer*

ALLIE PLEITER

Queen Esther
& the Second Graders of Doom

Steeple
Hill
Café

Published by Steeple Hill Books™

STEEPLE HILL BOOKS

ISBN 0-373-78556-9

QUEEN ESTHER & THE SECOND GRADERS OF DOOM

Copyright © 2006 by Alyse Stanko Pleiter

www.SteepleHill.com

Printed in U.S.A.

To Christopher John Pleiter
My Second Grader of Delight

And

To
Anyone
Anywhere
Who's ever taught
Anyone under ten years old
And lived

ACKNOWLEDGMENTS

Some books just come to you. The Doom Room and its burping crashed into my imagination one afternoon and simply refused to leave. Those are the books that are joys to write, because it is like unwrapping a gift of many layers—your efforts are filled with *ooohs* and *aaahs* as you discover what it is you've been given.

First, thanks should probably go to my own son, CJ, who was in second grade when his imaginary counterparts invaded my life. I must emphatically state that *none* of the antics portrayed in this book were from CJ's actual second-grade existence. Some, however, come *mighty* close. Any mother of any second-grade boy anywhere will attest to the universality of bathroom humor, bug fascination, airborne objects and the ability to start a tussle in seven nanoseconds. Still, son of mine, you remain as joyful as you are jumpy, and much of Esther's experiences comes from my own journey of motherhood—including Josh's non-stop teething. It seems like all too soon we'll be marching those pearly whites to the orthodontist....

The rest of my family, even if not so accurately depicted, shoulder the burden of living with me during the writing process. For that I will forever be grateful.

Rachel Young, my own personal New Jersey shot-put champion, served not only as a sparkle of inspiration, but also my resident expert on the athletic details. Any botching of the details is purely my own fault. Caroline Wolfe assisted me in several of the medical details—how many friends can help you pick out the perfect annoying geriatric female ailment?

I'm continually grateful to the team of professionals that keeps me on the bookshelves. My editor, Krista Stroever, always knows just when to let my wacky sense of humor fly, and when to...*ahem*... rein it back in. My agent, Karen Solem, continues to be the wisest of counsel in this wackiest of worlds that is publishing. Add those fine experts to the high-octane fuel of mocha lattes and Skinny Cow ice cream bars, fold in one kitchen counter and one laptop computer, and you've pretty much got the Allie Pleiter production mechanism.

And, as always, I'm grateful to the God who made me, wackiness and all. Who else but our Lord could create the marvelous surprises that have filled my life and gifted me with such wonderful stories? I am truly, abundantly blessed.

Blessings to all,

Allie Pleiter

Chapter 1

Of Salt Air and Soy Sauce

Essie burst into the room.

Well, that wasn't unusual—Essie always burst into rooms. It was the look on her face, though, that made Doug put down his hacksaw. It wasn't very often he saw his wife in a state of panic.

"Essie?"

She groped for words. It didn't seem to be about Josh: he was right there, tucked baby-perfect into her elbow and chewing on her knuckle, looking as content as a five-month-old teething baby could. Staying in the church nursery during Sunday school obviously hadn't done him any bodily harm. The walk home perhaps? Had something happened then?

"Promise me!" she blurted out finally.

Doug stashed the saw in its proper drawer and began walking toward Essie to take Josh. "Promise you what?"

"Promise me Josh will never make bathroom jokes, or

think crawling under the sanctuary pews is cool, or try to blow Kool-Aid out his nose because he was dared to, or draw the Apostles having a belching competition on his gospel lesson papers—*promise me!*"

Doug tucked Josh onto his shoulder, feeling his shirt dampen. His new son seemed to be a constant source of saliva. "Slow down, Essie...."

Which was useless, since Essie had now begun to pace the tiny workshop they'd carved out on the back porch of their San Francisco apartment. "Promise me he'll never see who can say booger ten times fastest, or bark like a puppy for ten straight minutes while someone's trying to teach him about forgiveness, and that he will possess the seemingly rare ability to *sit still for thirty seconds,* and that he won't turn into *one of them!*"

Doug wasn't sure there was a safe response to that. He tried to catch Essie's hand as she paced the short length of the deck, but she slid out of his grasp. She turned and crossed the length again, tugging at her ponytail. She looked like she had another hundred such laps in her.

"They're animals," she said to no one in particular. "They're little beasts in tiny khaki pants and itty-bitty loafers. They couldn't have been raised by humans. They're *animals.*"

"They're second-grade boys. That's pretty close to animals in my book."

"No." Essie turned to him, eyeing him like a biology specimen. "These aren't normal boys. Men who run companies and drive school buses and file tax returns don't start out like this. *Mobsters* start out like this, not nice boys."

"You just had a bad day."

"You know," she replied as she rubbed at a marker stain

on the cuff of her shirt, "I thought that. Last week. But this week was just the same. They're lunatics, these little boys. It's like trying to teach a band of chimpanzees on a sugar high."

She stopped pacing and leaned her body back against one of the support columns. Strands of curly hair had escaped her ponytail, and she pushed them aside with an annoyed gesture. "I don't why I ever let Mark-o talk me into this."

Doug offered Josh a knuckle, wincing as the tiny edge of a new tooth made itself known. "You were excited about this. Essie, you've always been great with kids. You're great with Josh. You were voted Teacher of the Year before we left New Jersey. You can do this."

She turned her gaze out over the alley, away from him. "No one in the hallowed halls of Pembrook High School ever called me Mrs. Poopy-head."

"Well, not to your face, maybe…"

"Doug…"

"Okay, okay." He came up behind her and kissed one shoulder. "So they're a rough crowd. And they lack certain social skills. That doesn't make you a bad teacher. From what I remember of second grade, 'poopy-head' is a compliment."

A tiny laugh escaped her lips. "So this is like kindergarten, where if I hit you it means I like you?"

"Not exactly. By second grade the 'cootie factor' comes into play. Look, Essie, Mark's under a lot of pressure from those private-school-types to get things right. He wouldn't have asked you to teach at his church if he didn't think you'd do a great job."

"I bet he'll get calls today. Mrs. Covington's gonna pop right out of her Guccis when she sees her son's 'Burping

Apostle Peter.' Where do those little minds dream up this stuff?"

"You were expecting them to line up and sing 'Jesus Loves Me' in harmony? Don't you remember second grade?"

She rested her head against the pillar. Josh reached out a chubby hand to grasp at his mother's curls, now within reach, and tried stuffing one in his mouth. Essie winced at the pull and turned to face them. "I thought I could handle them, Doug."

"You can. You're just going to have to work a little harder than you thought to pull it off."

"I don't know."

"I do. The Essie Walker I married can't be conquered. You could shot-put one of those kids across the room if you had to, and I bet they know it. Perhaps during next week's lesson you could mention that you are the New Jersey state champion."

"These boys don't even respect the laws of gravity. They're not going to respect the 1993 New Jersey state shot-put title."

"I don't know," said Doug, breathing in the particularly wonderful scent of his wife's neck. "It goes a long way with me."

"You," she said, her voice pitching a bit higher when he kissed her in just the right spot, "don't count."

"Joshua and I are insulted at that remark." Doug pulled away in mock indignation.

"I'll make it up to you."

She leaned in to kiss him, her hair glinting in the early afternoon sunlight. Doug inhaled in sweet expectation.

Only to hear his son fill his diaper. Enthusiastically. And then snort in manly satisfaction.

Doug rolled his eyes. "Boys and their bodily functions."

Essie sighed. "I'll change this one."

"No," Doug countered. "I think you've had enough of male physiology for one morning. I'll take this one. There's some pink lemonade in the fridge. I'll take care of Mr. Toxic Pants here and meet you back on the deck chairs." He used his free hand to nudge her shoulders toward the kitchen.

Essie didn't argue. Which could only mean those boys really *had* been beasts.

The second-grade boys' Sunday school class at Bayside Christian Church was proving to require stamina of Olympic proportions. Two weeks into the job—no, Essie corrected herself, into the *ministry*—and she was up to her earlobes in doubt. She was a fine teacher, but try as she might, she could not get the upper hand with this squirrely class. Essie was still shaking her head as she closed the fridge door and returned to the porch to sink into an Adirondack chair.

She loved these angled wood chairs. They barely fit on the deck, and their New England rustic charm clashed with the jazzy Euro-style that was San Francisco. Ah, but Essie wouldn't give these chairs up for the world. They were home. Barbecues in the backyard followed by walks to the beach. They were morning coffee cups steaming into the salt-laden air, they were lemonades on the lawn when it was hot and sticky. Essie let her head fall back against the wood and tried to conjure up a New Jersey Sunday from the scents that lingered in the grain. Of a life where she knew what to do and where she fit in. It worked a bit—just the hints, the barest fragments of a Jersey shore summer came uncurling out of her memory. Had they really been in San Francisco for a month? Had she really jumped straight from the shores of one ocean to the shores of another? The tang of soy sauce from the sushi bar on the corner floated in on the breeze as if to confirm her thoughts.

Josh's post-baby-wipe coos came through the doorway. "Wow!" commented Doug, wrinkling his nose as he tucked Josh back onto his shoulder. "Can all that come out of one baby at one time?"

"Please...not one more shred of conversation about body functions. Even from you. Even about Josh."

Doug chuckled as he eased himself and Josh into the other chair. "Deal. Hey, look, Essie, you've done your tour-of-combat duty for this week. Josh will practically sleep through couples' Bible study tonight, it'll all be grown-ups, and you've got six days before you even have to think about apostolic burps again. Just let it go for now."

Esther drank her lemonade, wishing it was as easy as that. "I wish you were right, but I said I'd come to their Christian education committee meeting on Tuesday morning. They even promised to get one of the committee member's daughters to sit for Josh if he got antsy so that I could attend. I'm gonna get grilled, I know it."

"That's your game-face talking, Essie. They are not going to hold up score cards to rate your first two weeks with that class." He turned to look at her. "Did you ever stop to think that Mark invited you so you'd get a chance to meet some of the other mothers in the church? To help you make a few friends out here? Did you consider that?"

"No."

"Well, you ought to. Your brother's no fool. He's smart enough to know that if we had to count on the finely tuned social graces of my coworkers at Nytex, we'd never meet a soul. Software engineers don't have a geeky reputation for nothing. I'm living in the land of the pocket protector here."

There was just a bit of an edge to his last remark, and Essie realized she hadn't thought about that. She'd just assumed that Doug had grafted himself into a ready-made circle of friends. She imagined him lunching with buddies and rehashing baseball games at the watercooler. They'd made this cross-country move for her more than for him—it was purely God's grace that he was able to land a job so easily after they decided to join her brother out here to help with her aging parents. Sure, he'd never once griped about moving to San Fran, but that didn't mean he was enjoying it. Doug wasn't the kind of man who complained. Essie wanted to whack herself on the forehead for being so self-centered.

"Office a little geeky this week?" She'd never even thought to ask before now. Nice wifely behavior. Way to be that strong support system, Essie.

Doug's sigh told far more than his words. "A bit. I'm fitting in." After a long pause he added, "Slowly."

"We did the right thing, didn't we? Made a good choice?"

Doug turned immediately and caught her hand on the armrest next to his. "Yes. Essie, I don't doubt it for a second. You know I agreed to this fully, of my own geeky free will. My parents in Nevada aren't so far away now—we're nearer to both our parents."

"Why isn't it *easier?*" Essie was amazed at how much the words caught in her throat. Josh stared at her, his wide gray eyes beaming love out from their perch on Doug's shoulder. He made a gurgling sound and waved a tiny fist in the air. She caught it, and reveled anew in how his minute grasp fit perfectly around her finger. She'd wanted to be a mother since forever. No book or magazine, though, did justice to how just plain hard it was. She'd never felt further out of her element than she did this past month.

"Let's see," said Doug, pushing his glasses up on his nose. "New job, new city, new baby, new home, new weather—well, okay, that's more of a fringe benefit. There's a hunk of adjustments in that list. I think we're doing pretty good. Most of my programs don't even adapt this well—and I design relocation software, remember?"

"Can you design a—what do you call it? An integration program—for one small family? Make a button for me, Doug. One I can push and make all the uncertainty go away."

Doug chuckled. "I did, sort of."

"No kidding? Where is it?"

Doug held up the cordless phone he'd evidently brought onto the deck with him. "Pepperoni pizza, really thin, New York-style. Coming up."

"I'm liking this."

"A guy at work—one of the less geekier ones—recommended a place. His uncle moved here from Manhattan, and called it his 'relocation coping mechanism.' I've been saving its implementation for just such a moment."

"Doug Walker, I love you."

He winked. "Nah, that's just the pepperoni talking. Is this a 'medium,' or a 'large' kind of day?"

Essie smiled, too. For the first time since she came home. "Do they make an extra large?"

Chapter 2

Zacchaeus Was a Wee Little Man...

She wasn't supposed to be this nice.

When Essie first spied Celia Covington—and even more so when someone called her "Cece"—she was supposed to fall easily into the well-to-do-nitwit category. The twinset was a dead giveaway. Essie was always suspicious of women who wore twinsets. Those bearing sweaters in pastel colors, and most especially when adorned with a string of tasteful pearls, were to be avoided at all costs.

Essie had her own personal classification system for the branches of womanhood. There were "the ponytails," which had a subset containing the unpretentious and practical, and another subset of the entirely-too-perky. This could usually be distinguished by height. Not of the woman, but of the ponytail. High ponytails signaled high-level perkiness. Low ones generally denoted practicality.

On another branch of the tree of womanhood sat "the headbands." There was a certain kind of woman, Essie sur-

mised, who wore headbands. Personality was then tele-
graphed by the type of headband selected—fabric, tor-
toiseshell plastic, wide, thin, etc. But it was the well-off,
well-bred, well-dressed woman who generally opted for the
headband as hair accessory. Or, on rare occasions, the headband became the tool of choice when the practical woman
wanted to dress up.

Put a headband and a twinset together, and a smart gal
runs quickly in the other direction.

Celia Covington, however, didn't fit the twinset mold. She
passed by the precise corner of pastel-sandaled women who
flanked the far end of the table and plunked herself down
in the middle, with a heavyset, friendly Japanese woman on
her left, and an Hispanic grandmother-type on her right.
This placed Celia directly opposite Essie across the rectan-
gular table. Essie had opted for the middle of the table as
well, seated next to Mark. As in her brother Mark-o, or as
everyone called him, Pastor Taylor.

"You've got to be Mrs. Walker," Celia said, smiling. "David
went on and on about you the other day. You've made quite
an impression on my little monster, and that's no small feat."
She had an authentic, squint-up-the-corners-of-your-eyes
smile that lit up her face. Essie tried not to like her—on account of the headband and all—and failed.

"Please, call me Esther. Actually, call me Essie. Everyone
else does."

"I'm Celia—Cece, actually. David, the little tornado in
your class, he's my youngest. He's a handful, especially after
he's sat through a Sunday service. There's only so much patience a roll of Life Savers can buy."

Well, it was a small headband, after all. And coral isn't
really a pastel. "He's a good kid. Very creative. I think he

really enjoys drawing, and he seems to be rather good at it. I could tell right away that his gray blob on Noah's ark was a rhinoceros. Most of the other blobs were undistinguishable. And no one else thought to put rhinos on the ark."

Celia laughed. "That's David. Always thinking out of the box. My oldest, Samantha? She's in the nursery with her nose in a book, ready and waiting should your little one get too squirmy."

Nice lady with babysitter daughter. No, coral is definitely not in the pastel family. "Thanks, but I think Josh is out for the count. You never know, though."

"Don't worry. Sam would consider it a treat to tuck a little cutie like that into her arms. Want some coffee?"

Essie sighed. "Oh, you wouldn't think Josh was so cute if you'd seen him screaming his adorable little head off at two-thirty this morning. Sugar, please."

"Teething?" Celia called over her shoulder as she walked to the sideboard.

"Like a pro."

"Have you tried a grapefruit spoon?"

A what? Why would you hand spiky silverware to your newborn? Who actually had one of those? "Uh, no."

Celia laughed at Essie's apparent shock. "I know it sounds barbaric," she said, bringing back the coffee, "but the metal stays cool, and as long as the serrated edges aren't really sharp, it helps the tooth break through the gum. It's all that straining against the gum that makes babies crazy. Once the full surface of the tooth breaks through, they settle right down."

"Really?"

"I've got four sets of healthy gums marching their way to the orthodontist to prove it."

Lean, lovely Celia Covington was way too toned to have

birthed four children. Not if Essie's own lumpy belly was any indication. Still, she had returned from the sideboard with java and cookies, not the spiffy-label bottled water that seemed to be the beverage of choice over in the corner. Those women looked like they'd not touched a cheeseburger since high school. "I'll take your word for it. But I don't own one. I don't even know where you'd get one."

"Well, you could go to TableSets and pay a ridiculous amount of money for some, or you could stop by Darkson's restaurant supply just down the block and pick up a half-dozen for peanuts. If Josh is crying as you walk in the door, they might even give you one for free out of sheer sympathy." She winked as she dipped a cookie into her coffee.

Essie decided that she might want to start liking Celia Covington.

"Now that we solved a few pediatric issues, here," interjected Mark, looking at his watch, "we need to get started so I can give you ladies as much of my time as I can before my eleven o'clock appointment. Dahlia, do you have an agenda for today?"

Dahlia, who looked like she'd just walked off the cover of a magazine, flipped open an expensive-looking notepad. "Just two items, Pastor, but they're hefty ones. One—" she held up her substantial silver pen and flicked it like an orchestra conductor "—I want to run down how things are going with Sunday school. It's been two weeks, and we ought to be able to see the problem areas bubbling up by now."

Essie gulped. Somehow she just knew this woman had a second-grade boy.

"Second—" the pen bobbed again "—it's time to start the ball rolling on the Celebration." That seemed to surprise some of the women around the table. "Now, gals, every January we're caught scrambling. I know we're all just getting our feet underneath us with Sunday school for the year, but I can't help thinking now's the time to start planning."

Celebration? Could that be that "little drama thing later in the year" Mark-o mentioned? That thing he distinctly described as "nothing you'll have to worry about"? She'd taught school long enough to know that any event requiring several months' worth of preparation could never be classified as "nothing much." Most especially when parents were in charge. Essie shot a look to her brother out of the corner of her eye. He knew this was just a trial stint. He knew she and Doug weren't sure they could make it on one income, and that Essie going back to work in the new year was a distinct possibility. Now there was this Celebration thing in the mix? If she did go back to work, Essie was pretty sure she couldn't handle this on top of it.

"Wise indeed, Dahlia," Mark said in a pastoral tone. "It does feel like we scramble just after the holidays, doesn't it? But I do think we ought to tackle the Sunday school stuff first, as I doubt my skills are really required for Celebration discussions."

Oh, yes, Mark-o, get out while you can. Remind me to thank you later when I'm hand-sewing second graders into sheep costumes....

"Sorry I'm late. Max forgot his trumpet again and I had to swing by school. I think I'm going to make him take up the piccolo and tie it around his neck." A woman in jeans and a red sweater dumped her large canvas bag on the floor next to one of the empty chairs and turned toward the coffeepots. "*One* of these days I'll make it on time to a meeting."

"We wouldn't recognize you if you did, Meg. Come on, you haven't missed much at all." Celia waved her arm and pulled out the chair Meg had chosen.

"Which reminds me," Mark said. "I've clean forgotten the introductions. Ladies, this is my sister, Esther Walker. She just moved here with her husband and baby to help us with Mom and Pop. Some of you already know her as the second-grade boys Sunday school teacher. Essie, these are my school soldiers. The fine ladies who keep Bayside's Christian education programs up and running."

"Pastor Taylor's sister, hmm?" said Meg, plunking herself down in the chair. "I was wondering how he'd wrangled a newcomer into that spot. You're either a brave woman, or you owe your brother a very big favor."

"Now Meg, be nice…."

"I taught the Doom Room one year. I speak from firsthand knowledge."

The Doom Room? The *Doom Room?* Essie swallowed hard. *Just exactly what is it I've promised to do?*

"Meg," said Celia, "no fair scaring our new friend here. Just because you've now upgraded to the compliant third-grade girls' class is no reason to think…"

"Ladies," interjected Mark for the second time that morning, "Essie can handle our little men. I'd say one state champion athlete against eight small boys is more than a fair fight."

"State champion athlete, is it?" said Celia, flexing perfectly manicured fingers. "Good. You'll need it. What event?"

"Shot put." Essie waited the obligatory ten seconds it took everyone on Planet Earth to realize all female shot-put champions did not necessarily look like pro wrestlers or have names like "Uta." It happened every time.

The pastel corner didn't seem to know what to do with that information. Nola nodded her head in a show of respect, Jan merely raised a dark eyebrow. Meg, however, looked downright tickled. "Shot put? Well, that ought to do nicely. Wow. How much does one of those things weigh, anyway?"

"About the weight of your average second grader." Essie amazed even herself with the zippy comeback.

"I'd share that with the class next week," Celia added.

"I just might." Even the pastel contingency managed a giggle at that. Adding his own voice of approval, Josh produced a loud, squeaky grunt and shifted in his carrier. "Excuse me, but it seems I have a little business to take care of."

"Want me to get Sam to handle it?"

"No, thanks, I think I'll spare her the joy of diaper changing." Truth be told, Essie wasn't even sure he needed a diaper change—she was just glad for a reason to leave the room before the dissection of Sunday school began. Those women in the corner looked like they were in possession of firm opinions on all kinds of subjects. If they had suggestions—those kind of parents always called them "suggestions" rather than the more truthful label of "complaints"—Essie was sure she'd rather hear them through Mark-o's compassionate filter than straight from the source.

Essie picked up Josh's carrier as a pointed "Well now!" from Dahlia signaled the evaluation starting gun.

Go easy on me, ladies. I haven't had a full night's sleep in twelve weeks.

"They gave it at least a seven-point-oh," whispered Mark as she returned. He accompanied that last remark with a discreet thumbs-up under the conference table.

"Bible Heroes' it is, then?" Dahlia was saying. "Arthur has a friend whose son is majoring in children's theater at BSU—a fine young Christian man, someone we can trust with a project like this. I feel certain we can draft him into scriptwriting." Essie was both impressed and baffled. This was a church play they were talking about, wasn't it? One of those little forty-minute drama things? Where she came from, church plays were bought from the script rack at the local Christian bookstore or whipped up by someone's good-natured mother. Drama penned by an advanced degree theater major; well, that was pretty hot stuff.

From the way Dahlia put it, however, it sounded as if the committee was going to request a statement of faith and four references from the poor young man. She could see it now: Dahlia's silver pen slashing its way through the poor young scriptwriter's first drafts, editing, cutting, changing. Asking for the theological reasons for dressing the wandering Israelites in blue, rather than beige.

Three years of teaching had taught her to spot this type of parent. Essie was glad it wasn't Dahlia's son who'd sketched the belching apostle. Dahlia looked like the kind of mom who would write a long letter over something like that. A *really* long letter. Anyone with a pen that formidable would know how to use it.

Twenty minutes of discussion followed. After they gave her class the story of Zacchaeus, Essie didn't catch much of the rest. Her brain was busy concocting the image of second-grade boys launching themselves off of piled-up classroom chairs while others shouted, "Zacchaeus, come down," in their best deep Son-of-God voices. Evidently, each classroom was being assigned their own hero. Mr. Scriptwriter would be given his detailed marching orders, and the "Celebration of Bible Heroes" was born.

Dahlia snapped the cap on her pen, signaling the end of the meeting.

"Come on," said Celia as she stuffed her notes into a canvas bag. "I've got a bit of time before I have to drop Sam off. We can go get you those grapefruit spoons."

"Just give me a second." Essie ducked back into the church's administrative offices, leaving Celia to grin at Josh as he made faces at her from his carrier. Waving at the harried-looking secretary, Essie snagged a Post-it note and pen off the woman's desk. She wrote, "Mark-o, call me" in her large handwriting and stuck it to Mark-o's closed door.

September in San Francisco was feeling complicated, but evidently it was going to make February look like a walk in the park...if she even lasted that long.

Chapter 3

Stinky Whale Guts

"You're not going to let Joshua chew on that thing, are you?" Dorothy Taylor eyed the evil implement Essie was about to hand the First-Ever Grandson.

"Actually, yes. It really works." Essie assumed the position she'd held every waking moment for the past two days. Josh in one arm, grapefruit spoon in other hand. Chew, drool, repeat. Sleep for thirty minutes, wail, then begin again. Essie had decided she was developing a healthy hatred for teeth. Teeth=no sleep. No sleep=bad days and worse nights. She had begun scouring the baby books this morning to see how much longer it would be before Josh could hold his own spoon, thereby buying her perhaps forty-five minutes of uninterrupted sleep. Evidently that precious mercy wouldn't be forthcoming for at least another month. She yawned involuntarily at the thought of so little sleep for so long. "He's having such trouble cutting this first tooth. I hope they're not all like this."

Dorothy Taylor eyed the handle of the grapefruit spoon, now wobbling with every gummy chomp as it stuck out of Joshua's tiny mouth. She frowned again. "I just don't know, Essie. I never gave you or Mark any such thing. I remember I just woke up one day..."

"And noticed we had teeth. Yes, Mom, you've told me." *And trust me, it's not helping to hear how you never went through any such thing. I'm already feeling so confident in my parenting skills. Really, it does wonders for you to hand me another reason to question things. Please, if you think of any more, don't hesitate to bring them up.* "How's Dad liking the new doctor?"

"Oh, he argues with this one just like he did in New Jersey. Yesterday he told Dr. Einhart that he walks thirty minutes each day."

"He *what?*"

"He spent ten minutes telling Dr. Einhart how he exercises each day."

"Mom! That couldn't be further from the truth. Why did you let him do that?"

Essie's mom blinked. "Do what?"

"Lie to his doctor? It's ridiculous."

"But he's supposed to walk each day. They've told him he should walk each day."

Essie shot out a frustrated sigh. "Well, he doesn't, does he? We both know he doesn't."

"Well, of course he doesn't. His knees bother him."

"Mom, we've been over this a gazillion times. If he'd walk more, his knees wouldn't bother him, then he'd drop some of that weight, then his knees would bother him less. It's just going to get worse if he keeps sitting there. No, no, it's not just that, but sitting there and lying to his doctor."

Mom crossed her arms. "I'm not going to make him look bad in front of his doctor."

Essie wanted to scream. "This is not a popularity contest, this is Dad and his doctor. What's the point of going to a doctor if you don't actually tell him what's going on?"

"How's Doug, dear?" Mom clipped that thread of conversation clean off. It was quite clear no further discussion on the subject of honesty with one's doctors would be allowed. Essie fought the urge to go find her father and shake him by the shoulders. *Lord, help me. They sure won't help themselves. Patience, just send gallons and gallons of patience. Right this minute, or I'm going to go out of my mind.*

Essie let out a long, slow exhale, rolling her shoulders back as she watched Joshua inspect his thumb. "Doug's doing fine. The new department has more people and more resources than he had in Jersey, so he's happy. It's been a good move for him."

"That's nice, dear. Have you talked about having another child? Soon?"

Essie popped her eyes wide open. "Mom, Josh is five months old!"

"I had you and Mark only a year apart. You played so well together."

Oh, yes, Mom, I have such happy memories of tearing Mark-o apart in joyful siblinghood. Not to mention I'd like to get acquainted with the sight of my toes again.

"Really, Mom, it's a bit early for that sort of thing."

"Nonsense. You're thirty-one. Life won't go on forever you know. An old woman can pine for grandchildren, can't she?"

Essie didn't quite know how to convince her mother she didn't want to be pregnant for every waking moment of her thirties. *Deflect the attention.* "You know, there's always Mark-o. He could have children. He's *married,* you know. Married people do that sort of thing."

Her mother waved a hand as if that were an absurd suggestion. "Oh, yes, but Mark is so very busy with that church. And Peggy—well, I just don't see Peggy being ready to have children soon. She's just not that motherly type."

So I should pop out a gaggle of grandchildren to compensate? And aren't Doug and I busy? Now that I'm at home with Joshua, is procreation my only purpose in life?

"You, my little Queen Esther." Essie watched her mother burst into a wide smile. "You were always meant to be a mother. I always knew you'd give me precious, beautiful grandbabies to love." She scooped up Joshua just as he was dozing off, and made loud snuggly noises into his neck.

Which, of course, sent him into a full-fledged wail.

"I just never thought I'd see the day my Essie fed her children silverware." Her disapproval of the now-revered grapefruit spoon trick was almost palpable. "Really. No wonder he cries so much."

He cries so much because you just did the unthinkable: you woke a sleeping baby. A sleeping cranky baby. My sleeping cranky baby that almost never sleeps. Mother-r-r...

"How can such a darling boy be so miserable?" Dorothy made a sour face and handed her "precious grandbaby" back to Essie, obviously unwilling to hold anything making that much noise, even if it was flesh of her flesh.

"He's teething, Mom. Don't you remember how miserable a toothache is?" Essie fished around on the couch for the spoon, mentally convincing herself it didn't need reboiling just because it had endured forty-five seconds on her mother's couch cushions. She returned it to Joshua's gaping mouth.

Within fifteen seconds Mount Joshua ceased to erupt. With a dying chorus of wet gurgles, Josh settled into a slow, relieved chew. Essie felt the spoon's handle wobble up and down as Josh's besieged gums found their solace. "I know it's weird," Essie replied to her mother's subsequent frown. "But it *works*. See? It works. I don't care how, I don't care why, I just know it works. If putting him in purple socks worked, I'd probably do that, too."

The front door pushed open and Essie's dad shuffled in, clutching a white paper pharmacy bag. Mark-o entered behind him, holding a paper bag of groceries. It took Bob Taylor four full minutes to make it from the front door to his permanent spot on the recliner beside the couch. He grunted with every step, and groused with every breath about "those knuckleheaded quacks and their useless pills."

"I'm gonna spend my pension at that pharmacy," he grumbled as he eased his large frame into the worn chair. "Every day and every dollar's gonna buy some drug executive a shiny new yacht."

"Now, Pop—" Mark-o had put on his counseling persona; Essie could tell by his voice. "If it weren't for those useless pills, you'd be in the hospital looking at a shiny new wheelchair."

"Baloney." Essie's dad tossed the bag on the coffee table in disgust. "I'm slow, but I'm still moving. Since when is it a sin to get old and slow?"

"At your young years," Mark shot back, his fraying patience beginning to show through the practiced calm, "it's a sin."

"So's lying." The words jumped out of Essie's sleep-deprived mouth before she could think better of it. "As in lying to your doctor."

"Oh, honey…" began her mother.

"Pop, all she's…"

Pop's next booming question stopped the argument in its tracks: "What *on earth* is that in *my grandson's mouth?*"

"Now, who knows the story of Jonah?"

Four cookie-crumbed hands shot up. Essie passed out a second set of napkins before she allowed Justin to answer.

"He got stuck inside a fish."

Essie smiled. "He sure did. You were listening in assembly this morning, Justin. Who knows how he got there?"

Stanton, a tall boy in pressed pants and gelled hair, strained to get his hand as high as possible. He yipped a series of small "Me! Me! Me!"s. Frantic to be picked, he seemed oblivious to the fact that his was the only hand aloft.

"Stanton?"

"I bet he was swimming. My dad, he took us swimming once, on vacation, and I was really worried about the fishes when we were swimming. I didn't want to swim where the fishes were, but he told me pools don't have fishes, 'specially hotel pools. And we were in a hotel 'cuz we were on vacation and stuff, 'cuz we went on vacation over Christmas and we got to go somewhere warm so we could go swimming, but my big brother got in trouble 'cuz he…" The entire speech whooshed out of him in a single breath.

"Okay," Essie cut in, placing her hand on Stanton's arm. The boy was wearing a watch. A fancy one. *Who buys designer watches for their eight-year-old?* Dahlia Mannington, of course. For all his dapper duds, Stanton was a sweet boy with tender green eyes and a near insatiable appetite for attention.

"Swimming is fun. But Jonah wasn't swimming for fun. Can anyone tell me why Jonah was in the water?"

"It's hot where he lives!" said Decker Maxwell, as he tipped his chair back far enough to send himself head over heels. The resulting laughter stopped any hope of education dead in its tracks for the next five minutes, as all the other boys tried immediately to follow suit. Essie finally had to resume her lesson on the floor in a circle, without the benefit of chairs. She tried to ignore the sensation of her legs falling asleep as she patiently suggested that Jonah was running from God's commands.

"Did Jonah get a time-out? I wanna do my time-outs in whale guts!" Peter, a smaller boy with wildly curly hair and an obsession with all things bug- and animal-related, pushed his glasses back up on his face as he joined the conversation.

"Well," replied Essie, catching a pencil as Stanton sent it through the air in another boy's direction, "it was sort of a time-out. In one way, God saved Jonah because he wouldn't have survived being thrown out into the middle of the ocean like that. But in another way, God gave Jonah a good long time to think about what he'd done."

"My mom does that," grumbled Peter. "In my 'Think It Over Chair.'" He crossed his arms over his chest in an exaggerated fashion that made his next comment almost unnecessary. "I hate my Think It Over Chair."

"Discipline isn't much fun, is it?" Essie passed around the large blue whales she'd spent two hours cutting out last night.

"What's dicey-pline?"

"Di-sci-pline." Essie made a mental note to strike any word over three syllables from her lesson plan. "It's what your mom or dad does to help you think about something wrong you've done."

"You mean like getting spanked?" Steven Bendenfogle offered. Essie continually felt sorry for a little boy with such a mouthful of a last name. She guessed Steven's meek demeanor came from endless teasing.

"That's one kind of discipline, yes."

"God spanked somebody?" Steven seemed scandalized at the idea. "Wow, I bet God hits really hard." Essie wondered if Steven even realized he was rubbing his backside protectively. Which made her wonder if Steven had considerable personal experience. Did people still spank their kids?

Would she ever spank Josh? It seemed hard to imagine. She couldn't fathom doing anything like that to her son. Then again, when Decker took the paper whale lovingly prepared for him, crumpled it without a moment's hesitation, and threw it straight into Steven's face—hard—Essie could see where a spanking might have its uses.

Well, she'd taken on this class as a chance to see what young boys were really like. *Oh, Essie,* she chided herself, *when will you realize it isn't always great when you get what you pray for?*

"God has never spanked someone, Steven. He— Decker, uncrumple that whale right now, you're going to need it in a minute. And say you're sorry to Steven. Nobody throws anything at anyone in this class. God's so smart, He can find different ways to let us know we've not obeyed."

"I still like the whale guts," said Peter, obviously disappointed that a stint in whale innards wasn't in his immediate future. "I bet they smell really gross."

The suggestion sent the boys into a flurry of stinky adjectives, each in a full-out competition to find the grossest possible description for how bad whale guts would smell. *How can I hope to teach obedience here, Lord, when I can't get past the stinky whale guts?*

Just when she thought she could restore order, Peter remembered the lyrics to "Gobs and Gobs of Greasy Grimy Gopher Guts," a revolting camp song Essie was horrified to discover had still survived even from her childhood. Within seconds all decorum was lost. Essie stood up as fast as her thirty-one-year-old knees would allow, bellowed out a menacing, "Settle down!" in her most authoritative voice and flicked the light switch. It sent the room into darkness.

That shocked 'em. All noise and movement stilled.

"When I turn these lights on, I want everyone to pick up their paper whale and come back quietly to the table. Okay?"

A few whimpered "Okay"s signaled her return to superiority.

"Now," Essie said in a calm voice as she turned the lights back on, "I want each of you to think about something that you know you should do, but is hard. Something that you know you have to do, but you don't always want to do. Those things are like Jonah's trip to Ninevah. We're going to write those things on your whales. Raise your hand when you have an idea of what to write, and I'll come help you."

Peter's hand shot up first. "I hate getting my allergy shots."

Essie nodded in agreement. "That's a good example. It's no fun, but you know you'll feel better when you get them, right?"

"Yep, but they hurt."

Essie wrote "allergy shots" in large letters on Peter's whale. "When you get them, you can remember that you're being obedient, and doing what you need to, even though it's tough. God is very happy when we do obedient things like that."

Soon the other boys chimed in with their ideas. "Practice piano.""Be nice to my new baby sister.""Go to bed." And a host of other examples until one little response gave her pause.

"Like my new stepmom," said Alex Faber quietly. "She's my third stepmom," he added, kicking his chair with his foot over and over. "I don't like her. And I don't think she likes me very much."

What do you say to something like that?

"It's hard to be the new person," Essie responded. "It's hard to get used to new people. What makes you think your stepmom doesn't like you?"

"She said so." Alex kept kicking the chair.

Oh, my.

"I wonder if that's really true, Alex. Grown-ups have a funny way of saying things sometimes that little boys don't always understand." Essie squatted down beside him, warning her knees to cooperate in the name of human compassion. "Can you remember what she said?"

"Well—" Alex took his crayon and began drawing swirly circles on his whale as he talked. "She was talking to Dad at night. I wasn't s'posed to be up, but I was thirsty so I got a drink and I heard them talking down the hall. You know, in Dad's room. Vicki—that's her name, Vicki—didn't have kids before she married Dad. She was telling him how she didn't like being a mom so quick." Alex looked at her with hard eyes. "But she's not my mom. My mom's in Minnosoda now."

"That's hard."

"Vicki doesn't now how to make peanut butter sandwiches or play Uno or do any mom stuff. My sister calls her Icky Vicki. That's when Vicki gets all mad and locks herself in the bathroom and tells me to go play outside."

Essie didn't think it would be wise to admit that she'd have liked to lock herself in the church ladies' room a couple of times in the last few Sundays.

She took Alex's hand, stilling the flow of crayon swirls for a moment. "You're right, Alex, that is a hard thing. And God would want you to learn to like Vicki. And I think He'll help you if you ask Him."

Alex raised an eyebrow. "I dunno."

"I do. Every family's got an Icky Vicki. Someone who's hard to like. But sometimes, the Icky Vickies turn out to be the nicest people if you just give them a chance."

"Yeah," offered Justin with sudden enthusiasm. "I thought my Uncle Arthur was really boring until he showed me how he can take his *teeth* out. *All* of 'em."

That brought a chorus of approving oohs and aahs—the gross-out factor of extractable teeth was a sure-fire hit with this crowd.

"Justin's right. People surprise you." Essie pulled the Children's Picture Bible off the shelf behind her where it lay open to the Jonah story. "Jonah thought the Ninevites were a whole city of Icky Vickies. He didn't want to go teach them to act better. He didn't want to care about them one bit. But God wanted him to care, and to go there. And so, when he did, the Ninevites changed their icky ways and Jonah learned it's a good thing to be obedient to what God wants."

And what do you know, those tiny faces actually registered understanding! Little heads were actually nodding.

If Jonah could work with the Ninevites, maybe there was a shred of hope for the Doom Room.

Chapter 4

How Many is the Norm?

Josh wailed every single moment of his doctor visit. This morning's fever had called a halt to any hope of Josh's grumpiness being "just teething." Essie was barely conscious. She couldn't remember if she'd brushed her teeth yet this morning, so she tried to smile for the doctor without opening her mouth. She tried to look like an intelligent member of the human race, even though she was feeling pretty much like an amoeba.

"Yes, there, Master Walker. That's one whopping ear infection you've got. Both ears, too. Overachiever, I see." Dr. Martin was trying to put a good spin on things. The man could even be called cheerful. But to Essie right now, twin ear infections sounded like the end of the world.

It must have shown on her face. Dr. Martin walked over and returned screeching little Joshua to her arms with an understanding smile. His appearance and demeanor were so completely, perfectly "doctorish," that the guy belonged on television. "You'll be amazed," he commiserated, "what a little pain medicine will do for the guy. Half an hour, a couple of squirts of pink stuff and he'll be snoozing in no time."

"Could I have that in writing?" Essie whimpered.

"Next best thing," replied Dr. Martin, scribbling off a set of prescription notes. "May I introduce you to your new best friend, amoxicillin? You'll be very well acquainted by the end of the year. There are two kinds of babies in this world. The kind who hardly ever get ear infections, and… the other kind."

"Josh is an 'other,' isn't he?"

"I could lie, but you look like the kind of person who prefers a straight story."

Essie juggled Josh onto her shoulder, which settled his wailing down into a low-grade, pitiful moan. "And the straight story is I'm going to see a lot of amoxi-whatever."

Dr. Martin touched her shoulder. "It does get easier. When he gets old enough to have good control of his hands—which should be soon—he'll grab at his ears and you'll catch on before it gets full-blown awful."

This was not comforting. Essie felt as if she might burst into tears. Some small part of her knew it was only the sleep deprivation, but right now Josh was looking disabled, scarred and victimized. "Okay," was all she could sputter out.

"Mrs. Walker, it's going to be fine. The first one is always the hardest. There's one thing you should know, though, if you don't already."

Your child will never hear again. His brain will be permanently affected. He will…

"This stuff stains."

"Huh?"

"Amoxicillin. It stains. Keep Josh in old onesies or whatever for the first couple of days because it seems to get everywhere, and it stains. You, too." He chuckled. "I'd lay off the evening gowns for the next few days so you don't end up pink, too."

"Yes, of course," Essie replied, but in her head she thought, *You wouldn't be laughing if you knew I've had this same shirt on for three straight days.*

"Mrs. Walker?"

"Yes?"

"That was a joke. A bad one, but still a joke. You're going to be fine, both of you. Make a follow-up appointment for two weeks from now on your way out. And if you don't have one of those tiny medicine things that looks like a miniature turkey baster, make sure you pick one up at the pharmacy—it might save you a lot of trouble and a lot of upholstery."

Josh had settled down to a grumbling whimper by the time Essie reached the pharmacy. "I need amixibillin and a turkey baster."

An older woman behind the counter blinked from behind her thick black glasses. "Pardon me?"

Essie shifted the baby carrier to the other hand and fumbled in her purse until she found the square of blue paper. She pushed it across the counter to the pharmacist. "This. I need this prescription filled." Essie's keys tumbled out of her purse and fell on the floor. She noticed the candy bars beside the counter. How many would it take to be considered a glutton? Sixteen?

"The amoxicillin I guessed. No problem, I have that. It's the turkey baster that has me stumped."

Oh, my, had she really said that? Essie pulled in a focusing breath, just like she used to do before she competed. "My doctor," she began, letting the breath out in a slow, deliberate exhale, "well, Josh's doctor, recommended a medicine spoonish thing he said looked like a miniature turkey baster. For the amoxicillin. Do you know what he means?"

The woman's face spread into a smile. "Oh, of course. Look down to your left. And if I were you, I'd get three of them. You can never find them when you need them, especially in the middle of the night. They work wonders, these little things, but don't use them if the baby's asleep. You always need to make sure they're awake when you give them the medicine. Even if you have to wake 'em up, which I know no one wants to do."

"Okay, good. Three of them it is. Thanks for the tip."

Essie noticed the pharmacist, who now seemed infinitely friendlier, was looking at her with an odd, knowing expression.

"How many chocolate bars do you want me to put in the bag with that medicine?" She winked. Really, she *winked*. It made her look like a great, gray owl with those magnified eyes.

Surprised into honesty, Essie blurted out, "How many is the norm?"

"I've seen one mom take eight. Of course, that was a case of scarlet fever, so extreme measures were called for. I don't usually recommend that many."

Scarlet fever? Didn't people get that in Dickens novels or something?

"I'll take four." Just then Josh let out an ear-splitting wail. "Five."

The pharmacist dropped the bars in the bag and leaned over to see the source of the five-alarm screech. "He'll be a

new man by tomorrow, you'll see. This stuff works wonders."

"The chocolate or the medicine?"

"Same thing in my book, sweetie. I'm a bar-a-day choco-
holic myself. Don't forget your keys."

Doctor Martin was right. Amoxicillin did get everywhere.
It looked and smelled like Pepto-Bismol, and trying to get
it into squirming, wailing Josh's mouth with that baster thing
felt more like target practice than medical care. This child,
who had no practical use of his hands yet, seemed to acquire
perfect aim and swatted the medicine away just as it hit his
mouth. Should any of it actually make it into his mouth—
which should have been simple because it was open in a non-
stop screech during this procedure—he coughed and
sputtered it back out in a shower of pink drops.

Finally, Essie fell back on deception as a tactic. She nestled him in her arms as if to nurse him, which of course
sent him into instant sucking mode. Before he knew what
hit him, she snuck the tip of the medicine dropper-thing
into his mouth and gave the bulb an authoritative squirt. He
coughed, and sputtered, but this time the actual majority of
medicine remained in the baby, where it belonged.

The rest, though, was just about everywhere. By the
time they were done with both medicine and baby aspirin,
Josh's onesie had more pink than its original blue. He was
verging on sticky from all the drips, and Essie's shirt was
beyond repair.

But he calmed. When he produced a yawn—an actual,
nonwailing yawn—Essie set the world's speed record for
quick baby wash-down and insertion into a clean onesie.

And the child slept. The silence was the most beautiful sound Essie had ever heard.

She threw her dank shirt off, grabbed a T-shirt of Doug's and collapsed on the couch. A glance at her watch told her over two hours had gone by when the phone woke her up.

"Hello?"

"Essie?"

"Anna! Oh, Anna, God must have known I needed to hear your voice today. It's wonderful to hear from you."

"Essie, no offense, but you sound awful. How's life on the other side of the continent?"

Even though she'd had enough sleep to take the edge off, Essie burst into tears. "Awful. Josh has ear infections and I haven't slept and Doug's been working late."

"Ear infections, ugh. Josh is going to be one of those, huh? Danny was one. That's rough—I'm sorry you're having such a tough go of it."

Essie nudged the box of tissues on the floor with her foot until she pulled it within reach. "How come nobody tells you this stuff? It's so hard…." Essie was trying to cry as quietly as possible, desperate not to wake Josh. She'd even stuffed the phone under her pillow so that only she would hear it ring. She walked out onto the back balcony, thanking God—again—for giving someone the idea for the cordless phone. "I miss you—all of you—so much."

Essie could hear Anna's voice catch. "I'd give anything to be able to pile in the car and come over there right this minute. I hate it that you're so far away."

"Me, too." It was more sob than sentence.

"But you know, Essie, this is where you're supposed to be right now. We went over this so many times. You're supposed to be in San Francisco. Your family needs you. But I hate it all the same."

Essie wished she had a pink medicine to make the ache in her heart go away. "I just can't see how it's good now. I remember being so sure." She ran her hand along the curved edge of the toy box Doug was building out here. "Now I'm not sure at all. Wait a minute...I needed to get the monitor thing, Anna, sorry."

"Monitor? How big is your apartment, anyway? I thought Doug told us it seemed like he could only afford something the size of a two-car garage out there."

"Very funny." Essie was glad to hear one of Anna Miller's wisecracks. She missed her more than she realized. "I need to know he's okay while I'm out here on the deck."

"He's got Walker-powered lungs. I could probably here him over here."

"Oh, yeah?" Essie found herself smiling, just a bit. "Well, then you didn't get any sleep last night, either, did you?"

"Okay," Anna relented. "Okay. Is he doing better?"

"I've learned how hard it is to get amoxicillin from the bottle and into the baby, if that's what you mean. It's working—he's finally sleeping. I even got to sleep."

"I woke you up, didn't I? Sorry."

"No," sighed Essie, easing herself into the Adirondack chair and wishing with every cell in her body that Anna was on the chair next to her and they were in New Jersey again. "No, I'm really glad to hear your voice. I'd have been sick if I missed your call."

"Listen, I'm sorry things are lousy right now, but I have some good news—it's one of the reasons I called."

"I could use good news right now."

"Kevin was at some athletic thing last night, one of those

association meetings or whatever those monthly things are, and he ran into someone."

"Yeah?"

"Some former college buddy who knows a bunch of people out in California. Essie, he says he knows of a junior college right by you looking for a women's track coach. Starting in February. Isn't that when you said you would need to go back to work?"

Essie took a deep breath. "It's too early to be making those kinds of plans. I'm lucky to be walking and talking these days, much less launching a job search."

"This could be God working things out for you. Think about it—what are the chances of Kevin bumping into this guy and hearing this kind of information?"

"No, you're right, it does sound like it's worth checking into." Essie thought that last bit sounded less comatose.

"Good. Check your e-mail tonight. Kevin is sending the details. And I want photos of my little godson. He must be growing like a weed by now."

"At the moment, he's just growing viruses. Well, I do think he's up a pound or two. I didn't take much notice at the doctor's this morning."

"You found a good doctor?"

"Yes, he seems great. Your standard nice-old-guy pediatrician."

"You mean they don't all look like George Clooney out there?"

"I wish. No, this guy looks closer to Ed Asner. Or that oatmeal spokesman—what's his name?"

"Beats me, I'm strictly a toast kind of woman. But I think I know the type."

Essie let out a long sigh. The kind of shuddering sigh a

body gives out after too many tears. "I want to come home. I'd never say that to Doug—or to Mom and Pop—but I want to come home."

"You are home, Essie. You just don't know it yet."

No, thought Essie, laying her cheek against the chair back, *I don't know it at all.*

Chapter 5

The Box Marked "Those"

Essie had barely caught her emotional balance when the phone rang again.

"Essie. Hi there, it's Dahlia. Dahlia Mannington. Glad to catch you at home. Is now a good time?"

A good time? That might take a six-month delay. "Now's fine. Josh hasn't been feeling well, but he's down for his nap. What can I do for you?"

"Well, you've had Stanton in your class for a few weeks now. I make it a point to get together with all Stanton's teachers early in the year. You know, a bit of a 'get to know each other' visit."

Wow, thought Essie, *this is one thorough woman.* She'd had parents like that at Pembrook High, but never ones who extended such thinking clear into Sunday school. Of course, the parents who make such heroic attempts at parent-teacher cooperation were almost never the ones who needed it. The parents of teens who terrorized classmates on the bus, or deliberately hit kids' heads in dodgeball, those parents would never offer to meet. Many times they often refused to meet, certain their splendid offspring could never do wrong.

Almost all the time. Occasionally, a clever, manipulative child had intensely cooperative parents. It was usually then that Essie discovered the thin line between "intensely cooperative" and "cleverly manipulative." The very thin line indeed.

"Essie?"

"I'm sorry. I'm just so surprised at your...commitment... to Sunday school. It's nice, actually." She really almost meant it. "Sure, I'd love to meet. Stanton's quite a boy."

If a mom could beam over a telephone line, Essie thought she could hear it right through the wires. "He is, isn't he? Boys can be such a handful as infants, but Stanton's turned out to be such a joy to us."

On impulse, Essie asked, "Did Stanton get a lot of ear infections when he was a baby?"

Dahlia groaned. "Is that what Joshua is facing? Oh, Stanton had dozens. I ended up seeing three specialists, all to no avail. Ears will do what ears will do, evidently. Even did the tubes, but they popped out—twice." Her voice changed as she suddenly caught the motivation for Essie's question. "How many so far?"

"Just one so far, but it's in both ears. His doctor tells me it won't be his last, though. He actually said I should be pleased he didn't get his first one until he was this old."

"How old is your son again?"

"Six months."

"Six months and this is your first infection? Oh, I'd have to say I'd agree. I think Stanton had been through at least two by then. Maybe even three."

Now it was Essie's turn to groan. "I want to feel lucky, really I do."

"By the fifth infection, you won't even flinch. I guarantee it."

Fifth?

"And if you have to do the tubes, I know a fabulous specialist."

Of that, Essie had no doubt.

"Well," continued Dahlia, "I'm glad you're amenable to a meeting. How does ten-thirty Thursday suit your schedule? I'll have Carmen whip us up some sweet rolls."

Essie could guess who Carmen was, and how much work might be involved in "just whipping up" some sweet rolls that met Dahlia's standards.

"I'd love to come. Ten-thirty is perfect—it means Josh will conk out in his stroller for most of the meeting."

"Splendid." Dahlia gave Essie the address, even though Essie had a class list with all kinds of contact information. Essie took it down, mostly to be polite. Sure enough, it was in one of the spiffiest sections of town.

Essie was just talking herself out of a case of nerves when Dahlia added, "I've got a few papers I was hoping you could read before we meet. You don't happen to have a fax machine at home, do you?"

"Uh, no." Fax machine? Essie was glad they'd managed to pay for Internet service. Forget about a fax machine. Then again, Doug did work in computers and Dahlia knew that, so maybe it wasn't such a stretch for some.

"Do you think I could fax it to your husband, or your brother, and have them give it to you?"

Obviously, Dahlia wanted Essie to do her homework before they met. On a quick analysis, Essie decided Doug was the better candidate, and she rattled off Doug's office fax number. "I'll just call Doug after I hang up with you and tell him to expect something."

"Marvelous." A cascade of Spanish erupted in the background and Dahlia let out an exasperated sigh. "*Uno minuto,* Carmen. Sorry, but I'd best get going. See you Thursday."

Doug chuckled when Essie called him to alert him to the incoming fax.

He was laughing out loud when he delivered the seventeen-page document into her hands that night. Seventeen pages.

Essie pulled off the cover sheet expecting to find half a dozen articles on the proper spiritual education of second-grade boys. What she found couldn't have surprised her more.

In her hands was an extensive analysis of Stanton Mannington's spiritual strengths and weaknesses. Dahlia had actually taken one of those books with tests to help someone discover their "spiritual gifts"—things like hospitality, wisdom, leadership, prophecy—and filled it out for Stanton. There were no less than ten pages of test scores, four pages of commentary and three pages of Dahlia's recommendations for Stanton's areas of potential ministry.

All this for a seven-year-old boy.

Maybe "thorough" wasn't quite the word to describe Dahlia Mannington.

Mouth open, Essie stared at Doug. He looked as baffled and amused as she felt. "That lady tied up my fax machine for eleven minutes. Next time tell her I'll swing by on my way home." He pointed at the packet. "What in the world is that thing, anyway?"

"Test results. Dahlia Mannington filled out one of those spiritual gifts tests for Stanton. Then she interpreted the results. Extensively. It's a what-you're-good-at, where-you'd-do-well kind of thing. For *adults.*"

Doug looked skeptical. "Like those tests we used to take our senior year in high school? To tell us what to major in?"

"Same principle, just applied to the different types of spiritual gifts Paul mentions in the Bible. Someone took the idea of Paul's that each of us is wired by God for different types of service, and applied the idea to those school tests." Essie narrowed her eyes. "It's fascinating, actually." She fluttered the papers. "But this is just crazy." She fanned through the thick, official-looking packet again. "Look at this—can you believe she did this?"

Doug smirked. "Somehow I think Mark-o has a thick file of paperwork on each of the Mannington children. Probably the parents, too." He parked his briefcase in its designated spot by the front-door umbrella stand and tossed his keys onto the hall table. "I admit, it's weird, but still, when is the last time you met someone who took their child's spirituality so seriously?"

"'So seriously'?" Essie cocked an eyebrow. "I think this qualifies as too seriously. Stanton's only seven. How's anyone supposed to have any idea what his spiritual gifts are? Why does anyone even need to know? I'm sorry, but this qualifies as wa-a-ay over the top."

Doug crossed his arms over his chest and laughed. "This, from the woman who spent the last year groaning to me about parents who didn't care enough, who wouldn't get involved, or didn't think track and field ranked anywhere near football in importance. Now you've got yourself a parent who pays a boatload of attention and you're griping?"

He was teasing her, she knew it, but it still got under her skin. "This is overboard, Douglas Walker, and you know it. I can spot this kind of parent a mile off, and it's never good. I'm going to have Dahlia Mannington and her spiritual recommendations breathing down my neck and I'm not happy about it."

"Well, I was wondering if she'd pull something like that." As they sat in his office the next morning, Mark-o's reaction told Essie that this was not at all out of character for Dahlia Mannington. With a wince, Essie remembered that it was Dahlia who had "commissioned" the Ph.D. student to write a simple Sunday school drama. Simple, it seemed, was not in Dahlia's vocabulary.

Essie shot her brother a sidelong look. "You knew she would do this. She's done this before. Mark Andrew Taylor, you knew exactly what you were letting me in for. Shame on you, duping your little sister."

"Hey, you're the one who told me you wanted to learn about raising boys. I distinctly remember you saying during some dinner at Mom and Pop's that you knew enough about teenagers, but needed to figure out how little boys worked. That's a wide-open door in my book. I just figured God was being obvious."

Essie leveled a look at her brother that she hoped told him such a story wasn't working. Understanding little boys was one thing. Corralling them into higher levels of spiritual development without major bloodshed—well, that was quite another. "You knew about Dahlia."

He acquiesced. "Okay, I knew Dahlia was a handful. But I also knew Cece Covington was in there, too, and you two have seemed to hit it off."

Essie couldn't argue with that. She and Cece had met for coffee twice since that first committee meeting. Every minute of happy grapefruit-spoon quiet proclaimed that Cece was a mom who knew her stuff. Plus, it was just plain fun to be with someone who declared for certain that children aren't in diapers forever and they do actually sleep through the night eventually. "Still...Mark-o, Dahlia's one of those. You know how I hate them. Next thing she'll be telling me I can only use recycled drawing paper or organic crayons. Soon, I'll be getting magazine articles in the mail, and then it will be e-mails with links to Web sites helping me to teach The Lord's Prayer in Latin to grade-schoolers." She was on a roll now, imagining all kinds of havoc Dahlia Mannington and her kind could wreak in her classroom. "She's one of those, Mark-o, and you did this to me!"

To her surprise, this got his back up. She'd gone too far— she knew it the minute he set down his coffee mug with a loud clank. "I think, Esther—" and it was never good when he called her Esther "—that you ought to give Dahlia half a chance before you stick her in some box marked 'those' and write her off as nothing but a nuisance."

Mark-o had always had the ability to halt one of her tirades in a single sentence.

"If one quarter of the people in this church cared half as much as Dahlia and Arthur do about spiritual growth," he continued, lowering his voice again, "Bayside would be an astounding place. Sure, Dahlia's a bit of a pain, but I tell you, Essie, we're all a bit of a pain. If I had a dozen more like her there'd be no telling how much we could do here. No telling. Don't label her. It's not fair."

Since when was life fair?

Chapter 6

Play to the Strengths

Essie changed her own clothes twice, and Josh's three times, before declaring herself ready for the Manningtons'. For all its exclusivity, the area wasn't hard to get to—Essie was still surprised at how easy it was to navigate San Francisco. Most of her home state couldn't be called pedestrian-friendly— a car was essential to one's very existence. She'd been reluctant to take only one car to San Francisco, but everyone's insistence that she would rarely need it finally won out. Even encumbered by baby, stroller and diaper bag, it was still unbelievably easy to get around—except for pushing the stroller up all those hills.

Dahlia's house was on the ritzy side of town, away from the T-shirt shops and silkware stands of the tourism center. Here, tourism rarely crept in to spoil the carefully crafted atmosphere. Each house looked like its own perfectly composed watercolor painting. Charming little gates and artistic walls tucked each family into its tiny, manicured kingdom. No one had a mere yard and house here—no, here it was all "landscaping" and "architecture."

Essie maneuvered Josh's stroller up the small, curving walkway, then took a deep breath and pressed the doorbell. A dignified chime echoed from inside the artfully carved door. Essie checked her own outfit and made sure Josh hadn't repeated his favorite trick of removing his socks. After a short pause, the locks began to rattle and a small woman in a blue dress pulled the massive door open.

"Hello," Essie blurted out, her voice revealing more tension than she would have liked. "I'm here to see Mrs. Mannington. I'm Esther Walker."

The woman produced a rehearsed smile and reached down to help hoist the stroller over the threshold. "She's expecting you. I'll show you to the sunroom."

The sunroom. Uh-oh, that sounded far too spiffy. Maybe she should have worn a skirt or something. Or a twinset. She should probably have gone out and gotten a twinset.

Now wait a minute, you hate twinsets. Essie gave herself a little pep talk as she went through the rigors of detaching Josh's carrier from the stroller mechanism, removing his sweater and all the other details involved in transporting a now sleeping Josh into the sunroom.

This is a parent, Essie, plain and simple. You've gone into battle with football dads who can't understand why their son isn't captain of the track team as well as starting quarterback, you've dealt with schedule-crazed moms who want you to excuse their little darling from practice so she can get the only open manicure appointment; you've dealt with far worse with far more at stake. Don't tense up now. You're going to spend twenty minutes listening to every good and perfect character trait of Stanton Mannington, eat some free pastries, drink some decent coffee and nod a lot. That's all you have to do.

As she walked through the well-appointed house, devoid of undone laundry, strewn toys, or any other signs of juvenile life, Essie couldn't shake the feeling that this wouldn't be that simple at all.

"Oh, Essie, I thought that'd be you. Did you have any trouble getting here?" Dahlia rose elegantly from her wrought-iron bistro chair and reached out a hand to take Josh's carrier.

"Not at all. I'm still getting used to how easy it is to get around here."

"And your little one is out cold, just like you said." She smiled warmly down at Josh, touching a little green sock with a tender hand. "I miss the socks most of all. The tiny little socks in such fabulous colors. He's darling." She settled the carrier into a chair placed beside the table—just for the purpose of holding Josh, Essie suspected. The woman never missed a detail. "Now, Pastor Mark told me you drink coffee, so I had Carmen brew up some decaf because I remembered you're still nursing. Carmen makes fabulous coffee—even decaf—so drink the whole pot if you like." Dahlia motioned for Essie to take a seat in the other chair. The table was set like something out of a department store display—fresh flowers, starched napkins, rattan place mats, gorgeous china.

On cue, Carmen reappeared, bearing a tray of goodies. The scent of the sweet rolls could have made a grown man salivate, much less a mom who'd quickly downed a plastic bowl of wheat flakes an hour ago. A set of twin miniature coffee carafes took their place at the table—one with the universally recognized orange "decaf" marking, only this one was an elegant beaded clip rather than a plastic dot. Dahlia's idea of "just whip something up" was a lot different than most of the world's standards. Well, most of Essie's world, anyway.

"Wow," Essie commented. "This looks great."

"Carmen knows her way around the kitchen, that's for sure." Dahlia tossed Carmen an efficient nod. *"Gracias."* She poured herself coffee and whipped out the familiar Montblanc pen and leather notepad.

"Yes," added Essie, looking up at Carmen. "Thank you."

"So, *how's* the class?" Her voice had the musical tone of someone who was being polite, but taking mental notes. Lots of them.

"They're a…spirited lot, that's for sure. It's not hard to see where the nickname came from."

That got a look from Dahlia. "I've never liked the nickname myself. I believe children rise to the expectations you set for them. Call them doom, you'll get doom. I've never been asked to teach the class myself, but I can't imagine that all that energy can't be channeled with the right techniques."

Essie had heard some version of that speech dozens of times in her teaching career. The women's-magazine-TV-talk-show lingo of the enlightened parent. The parent who didn't believe in "C"s. Who felt that defiant children simply "weren't being challenged." The kind of mom who would never let their child mix cookie dough with their fingers or roll down a hill that might cause grass stains, but signed them up for French lessons when they were five. The parents who inserted their children—whatever their shape—into neat, successful, boxes chock-full of brilliant potential.

"Seven-year-old boys are bundles of energy." It was a poor response, but it was all Essie could think of to say. Last week Stanton had pushed up the tip of his nose with his finger and made pig sounds through the entire reading of the Bible story. She wasn't sure "the proper channel" had anything to do with that kind of behavior.

"Well, Stanton certainly is high-spirited."

Ah, there it was. That phrase. "High-spirited" was one of Essie's favorite euphemisms. Kids weren't bouncy or hyper or fidgety anymore, they were "high-spirited." As if the inability to sit still for thirty seconds was an early symptom of visionary thinking.

"I hope you're not finding him too challenging." There was an edge to Dahlia's voice. Not quite a challenge, but not quite an actual question, either.

Essie had long since learned that such a remark was a cue to gush about a child's outstanding class behavior. Anything else would be viewed as a deficiency in one's teaching skills. In her high school career, this remark—or anything close to it—was a parental "weather balloon." Something lofted by a parent to see if Essie was up to the challenge of their brilliant but slightly misunderstood progeny. Evidently, it was no different with the younger set.

Taking a sip of coffee, Essie did what was expected. She launched an enthusiastic rendition of Stanton's admirable qualities, concluding with, "Those papers you sent over didn't surprise me one bit." Okay, not exactly the truth—it floored her that Dahlia'd done what she did—but it was optimistic. Sort of.

They played this verbal game for the next twenty minutes, taking turns identifying Stanton's strengths and talents. Here and there each of them cited the lengthy paper, using the data as the springboard to a compliment. It was a taxing, almost choreographed conversation. Essie was used to it, but mostly involving the complexities and large-scale behaviors of teenagers. Trying to make the case for Stanton's often-violent obsession with being first in line as a precursor to leadership skills, well, that took a little more verbal agility. It was always a precarious knife edge on which to balance a conversation; when to be direct, when to hint at a problem, when to tell the parent what they wanted to hear. Essie was exhausted by the end of her third cup of admittedly excellent decaf. *Come on, Josh, wake up and give me a diaper change to catch my breath here.*

"What does the class need, in your opinion?"

Sedatives, Essie thought before she could stop it. Instead, she attempted a braver course. "In all honesty," Essie ventured, "another set of hands would make things much easier."

Dahlia didn't even recognize the veiled request for her time. "Well, yes, of course," she said, as though it were obvious that it should be someone's—but clearly someone else's—job to take care of such details. "It's church policy to have two teachers. I'm sorry your co-teacher moved on such short notice and we've not yet found a replacement. I was thinking, though, more in the way of equipment, materials, that sort of thing." In other words, what can I buy you? Because I have no intention of coming in there and helping you myself. Nope, no surprises here. "I am very busy with coordinating the Celebration, of course, but I do want to do my part in helping out the class."

No, you don't, thought Essie, *you want me to give you an out.* "I know it's a lot to ask, but do you think Carmen could whip up some of these goodies for the Harvest of Witnesses event in a few weeks?"

Bingo. She'd hit the target. Dahlia fairly beamed. "Why,

of course. Something a tad more nutritious, of course, but goodies nonetheless."

"That'd be great. And I know we need someone to make up little baskets—nothing too girly, but still creative—for the class to use that day." The children had an event where they went around the church "harvesting" goodies and information about great figures of the church. A few years ago, at Mark-o's suggestion, a group of moms had created this event—a combination of scavenger hunting and gift-giving on the first day of November. It had become one of the things the church was known for, one of those things that drew new families to the church. Essie had always considered it one of the coolest things her pastor brother had ever done. "Can you think of someone who's got those kind of talents?"

Dahlia's pen bobbed again. "Oh, I've just the person. Vicki Faber—Alex's new stepmother? She has a decorating business. She's redone the house beautifully. I'm sure she's got someone who could whip together just what you need."

Alex Faber's stepmother. Icky Vicki. Vicki and Alex's dad had been one of the class's invisible sets of parents. Alex's older sister Sharon—the one who'd come up with the "Icky Vicki" moniker—always collected Alex from class.

"Here're her numbers, why don't you ring her up?" Dahlia said, handing her a thick card with the heading "From the desk of Dahlia H. Mannington" across the top. Pouring more coffee, her voice took on an "I don't mean to be unkind" tone. "She is a bit younger than you, but I do think you might enjoy getting to know each other."

I'll just bet she's "a bit" younger than me, Essie's thoughts replied. *And probably looks like she walked off the set of* Baywatch. *What am I doing with these people?*

"I think Vicki has had difficulty adjusting to her new role. It was a nasty divorce, really. Vicki's had her hands full trying to smooth things over. I imagine she'd welcome a little project to do for the class— I'm sure she knows loads of designers who could whip up a dozen or so perfectly manly baskets. I'd try the cell phone number first—Vicki is out and about most of the time."

"Thanks, I'll call her."

Dahlia closed her organizer and notepad. Again on perfect cue, Carmen appeared in the French doors with a small white bakery box. "I had Carmen pack up a few of these rolls for you to take home. They're far too good for me to keep in the house without gaining a dozen pounds, and I wonder if that husband of yours can help finish them off?"

Dahlia Mannington did think of everything.

"Oh, Doug will be more than happy to have these. That's really nice of you." And, believe it or not, she meant it.

Chapter 7

And on Some Sunday Afternoons...

"I'd never eat fish for lunch. Yuck." Decker made a face as the Doom Room pondered the Bible story of the loaves and the fishes.

"Not even fish sticks?" Essie ventured. She fondly remembered the special days of fish stick and French fry frozen dinners on folding trays in front of the television. They were one of the great treats of childhood to her. She and Mark-o would usually have a competition of sorts as to who could glob more ketchup on a fish stick. Essie usually won.

"Fish sticks are gross," Decker replied. "Besides, Mom says they're fattening. She makes me eat Sam Man—you know, the pink fish—every Tuesday for dinner, but I hide it in my napkin and give it to Sparky. What's 'brain food' anyway? I'm not eating that Sam Man's brains, am I?"

Essie guessed that either Decker's dog or cat was eating very well on Tuesdays lately. Salmon versus fish sticks. It sounded like a bad country song—

I'm just a fish stick gal,
Caught in a salmon fillet world…

"Salmon, Decker, is a fish, you're right. But, no, it's not brains. It's good for your brain like lots of other kinds of protein—those are the types of foods that give your brain the energy it needs to do its job."

"I think better eating cookies," Dexter proclaimed, clearly unswayed.

Essie dragged the discussion back to the topic at hand. "Well, then, it's a good thing you've all had a cookie or two, because we have lots of thinking to do today." She clasped her hands. "Now, we've already read the story about this boy and how he brought his bread and fish to Jesus." Decker opened his mouth, presumably to start up again about the grossness of fish for lunch, but Essie held up a silencing finger. "Almost everyone's dad was a fisherman there, so bread and fish would have been like…like peanut butter and jelly to us. Everybody ate it."

"I'm yullergic to peanut products," pronounced Peter with a resigned voice. Just as Essie knew he would. Peter, it seemed, was "yullergic" to just about everything. Some days all Peter could add to a conversation was a list of relevant items to which he was allergic. On those days he would sigh, speak without enthusiasm and generally look as if the entire world was gunning for his immune system. How he reconciled such an outlook with his love of bugs and other slimy creatures, she couldn't really say. An image of Peter, foraging under a rock with latex gloves on, flashed uninvited in her brain. *Focus, Essie, focus.*

"Okay," she continued, "what he ate isn't really the point here. The point is that he gave what he had for Jesus to use, even though it didn't seem like much at the time. "David," Essie said, turning to Cece's son in an attempt to get things on the right track, "do you think five loaves and two fishes is enough to feed thousands of people?"

David scrunched up his forehead in thought. "You'd have to break it into really tiny pieces."

Essie had to laugh at that one. "Even then, what that boy had just wasn't enough to go around. Remember, it said that there were baskets of leftovers even after everyone had eaten. That's why it was a miracle. Jesus took that food and made it able to do something very special. Something only God could make happen." She looked around the room, trying to catch each boy's eyes. "Sometimes the stuff we have to do in life feels like more than we can handle. Like we don't have what it will take to do what needs to be done. Does anyone have an example?"

Justin's arm shot in the air. "My baby sister. Sometimes she cries so much, I think I'm gonna explode."

Essie thought about Josh's most recent teething episode and could only nod in sympathy. "Babies are a handful, aren't they?"

"I heard Mom telling Dad she thought she'd never, ever get to sleep again. When I told Dad we ought to make baby Megan sleep in the garage, he told me not to say that in front of Mom, but he was smiling when he said it, so I know he thinks we oughta try it."

Essie could only imagine.

"My dad has a new job this month, and it's making him really nervous," offered Steven Bendenfogle. "He gets grumpy a lot. And sometimes he doesn't come home till way after my bedtime. And he brings home lots of homework, besides. I think he feels like it's too hard."

"New jobs feel too hard lots of times. You could really help cheer him up, Steven."

"I don't know." Steven shook his head. "He's really grumpy some nights."

"Well, now you've got something that feels too hard now, too, don't you? It feels like it may be too hard to cheer up someone who's really grumpy, doesn't it? That'll take Jesus' help, too."

Steven thought about that for a while, but then nodded.

"It'd be too hard," said Stanton loudly, "to beat Jesus in a jumping contest, 'cuz He's God and He's got superpowers and stuff. He'd beat you at anything!"

Well now, superpower was an odd definition of deity, but it must have rung true to the average eight-year-old, because the other boys all immediately agreed. Instantly, boys began shouting examples such as "I bet He could spit a watermelon seed around the world," or "He could kick a soccer ball through a brick wall," and even several instances of X-ray vision.

"Or," interjected Essie in a voice loud enough to cut through the din, "transform one little boy's lunch into enough food to feed thousands of hungry people."

Everyone had to think about that for a moment. Then, very quietly, Stanton said, "Yeah. Cool."

Was it okay to think of Jesus' miracles as superpowers? She hoped God didn't mind a little creativity, because clearly Jesus just went up a couple of notches in the "cool" department for a few of these boys. And that was the whole point, wasn't it?

"Superpowers aren't real," she said, because she felt it ought to be said. "But Jesus, and the things He can do with us when we believe in Him, those are real. And yeah, Stanton, they are cool. The older you get, the more you believe, the cooler it gets." Nods and a few amazed faces.

Zing. It sunk in. Score one for the crazy mom from New Jersey.

And the very cool God who brought her here.

As she put away the workbooks after class, Essie pondered how overwhelmed she had felt about this "Doom Room" class. Hadn't she felt like it was way too much to handle?

Suddenly, it wasn't exactly clear who was teaching whom. Cool.

Oh, it was cool all right, right up until Mark-o's phone call that evening.

"Congratulations, Essie, you made it four whole weeks before the first call. That may be a record."

Essie put down the stain stick she was using to try and get the Baby Tylenol stains out of a batch of Josh's onesies. "What?"

"I was just congratulating you on going a full four weeks before some parent found something to gripe about it. That's a pretty neat trick in my book."

Essie sunk to the couch, deflated even before she heard the details. "Yippee. What is it?"

"Do you want the pastor version, or the brother version?"

Essie found the sheer fact that he had versions to be mildly annoying. "Which one's more amusing? I gather this isn't exactly good news."

"Well, I admit to some level of bias, but I think the brother version has a bit more humor to it."

"Ooo, I can hardly wait. Okay, let's hear it."

"Steven Bendenfogle's mom is concerned that her son now accredits our Lord and Savior with the powers of X-ray vision." He was laughing when he said it.

"That's the brother version? And no, I did not say that Jesus has X-ray vision. As a matter of fact, I went out of my way to point out just the opposite."

"I believe you, relax. How did the subject of X-ray vision come up, anyhow?"

Essie wanted to hold her head in her hands. Here she'd been spending the afternoon in a glowing joy about how the kids had really grasped the truth of miracles, and it was all coming undone in the space of one disgruntled mother's phone call. "We were talking about the miracle of the loaves and fishes. They were really getting into it—you know, trying to figure out how that little bit of food fed all those people. We talked about God's power, and what miracles are. They saw Jesus' power as a sort of superpower. I think that's a pretty good grasp for kids of that age. Oh, Mark-o, you should have seen their faces. They began to think of Jesus as cool. As someone to help them when they felt overwhelmed. It was great. And now this. I could just scream."

"Look, Essie, don't get worked up about this. You need to remember that we're working on thirdhand information here, with one of those hands being eight years old. Things are bound to get twisted. You can't let it get to you."

"Then why am I suddenly envisioning 'This session may be recorded for quality control purposes'? She doesn't really think I told them Jesus has X-ray vision, does she? It's…she can't…"

"It's no big deal. Actually, I think it's rather funny."

"You would, but…"

"What it does tell me, is that you have these kids thinking. Engaged. Working through ideas in their own terms. Surely the educator in you can see what a good thing that is. I'd much rather have this than a group of kids who can recite the books of the Bible in bored voices."

"But…"

"It's an imperfect system. We're imperfect teachers. You're not going to get perfect scores on this, Essie, ever. You're going to miss the target lots of times. But it seems to me you're going to hit the mark lots more times, and in the end these kids will be the better for it. Will you believe me if I tell you that this phone call just reinforces for me that I got the right person for the job?"

"Oh, yeah? Then why'd you call me to tell me Mrs. Bendenfogle believes I'm bordering on blasphemy? Why didn't you just keep your satisfaction to yourself?"

Mark-o's reply was a frustrated groan. "Be-cause, Mrs. Ex-treme Drama, I need you to tell Steven Jesus doesn't have X-ray vision so he can go home and put his mother's mind at ease next week."

"I already told Steven Bendenfogle that superpowers aren't real."

"Then be more specific. Something along the lines of 'Steven, Jesus does not have X-ray vision' ought to do just fine."

"Mark-o…"

"One kid got his information twisted. Now stop getting all worked up, simply set him straight and get on with it, no matter how ridiculous it seems. You missed one shot, Essie, not the whole track meet. And it's not a competition. Look, if you knew how many calls like this I get a week, you'd see this for the minor detail it is. I get notes about how I don't comb my hair, or how I don't use the Bible translation they like, how the organ's too loud or the praise band isn't loud enough, or that we should be using white bread instead of wheat bread for communion—all kinds of tiny grievances."

Essie moaned. "How do you stand it?"

"I try to remember that if they care enough to make a comment, then I'm at least getting them to care at all. In my business, opinion isn't the enemy, apathy is." He paused for a moment before adding on a sigh, "And some Sunday afternoons, you hit the golf ball really, really hard."

"Okay. Young Master Bendenfogle will get his X-ray vision thing straightened next week, count on it."

"I knew I could. And promise me you're not going to get all worked up about this. It's one detail in a whole stack of successes. Got it?"

Essie sighed. "Got it. Hey, wait a minute! Doesn't seeing into our hearts, seeing past our actions into our intentions count as a spiritual sort of X-ray vision?"

The Pastor Taylor tone came back into his voice. "Essie…"

"Okay, okay, point taken. I'll be crystal clear next week. By the way, what did Dr. Einhart say about Pop's latest blood work?"

"The appointment got moved to this week. I…uh… meant to talk to you about that."

In Mark-o's world, "I meant to talk to you about that" translated directly to "I need you to take care of this for me." Esther didn't even have to guess what was coming next.

"The appointment was moved to this week on Wednesday at eleven o'clock, and I had to book a counseling session for that time. You can take Pop, can't you?"

Essie fisted her hands around an unsuspecting bath towel. "We agreed to split these. I've done the last two. I've got something going on Wednesday."

The silence on the other end of the phone spoke volumes about how much Mark-o thought Essie might actually "have going." He didn't even have to say "can't you move it?" His pause said it for him.

She beat him to the punch. "And no, I don't want to move it. It's an appointment, by the way, that I've had to bail on twice because you called me to pick up your end with Pop." She stood up off the couch, pacing the room now, her agitation growing. "You keep saying 'it's just this once,' but it never is. Both of us need to deal with this, whether you're off saving the world or not."

"I thought you came out here to help with Pop."

"Hold on there. I came out here to help, not to take over so you could get back to your oh-so-busy life. I know you did lots of this before, and I know you're an important man, but don't go dumping all of this in my lap just because I showed up on the West Coast."

"So you want me to tell this woman that I have to put off her counseling session—with a depressed daughter who has resisted counseling for six months and has finally relented—because I have to drive my Pop for a checkup?"

Oh, she hated it when Mark-o played the emergency card. Yes, lots of what he did was urgent, but it was always urgent. She hated how he made her life feel mundane and insignificant. How he made her feel selfish for wanting to keep a much-needed lunch with Cece. She'd already had to cancel twice on Cece in order to cover for him. He was a lifeline to lots of people, but did that mean she had to go without her own lifelines? "I want," she said slowly, "for you not to have said 'yes' in the first place. To have found another time because you had a prior commitment. What about Peggy? Can't she help you out?"

"Peggy's got a sales meeting in L.A. for two days. I just

thought…" His voice was so annoyed that he didn't even finish the sentence.

"I know exactly what you 'just thought.' It starts with 'since you're not working anymore and babies are so marvelously portable.' Taking Pop to the doctor's is a pain, but when will you to realize it's just as much a pain for me as it is for you?"

His silence told her he didn't exactly see it that way. After a long pause he said, "So will you do it or not?"

Essie rolled her eyes in exasperation. "Were you listening *at all?*"

"Look, Essie, I just need you to cover for me…"

"Don't you dare say 'just this once'!" she yelled into the phone. Loudly enough, unfortunately, to wake up Josh, who was napping in the swing beside her. "Oh, great. Thanks, Mark-o, this is really how I wanted to end my afternoon." Josh wailed, angry at having had his late afternoon nap cut short. "I'll talk to you at adults' Bible study if I see you. I've got to go take care of Josh." With a growl, she stabbed her finger onto the off button of the cordless phone.

Chapter 8

The Downpour of Demands

The clock seemed to delight in clicking over another digit to the brutal hour of 1:30 a.m. Essie let out a sigh as she dropped her bathrobe to the floor and climbed back into bed. Doug, to her surprise, was wide-awake.

"Josh nod off finally?" His voice sounded as tired as she felt.

"We can only hope. I think I'm gonna die if he's working on another ear infection. I finally gave him some Tylenol, and he seemed to calm down, so it's either his ears or his teeth keeping him up."

"Or both." He tried to make it a joke, but didn't quite pull it off.

"Oh, no you don't. I don't even want to think about that." She let her head hit the splendid softness of the pillow, felt the warmth of Doug beside her as she drew up the covers. "He woke up too early from his nap because of dear Pastor Mark-o—" she gave the words a nasty edge "—and he's tired and cranky. The lady in the church nursery said he fussed most of the evening. I don't know how she can stay so calm when those babies get like that."

"Easy," yawned Doug, pulling her into the curve of one arm, "she gets a full night's sleep."

Essie managed a weak chuckle and laid her head on his shoulder. Getting back into bed felt so good. Who knew a woman could become so enamored with the simple act of getting under the covers?

A mother of a cranky six-month-old, that's who.

Suddenly, she realized Doug hadn't managed his usual feat of falling right back to sleep even with a howling baby in the next room. She turned her face to him. "What are you doing up, anyway?"

"Oh, I don't know, I couldn't get back to sleep." He rearranged the pillow under his head.

"Work?" she ventured. She ran a hand down his arm and realized how tense he was.

"It's been a rough couple of days. We're launching a new upgrade this week. I don't like how it's going. These guys don't do nearly the same level of pre-testing that we used to do in New Jersey. I'm nervous about how things will go."

New products or upgrade launches always meant long hours for the first couple of weeks. Essie usually knew about them far in advance, and often planned for Doug to be gone a lot and be rather cranky. How had this one caught her by surprise?

"Big upgrade or little?"

Doug groaned. "Big. And now we have to do it with three less people. I can't believe they let tech support people go before an upgrade. That's about the dumbest thing you can do."

They'd had layoffs at work? She really was clueless. Sighing, Essie noted that she could now add "guilt-laden" to her current state of being tired, bloated and irritated with her relatives. "Did you tell me they laid off staff recently?"

"Two weeks ago. I mentioned it at dinner." He turned to look at her. "You know, dinner? That thing we used to eat in peace and quiet? Sitting down?"

Dinner had been anything but quiet and seated in the last couple of weeks. Josh had adopted early evening as his new time to fuss, and they spent most dinners tag-teaming it between eating and holding a bawling Josh. Conversation had grown near-impossible, but that was still no excuse for her missing such a major bit of news. "I'm sorry. I swear, I'm not sure I have any brain cells left at the end of the day anymore."

"Get in line." His voice was weary. "This week'll be long days, Es."

She was again reminded of the heavy load Doug was carrying. He deserved to come home to a peaceful, restful home, not a wife at her wits' end squabbling with her brother or griping about her impossible parents. Or complaining about Sunday school parents. It was like everyone needed something from her, and deserved to get it, only there didn't seem to be enough of her to go around. Some part of her brain thought that if she just got seven hours of uninterrupted sleep, even once, that she'd find the resources to meet all those demands. Another part of her insisted that such a notion was wishful thinking—the pulls on her weren't going anywhere anytime soon, not even if she got a dozen hours of uninterrupted sleep. No, this downpour of demands was Essie's new world.

And this week she'd be facing that world alone.

"I'm sorry," was all she could think of to say, which felt so far from adequate. "Don't worry about Josh and me—well, Josh and me and dumb old Mark-o and Mom and Pop and Jesus' X-ray vision. We'll muddle though. We may even surprise you with a new tooth."

"Whoopee." It had all the enthusiasm of a funeral march.

Essie ran a hand over his stubbly chin. "You won't think so poorly of teeth when you're gumming your puree in the nursing home. You'll be lucky if you can convince Josh to come feed you."

"Oh, let him feed me. Then I can spit my pears back at him in retaliation for all the pears he's going to spit at me soon."

"Yeah. Josh, eating food. That'll be amazing, won't it?"

"No, that'll be messy. Hey, I bet I can get you a hazardous materials suit from the office. Head-to-toe protection—right down to the molecular level."

"And have Josh think he's being fed by one of the bad guys in *E. T.?* No way. Momma's going to brave those pears unarmed."

"Well, then, do it this week so I'm not around to get caught in the cross fire." She knew he didn't mean it. After a moment he said softly, "You won't will you? Start him when I'm not around?"

She snuggled into him, loving his devotion to fatherhood right down to the airborne pears. "Never." She heard him exhale.

Closing her eyes, Essie sent a plea heavenward. *If my men can sleep until morning, Lord, we may just make it.*

Come Wednesday, Essie didn't know whether to pride herself or smack herself for the fact that she ended up tak-

ing Pop to the doctor's office. When Cece had called and
asked if she was free for dinner instead of lunch because Mr.
Covington had been called out of town, Essie could only
surrender to the tsunami that had become her schedule. In
truth, she relished the thought of having another adult to
pass off Josh to during dinner, even if it meant subjecting
Cece to a wildly grumpy Josh. Somehow Essie got the sense
that Cece would be unfazed, no matter how bad Josh got.

Even with all of that, Essie thought twice before calling
Mark-o to say she could pull doctor-transport duty. After
all, just because God had cleared her schedule and shown
her a better plan didn't mean Mark-o got off the hook.
Right? Maybe. As far as Essie was concerned, it was a tough
call between whether God was providing or Essie was caving. Honestly, she'd stood in the kitchen debating the issue
with Josh—or rather, debating the issue out loud with herself while Josh "supervised"—for twenty whole minutes before dialing Mark-o's office.

She made him promise, promise, promise to take the next
appointment. Maybe God was providing and Essie was
merely "setting healthy boundaries." She'd received such
advice in one of those parenting books. Yes, it felt much better to look at it that way.

"Glad to see you're not stuffing that boy with silverware anymore, Esther." Her father blew out a stream of
air after the twenty-two minute fiasco that was getting Pop
out of his town house, down the elevator and into a cab.
It didn't matter that there was a trolley that ran nearly from
his front door to the steps of the doctor's office—evidently
seventeen extra steps were too much hassle. All of her reminding that walking was one of those things Dad was
supposed to be doing proved fruitless. The guy could

gripe a blue streak about the high price of his prescriptions, would drive an extra ten miles to get a better senior discount, but broke his wallet wide to avoid a little public transportation.

"I've got a grapefruit spoon in my diaper bag, and I'm not afraid to use it." She forced a smile into her voice, determined not to let the frustrations of the day get the best of her. "So no complaining, or I'll break out the heavy metal."

"Too cold in this city. Who knew California could get so cold?"

"You moved here first, Pop. I just followed."

"We should have gone to Arizona or something."

"Oh, then you'd just be complaining that it was too hot. Really, Pop, I'm starting to like San Francisco. I think Mom likes it, too."

Her father grumbled. "Not enough to drive through it, that's for sure. I don't know what's gotten into her. We drove that Buick clear across the country and now she can't drive me twelve blocks to the doctor's? Why am I forking over money for car insurance?"

"Maybe that's because you ought to be *walking* the twelve blocks to the doctor's. And driving here—the city traffic and these monster hills—is a whole lot different than tooling around suburban New Jersey."

He shot her a look over his thick glasses. "Don't you go taking her side."

Essie rolled her eyes. "I don't want to be taking anyone's side. I…"

"Will you look at that meter already? I don't knowwhy they don't have a senior discount program in this city… you'd think…"

She'd vowed up, down and sideways not to get into it with Pop, but Essie was helpless against the frustration. "They do, Pop. It's called a bus. If you got a senior card and took it you could ride ten times for what you're paying to take a cab."

Pop banged on the Plexiglas divider with the handle of his cane. "You're not charging us for the baby to ride, are you?"

Essie tried to communicate "I'm so sorry" with her eyes when the driver caught her glance in the rearview mirror.

"What you say?" Essie knew the driver's heavy foreign accent would only make things worse.

"I said," replied her father, speaking in an embarrassingly slow and over-enunciated way as if he were addressing a two-year-old, "you're not charging us for three people, right?" He held up three thick fingers as if visual aids were required to get the point across.

"Three passenger?" The driver looked confused.

"No!" her dad bellowed, who'd already decided he was being cheated. "You can't count the baby. I'm only paying for two passengers, you…"

"Pop…"

"He's not gonna charge me for Josh, I'm not going to…"

"Pop…"

"Three passenger?" The driver was actually looking around the car now, clearly wondering where the invisible passenger was or if he was supposed to be picking someone else up. Essie was making herself promise that Mark-o would take the next dozen appointments. Forget the second graders, it was the senior citizens in her life who were driving her crazy.

"Oh, no, you don't…"

"*Pop!* Look at the meter, Pop. It says 'two passengers.' No one's charging you for Josh. Now will you just calm down and let us get there before you have a heart attack or something?"

Honor your mother and father, so that it may go well with you. Essie was certain that was the verse. If this was "going well," then it was time to pack up and head back to Jersey. Why was she even surprised when Josh started to cry? She wanted to cry herself.

She stared her dad straight in the eye as she reached into her diaper bag and pulled out a grapefruit spoon. He rolled his eyes as she popped it into Josh's mouth and he settled down.

"Next thing I know you'll be handing him steak knives."

There wasn't even a reply for that one. Essie wondered if she'd get arrested for leaving the doctor's office without her dad and telling him he should walk home. That's not technically abandonment, is it? *No really, officer, I'm just setting healthy boundaries. He's supposed to be walking, and when he started talking about steak knives…*

It was hard to tell who was more pleased that they spent the rest of the ride in silence—Essie or the driver. When she noticed Pop had neglected to tip the driver, she doubled back and pressed a five-dollar bill into the man's palm. He mumbled something in an Asian tongue that Essie was sure translated to "Don't you bring that man back into my cab ever again, lady." She'd refused to drive her dad in his car, not only because she was unsure of her own ability to navigate that boat of a car through the San Francisco streets, but because she knew that would open her father up to an endless list of errands he'd want to run with her. A one-hour doctor visit would turn into a four-hour festival of frustration. No, the only way to keep Pop from sucking up every waking moment today was to use a cab and try not to flinch.

She loved him. She loved her Pop and the enormous treasure chest of memories she had stored up over the years. The shoulders for boyfriend breakups, the golden afternoons on the beach, the cold rainy Saturdays endured on track-meet bleachers. She loved him.

She just wanted to strangle him at the moment.

Walking into the doctor's office, watching Pop tense up like he was walking into battle, she knew that feeling wasn't going away anytime soon. Why could he not see this professional, this marvelous doctor God had provided, as an ally in his health, instead of some enemy itching to cart him off to the nursing home? No one wanted Pop to move out. She'd moved clear across the country to help make sure he stayed at home for as many years as possible. Still, he couldn't seem to see that. Her father was a walking ball of defensiveness and irritation.

It went like every other doctor visit. Dr. Einhart, who Essie was sure was related to Josh's homey, friendly Dr. Martin, started out with a hearty, "How's it going, Bob?" Pop would reply with monosyllabic answers fit for name, rank and serial number. Dr. Einhart would ask about diet, and Pop would fudge his answers. Dr. Einhart would ask about exercise, and Pop would out-and-out lie. Dr. Einhart would ask about medications, and Pop would launch into a ten-minute diatribe about the price of drugs and ask for as many sample packets as he could fit into his pockets. Essie stopped counting how many times the phrase "Do you know how much this stuff costs?" entered into the conversation when the tally topped eleven.

"Now, Bob, Karen here is going to take you down the hall to get weighed and measured. We're not taking any blood today—we did all that last time." Dr. Einhart caught Essie's eye. "I want to take a gander at this fine, healthy grandson of yours."

Karen, it seemed, had done this before, because she had an arsenal of replies to Pop's resistance. She was a woman who wouldn't take no for an answer, and before Essie could take a breath she'd ushered Pop out the door and down the hall.

"Are you concerned about his weight?" Essie was sure the doc wanting to see her alone could only mean bad news.

"No." He smiled, picking up Josh with the practiced hands of a grandfather many times over. "It just makes him walk down the hall, and we'll take all the steps we can squeeze out of your ornery old dad."

"He's not telling you the truth about any of it." She blurted out, suddenly trusting this doctor and needing someone to know.

"I know."

"I'm not even sure he's taking his medication."

"I know."

How did he say that so calmly? "Dr. Einhart, we have to do something!"

"No, Esther, we don't. Your father, he's the one who has to do something. And he is still an adult capable of making his own decisions. No, I don't like them any better than you do, and yes, I've done everything I can to convince him that he needs to take ownership of his own health, but the bottom line is that he's the one who needs to make that decision."

Essie didn't know what to say. Why wouldn't this non-stop frustration with her Pop go away? "I want him around for a long time," finally whimpered out of her.

"I know. Let's talk about you for a moment. How are you holding up under all the strain?"

That was about the last thing she expected to hear. "Okay, I guess."

"And your mother? How are things going with her?"

"She's having a little trouble adjusting to city life. I know she's the one who wanted to come out here, and she did fine for a while, but that car accident a few months ago really spooked her and now she won't drive anywhere. Pop's on her about it all the time."

Dr. Einhart chuckled. "Bickering like kindergartners, are they?"

Essie smiled. "Exactly."

"That's good, you know." He tickled Josh as he settled him back into his carrier. "When they stop bickering, that's when you have to worry. Just make sure you don't get caught in the middle. You've got three generations of caregiving going on here, and it's easy to let that get the best of you." He handed Essie a paper bag stuffed with samples of Pop's medications. "This'll keep him happy for a while—your dad does love a good 'freebie.' Keep on him about his meds, find ways to make him walk a few steps—things like not being able to find a closer parking space, seeing a better bargain over on that other shelf, stuff like that. Just keep getting him out."

"But I…"

"Yes, I know it takes hours. Hours you may not have with that little one taking your time. I'm not saying you can solve his problems. Just do the best you can without wearing yourself out."

"I'm already worn out."

Dr. Einhart paused, looking at her with wise eyes. "Then do something about it."

As if it were that simple.

Attack of the Ph.D.

Cece dropped the thick, bound booklet on the table between her and Essie. "Well, there it is."

"There what is?"

"The Bayside Christian Church Celebration of Bible Heroes script."

Essie tried not to choke. She put Josh in his bouncy seat to buy another five minutes of calm while she pulled dinner together. "I think I've read shorter novels. It is always like this?"

"Well, you know, the footnotes do take up a lot of space."

"It has footnotes!?"

Cece crossed her arms. "Send a Ph.D. to do a mom's job and…"

"And *this* happens." Essie picked up the missive. "Oh, come on, someone must realize this is over the top." She thumbed through the huge document. "There's twenty scenes in here."

Cece took the container of salad she had brought out of its paper bag and opened the refrigerator door. "Well, one scene for each class. We've got over 250 children in Sunday school, you know. A big church needs a big program."

"Big, I can see. But this, *this* is epic." Essie grabbed plates and forks, trying not to cringe at the condition of her "casual" dinnerware. She and Cece had met often over the past weeks, but this was the first time Cece had eaten here in her home. Who were they kidding, calling this stuff "dinnerware"? It was one coat of shellac away from a paper plate. And, despite its many claims to unbreakability, she and Doug had managed to chip the majority of the plates. Cece had lovely dinnerware imported from Tuscany. And a kitchen you could actually turn around in, not this closet some real-estate broker had deemed "cozy." She forced her thoughts back to the conversation. "Bayside isn't one of those churches that does nativity scenes with live camels or anything, is it?" Cece, never one to stand on ceremony, began rooting through the kitchen to help set the table.

"They actually tried one year." Cece pulled out a pair of glasses seemingly oblivious to the fact that they didn't match—and went to the freezer for ice. "Well, not camels. I think it was a donkey and some sheep. But, naturally, we had a couple of parents complaining about sanitary and allergy issues, so that put an end to the live animal thing. Tom jokes that if we'd done it another year, we'd have had some parents writing in about animal rights issues or something else. When you involve that many people, there's always something someone can gripe about."

Essie stared at Cece. "Doesn't that bug you? I mean, doesn't it drive you nuts that you can't seem to turn around here without someone getting upset?"

Cece smiled. "Mrs. Bendenfogle, I presume?"

"How'd you know?"

"Getting a complaint from Alice Bendenfogle is a badge of honor around here, Essie. No one's made it though a semester of teaching a Bendenfogle—or coaching a Bendenfogle, or whatevering a Bendenfogle—without somehow getting under Alice's skin." She took the container of salad dressing out of the fridge again and shook it. "Honestly, I'm not sure Alice knows how to communicate outside of complaint mode." She arched her eyebrows playfully. "Okay, so what'd you do?"

Josh started fussing, so Essie picked him up again. "Let me simply start by saying that I am quite sure I never told anyone that Jesus had X-ray vision."

"Oh, the Jesus' miracles as superpowers thing. David just loved that. I thought it was a very creative concept." Josh broke into full-scale wailing, and Cece stretched out her arms to take him while Essie pulled the lasagna out of the oven.

"Thanks," Essie called over her shoulder as she opened the oven door. "However, you seem to be the only person over twelve who gets it."

"I'm going to take that as a compliment, aren't I grumpy little Joshua-boy?" Cece began bouncing around the kitchen, singing, "Joshua Fought the Battle of Jericho" in a sweetly off-key voice.

To Essie's astonishment, Josh stuffed his fist into his mouth and settled down quietly on Cece's shoulder. "Whatever you do, don't stop. I'll feed you standing up if I have to, but keep up that singing. I can't believe he settled down."

"And the walls came a tumblin' down. Don't let her get under your skin, Essie. She does this to everyone. Joshua fought the battle of Jericho…Jericho-o-o-…"

"That's just what Mark-o says."

"Your brother's right. Jericho…Jericho… And he's taken more than his share of shots from Alice, too, so he knows. Mmm, smells great. Just shake that dressing up one more time and put it on the…" Josh geared up to wail again so she sang the rest of her sentence to the tune of Jericho, "…sa-al-ad and toss it around a bit."

The tang of vinaigrette mixed with the cheesy scent of lasagna to make the kitchen smell wonderful. Essie realized she hadn't eaten an actual dinner all week—mostly just catching bites of things here and there between Josh's evening fussing. When she gave thanks for the food a moment later, it was with true sincerity. Her eagerness must have been evident, for Cece insisted she sit and eat while the older woman bounced around the kitchen in endless choruses of "Jericho."

"I remember," Cece argued when Essie tried to take Josh back. "I remember what it's like to think you'll never have an actual meal again. Josh and I are having fun providing your entertainment, aren't we, Josh?"

"Guwabaaaa!" Essie could only laugh, and hope Cece's lovely sweater didn't require dry cleaning.

"And how about Doug? Things let up at work yet?"

Even though her mouth was full of lasagna, Essie's eyes must have broadcast her guilt and worry.

"Ah, not so good, hmm?" Cece turned to Josh. "Mommy's got two grumpy men on her hands?"

"Three, if you count Pop." Essie glanced at Cece. "It feels like the whole world needs something from me all the time."

Cece sat down with Josh snuggled into one shoulder. Essie waited for Josh to explode in his usual objection to anyone actually being seated while holding him. He didn't. He didn't seem to mind at all. Essie tried to let herself feel purely grateful, but it didn't work. She just ended up feeling like Cece was somehow a better mother than she was, that Essie didn't have that "knack" everyone talked about. The mothering instinct.

She's got it, Essie's brain chanted, despite every logical argument against such a statement. *She's got it, and you don't.*

"Essie?"

Essie could not believe she was going to cry. It seemed like that was all she did these days—cry and feel like if one more thing was thrown her way she'd simply explode.

Cece put her free hand on Essie's arm. "Come on, out with it. I didn't just come here for the lasagna, I came to help you out. What's up?"

Essie plunked her fork onto the table. "How come this is so hard and you make it look so easy?" It seemed mean and ridiculous to say, but it jumped out before Essie could stop it. She wanted to know. Really. Wanted someone to give her the secret mother handshake. The tip that made all those other mothers look so in control. So pulled together when all she felt was pulled in a million different directions.

"It *is* hard."

"I haven't slept well in weeks. No, in months. Doug's a pile of knots and I didn't even know they'd had layoffs at work or they were launching an upgrade. He told me, but I didn't even *hear* it. What must he think of that? Josh is a crying time bomb every night and just, *just* when I get him settled down and think I'll have a single minute of quiet Doug comes through the door all tired and complaining. And my mom's suddenly freaking out over driving in the city and Pop…well, let's not even start on that one because he's just so impossible right now and…and…and Mrs. Bendenfogle is a fruitcake!"

Well, now it surely would only be a matter of seconds before Cece collected her gourmet salad dressing and bolted for the door.

She never moved.

She didn't even looked surprised. As a matter of fact, she took a forkful of lasagna as if Essie had just told her the evening's weather report. Except for the look of true compassion in her eyes.

Essie sniffed. "I don't know where that came from. I'm sorry. I…"

"Don't you dare be sorry for that. If I didn't throw at least one good fit a week, I think I'd explode." Cece pointed her fork at Essie. "Granted, you may want to choose your targets wisely, but you'd better get used to letting that stuff out every once in a while or it'll eat you alive."

Essie tried to imagine cool, calm, color-coordinated Cece pitching a hissy fit. Nope. She just couldn't see it.

"And just for the record," continued Cece, "Alice Bendenfogle is not a fruitcake. A bit excessive, yes, but I give you three months in pre-school before you see how hard it is to bite your complaining tongue over something they're doing to your precious baby that you don't like." She took another bite of lasagna. "Good choice of words, though. I like that one." She chuckled. "Fruitcake. Yep, that's a good one."

Essie wasn't quite sure what to say.

"Well, you feel better now, don't you? Let off some of that steam?"

"Actually, yes."

"Good. You call me whenever you need to rant and rave a bit, I'll be happy to come listen. What are friends for?"

Essie smiled and wiped her eyes. "To keep someone from calling Mrs. Bendenfogle a fruitcake to her face?"

"Exactly. Welcome to motherhood, by the way. Everybody wants everything from you every waking moment. It gets better when you get used to it, but you still need to protect yourself."

Essie thought of the Hazmat suit Doug had suggested. "Meaning?"

"Meaning, how old is your son?"

"Seven months tomorrow."

Cece started in on her salad with Josh still happily gnawing his knuckles on her shoulder. "And when is the last time you went out with your husband? As in 'on a date.' As in 'just the two of you.' Or even just gone somewhere all by yourself?"

"Not since we moved. Mom's offered a dozen times, but she's so..." Essie found herself without a good end to that sentence.

"She might do something not exactly the way you'd do it?"

"Oh." *Fruitcake for all.*

"Babies are boot camp, Essie. They suck up your time and your energy and your sleep. That's why God made them so cute, to make up for all those relentless demands. But they are demanding, and if you're not careful you'll pay the price."

"But I'm at home. I mean, I get to be at home, and not working. Surely..."

"Now wait a minute," interjected Cece sharply, "who says you're not working? Babies are the hardest job I know. And you, you've got all those parent issues to worry about on top of things. Where'd you get the idea this was going to be one long vacation?"

"I…I don't know, actually. I just didn't think it'd be so hard. I mean all those other moms, they make it look so easy. You make it look so easy."

"My kids are older, and it's just less messy, not any easier. If you saw me last Thursday just before Sam's social studies project was due…well, you'd change your tune. Anyway, that's hardly the point. I keep hearing you say 'all those other moms.' You'll have to stop spending so much time comparing yourself or you'll go crazy. Remember, my competitive friend, that you're only seeing what those women want you to see. What they've worked hard to make sure you see. Sure, Bayside likes to put on a pretty face, but don't be fooled, we're all just hanging on by our fingernails. Figure that out, and then the Alice Bendenfogles of the world won't get to you so much."

"I don't know."

"I do." Cece suddenly straightened in her chair. "You know, there's no time like the present. You finish this marvelous lasagna and then you are going to walk down to Ghirardelli's for chocolate ice cream. *Alone.* As in without this child. I am going to stay here and watch your baby and remind you that even if he screams his head off for the entire time you're gone, I've seen worse and he'll still live to see the morning." Cece narrowed her eyes when she saw Essie's hands go up in protest. "I'll pay for the ice cream myself and kick you out the door if I have to, so I suggest you go willingly."

"I…"

Cece shot her a look that could have stopped any teenager dead in their tracks. That all-powerful, "don't mess with me" look that was the weapon of all seasoned mothers.

Essie would never be able to say if it was desperation or

wisdom that said in her ear, *the woman is handing you choco-late ice cream and thirty minutes alone. Hush up and say yes, you fool.*

"I...um...I guess I'll just finish up here and be on my way."

Cece's face transformed into a warm smile. "Yes, you will. But, now that I think of it, you'll nurse your son before you go. Some things I can't help you with."

Even Hawaii couldn't have been more of a vacation than Ghirardelli's was that night. And true to Cece's word, Josh did live to see the morning.

Just fine.

Chapter 10

The Myth of Just Watching

Essie stood staring at the young athletes practicing on the field. One hand pushed Josh's stroller back and forth to keep him happily dozing, the other hand laced itself through the chain-link fence.

It scared her how much she ached to be on the other side of that track-and-field fence where she knew what to do. The world where lesson plans stayed planned and equations such as work+determination=success still held. Her neck felt naked without a whistle hanging from it, her hands empty without a clipboard holding team rosters and heat schedules. Oh, to return to a world where running from point A to point B meant reaching the finish line. Where efforts showed up in farther distances, lower times and tangible things like First Place. Where you got to win.

She wasn't sure how she ended up here, staring at the track field of Bay Area Community College. She could remember looking it up on a map, folding the e-mail from

Anna's husband into her back pocket, but not much else. It wasn't as if she made the conscious decision to come here; it was more like she floated along with a current determined to bring her here.

It was a small campus, but Essie liked small schools. The equipment had seen better days, but she knew how to work with such limitations. She watched a girl pick up a shot put and take her position. *No, you're grasping too much with your fingers, you've got to use your palm and follow through.* Essie watched the throw fall short, feeling the disappointment that hunched the young woman's shoulders.

Josh gurgled to announce his waking, and Essie picked him up. He smiled a crooked, toothy grin at her, grabbing a handful of her hair. She could see Doug in his eyes—they had the same greenish-gray tint even now. Surely he was the most handsome baby in the whole wide world.

I love this baby, Lord. I've always wanted to be a mom. And now You've given me this child. So why am I sitting here outside the fence wishing I were inside? You know me. You made me. Why aren't I thrilled and happy and content? Why do I feel like I've got everything I've ever wanted and nothing I wanted at the same time? Should I be here? Should I be somewhere else? I'm aching and I don't know how to fix it. You know how much I hate to muck around in all this confusion. I'm not going on a lot of sleep here— some very clear direction would sure help.

Nothing came.

The e-mail burned in her back pocket, feeling partly like a solution, and partly like an easy out. She'd reviewed the checkbook last night—the expense of West Coast living was catching up with them. Doug had been promised a year-end bonus, but who knew what it would be and if it would come at all now that they'd had layoffs? The bottom line still was that his salary might have been sufficient for life in New Jersey, but it was barely enough to get by in this expensive city.

Could they make it on one income? Lots of families had two working parents. It had its stresses, but life was already stressful now. If Essie had thought her being at home would get them peace and domestic bliss, it wasn't happening.

She pulled the e-mail from her pocket again. Maybe it would be a good idea just to call. Find out the details, see what's involved, get a feel for the position. It'd be rude, after all, not to follow up on the lead Kevin had given her.

Then why did it feel like dipping her toes in very dangerous water?

She felt Josh's fingers tug at her hair, and turned to look into those fabulous green-gray eyes. "Who knows, Josh baby, who knows? Do you know? What should I do?"

Josh looked as though he were actually pondering the question. His tiny blond eyebrows furrowed and his pink lips puckered into a sour face. Then his face brightened, his eyes looked right into hers, and he pronounced, "Umgababa." Truly, it sounded as if he had just offered her his take on the whole matter. There was even a tiny nod of his head when he was finished, as if to say, "The Great Joshua Has Spoken."

"Marvelous." Essie laughed out loud to no one in particular. "My son has just handed me the secret of life, and I'm stuck here without a translator. And I left my Infant-English dictionary back at the town house."

She suddenly realized that she was talking out loud to herself, and shook her head in resignation at the craziness of her world. Still, talking to Josh—even about grown-up issues like finances and crises of identity—seemed to help.

He was a good listener, a loving touch, and despite the fact that she could never interpret his commentary, she welcomed it anyway.

"Well, Josh, it seems I'm not going to get to know today. Trouble is—" she placed him back into the stroller and began to work her way around the fence to the other side of the campus where the bus stop was "—I don't think I should bring this up with Doug just yet. He wants to provide for you and me, kiddo, and maybe we need to give him the chance. It's only been a short time, and we don't know what the end of the year will bring. One thing is sure, your dad would stress out big-time if we put this on the table, and your daddy is one big pile of stress as it is."

She turned the corner, her eyes scanning the two dozen students on the field. "Nope, this one's gonna have to be between us for a while." As she passed a set of benches near the far end of the field, she noticed the team jacket lying there next to a pile of papers and a pair of notebooks. "Coach Jemmings" was embroidered on the back.

Coach Jemmings.

Essie ripped the e-mail from her pocket, scanning the text until she read the contact information. Coach Lyle Jemmings. "Whoa," she said under her breath, suddenly feeling the issue creeping up far too close for comfort. That guy over there was the man Kevin had talked to. She stared at the jacket as if it were some portent, some…sign.

She must have stood there far too long because she didn't even hear him come up to the bench. "You look a bit young to have a kid on this team."

Essie nearly jumped. Lyle Jemmings was the quintessential coach—stocky build, buzz cut, sweatpants, whistle, clipboard. "No, no," she countered, "I was just…uh…watching."

Jemmings snatched up a notebook, pulling the pen from behind his ear. He spoke while making some notations. "Been watching a while. Did you used to run?"

"No, throw. Shot put. In New Jersey." She took a deep breath, deciding that this was a fated meeting, and added, "I'm Esther Walker, the friend of Kevin Miller's. He told me you were in the market for a women's coach, and I…I sort of ended up here watching."

It took a moment for Jemmings to put the pieces together. "Walker—oh, I remember now. Kevin sent me an e-mail about you, saying you'd just come into town and might be looking for a position." He stared at Josh. "Didn't mention the new baby. Congratulations. Looks like a fine young guy."

"Oh, he is. When he's not teething, that is. Which is, well, most of the time." Essie wanted to say something else, something clever about his team or his field, but she was so stumped at the prospect of meeting him just now that her brain went blank.

"Kids can be a handful." He swept his arm around the field. "At any age. But hey, you used to teach, you already know that."

Used to teach. Essie found she did not like the sound of that phrase at all. "Yep," she replied, but it was really more of a gulp than a word.

"So," he said, scratching the side of his chin with the top of his pen. "We're still looking. You still interested?"

"I…um…I don't know."

"Hey, coach, the hurdle's broke again! Where's the duct tape?" A lithe young man in shorts and a ripped-up T-shirt trotted over to Jemmings with his hand out.

"In the bag, Newman, the one with the screwdrivers."

Jemmings pointed to a crate of equipment on the far side of the benches.

"Got it." Newman pointed a finger at the coach, then veered off toward the crate without breaking stride.

"High-tech equipment," joked the coach, cocking his head toward the boy, who was now trotting off toward the hurdles with a gigantic roll of duct tape in one hand.

"Been there." Essie basked in the familiarity of it all.

"Coach!" The cry came from another corner of the field.

"Hey, look, you got a lot on your plate there, Mrs. Walker. You give it some thought." He dug into his sweats pocket for a wallet, producing a battered business card. "Now you know how to get a hold of me if Kevin hasn't told you already. Mull it over and give me a call. We're looking to start someone in the spring, so you don't have to know now."

You don't have to know now. If Essie could have picked the one element of her whole world that made her most uncomfortable, it was that she didn't know. Not now. And she wanted to know. *Now.* Not having to know now was making her crazy. How like God to put just those words in Coach Jemmings' mouth.

If God had put them there at all. Which she, of course, didn't know.

She took the card as he poked it through the fence.

"Gotta go. Nice to meet you and…" He smiled at Josh.

"Josh, his name is Josh."

"And Josh there. Call me and we'll lay out the details if you're interested. It ain't the Olympics, but it's a solid program."

Essie wasn't sure how, but she knew that it was a solid program, just by watching them. "Thanks."

"Edwards," Jemmings yelled across the field as he turned back toward the students, "take those blocks over to the far track and set 'em up!" In a burst of clipboards and whistles, he was jogging back onto the field, stuffing his wallet back into his pants pocket as he ran.

Essie watched for a few more minutes, both anxious and entranced.

And thoroughly confused.

"Well now, Josh," she said as she turned the stroller back onto the sidewalk. "If I needed the matter all cleared up, that couldn't have been less productive."

"Gobawaaa."

She cocked an eyebrow at his loving gaze. "Some help you are."

To which Josh simply smiled and stuffed his fist in his mouth.

Traveling home on the bus, Essie pulled out the epic script of the Celebration. Riffling through the lengthy table of contents—which she noted contained scary sections entitled "Historical Context," "Major Theme," and even a "Bibliography"—she found the seven pages devoted to the Doom Room's presentation of Jesus meeting Zacchaeus. As she scanned through to find the necessary page, Essie decided that this poor student had either lost all perspective, or had had it snatched from him by the colossal expectations of Dahlia and her crew. *They're just kids,* she thought as she found footnote after footnote on the pages—*just kids putting on a play. Kids with parents who are plain nuts.* She frowned at the ridiculous lengths to which parents go.

Mark-o's words came back to her. *"I'm just happy to get them to care at all. Opinion isn't my enemy, apathy is."*

Well, Mark-o, you win this one. No apathy here. No, this is pretty much an avalanche of attention. It came to her like an Oprah commercial, with Oprah's perky voice announcing, "Here's what we're working on for next week's show—parents who care too much. If you are obsessed with your child's spiritual development, call our hotline now." This was something different. This was somehow not seeing the forest for the trees, somehow being caught up in the trappings of faith at the expense of the faith itself. This was just plain wrong.

Right?

I don't know, I don't know, I don't know!

All she did know was that when the stage notes called for a ten-foot tree with hidden scaffolding and a safety harness—a safety harness!—it was clear that this was going to be crazy.

Not knowing whether to laugh or groan, Essie read through the dialogue. It wasn't too bad. No big words, short sentences one could reasonably expect a second-grader to be able to memorize and, of course, rock-solid Biblical content. The crowd got lots of fun things to say, Jesus had compelling dialogue, and Zacchaeus was given a very sympathetic treatment. It wasn't until she read the final page that she realized the greatest challenge of this little escapade.

Eight boys. Eight boys' oh-so-invested mothers.

And only one Jesus.

She could see it now: Every mother would want—no, *expect*—their son to be given the role of Jesus. The only possible exceptions were Cece, who knew enough not to care, and Vicki, who probably didn't know enough to care. She could almost feel the disapproving glances of parents when scripts where handed out and they discovered their precious baby would simply be a member of "the crowd" rather than one of the two starring roles. Why didn't she have enough sense to land a class with twelve boys and request the story of Joseph? Telling a parent their child didn't have the skills yet to make the varsity team was one thing, telling a parent their son hadn't made the cut to be Jesus would be quite another. And really, who deserves to play Jesus anyway? How on earth do you decide something like that?

Talk about your no-win situations.

The Doom Room was going to live up to its name.

Chapter 11

Thou Shalt Never, Ever, Ever!

Essie was ten minutes into the lesson on the Ten Commandments, and was ready to add "Mind Thy Teacher" to the top of the list. Peter had brought a large plastic spider to class, and was smashing it with his fist repeatedly while she read the lesson. Essie supposed this was better than him placing it on his classmates, but the ferocity with which he was squashing the bug was disturbing. Peter was obviously working out some sort of aggression. She made a note to ask him about it after class—if she made it that far.

Steven Bendenfogle, having been duly corrected on the subject of Jesus' X-ray vision, was proceeding to stare around the room through his fingers "Junior Birdman" style, as if the gesture would gain him X-ray vision of his own. He's mocking me, Essie thought. *Nonsense,* she argued with herself, *these are second graders; they don't have the mental capacity to mock.*

"Oh yeah?" Alex yelled as if hearing her thoughts,

whereupon he immediately snatched Peter's spider and threw it across the room. That, of course, sent Peter into a nasty fit. Before she could say "Thou Shalt Not Kill," her entire class was piled into a wrestling match on the classroom floor. It seemed to take mere seconds for the boys to tumble into a writhing mass even an NHL hockey ref couldn't have undone. She ducked just in time to miss being hit by Stanton's airborne loafer. It flew into the bulletin board and sent Noah fluttering to the ground.

"That's it. That's *it!*" Essie reached into the tangle of arms and legs to find the one socked foot. When she found it, she grabbed it and pulled. Hard. Stanton's panting face appeared from the mob, eyes wide in shock that nice Mrs. Walker would actually stoop to such measures. "Over there," Essie growled, pointing to a corner of the room. "Now!" Stunned, Stanton sulked over to where she had pointed.

With a deep breath, Essie reached into the huddle and pulled the next appendage she could grasp. Decker, whining "he started it," was condemned to a corner of his own. Essie repeated the procedure until every boy was sent to a chair, corner, or bench. When they began to argue their innocence, she stared them down with a look she hoped would have made even Pharaoh cower.

Essie looked at her watch. Three-quarters of the classroom time was already gone. She'd have to do something fast if the Ten Commandments weren't going to be a total loss today. *A little inspiration would be nice, Lord. I'm at the end of my rope, here.*

As if she'd had a hotline to the Almighty, the idea hit her. Perfect and powerful. Without a word, she lined the boys' chairs up in a straight line, putting a few feet between each of the chairs so that no wayward arms or feet could find their way to a neighbor. Taking each child silently by the shoulders, she planted the boys in the chairs. Her quietness spooked them, and they caught each other's eyes in unspoken questions. The internal instinct all children have—the one that lets them know they've gone one step too far—had kicked in, and they were nervous.

Once settled, Essie turned her back to the boys and counted to ten. When she turned around to face them, she hoped her face showed every ounce of her frustration. "Today, gentlemen, I'm not just friendly Mrs. Esther Walker. As of this minute I am *Queen* Esther." That certainly got their attention. "And today, for the last few minutes of class, we're going to talk about Queen Esther's Commandments. Queen Esther's Commandments had better be obeyed in this classroom in the future. Do you know why?" She pointed at each child down the line of chairs, to which each boy silently shook his head "no." Good, that was the effect she wanted.

"Because Queen Esther decides who gets which parts in the Celebration. Queen Esther decides who gets to play Jesus and get lots of good lines. She gets to decide who will play Zacchaeus and get to climb the ten-foot *real* tree with scaffolding and a safety harness." Ooo, that really got their attention. "She gets to decide who will wear the nifty robes, and who might have to wear the dorky ones in front of the whole church. In short, gentlemen, she gets to decide *everything.*"

The Doom Room had never been so silent.

"Each of you will help me decide these things by how you act over the next three sessions. I'll be keeping track of how well you obey Queen Esther's Commandments, and the one who does the best job will get the best part. So, everyone who thinks it would be cool to be Jesus or be Zacchaeus and climb the tree—the real tree that's ten feet high—had better be on their best behavior. What you do in the play is up to you now. Everyone understand?"

A little chorus line of nodding heads ensued.

Essie walked over to the whiteboard and picked up a marker. She wrote "Queen Esther's Commandments" at the top and underlined it.

"Commandment number one is that everyone will keep hands and feet to themselves. *At all times.*" She wrote it on the board.

"Number two is to respect other people's stuff, their feelings and their opinions." She wrote that down. "That means no taking stuff, no interrupting, no saying bad things to each other and no telling other people they're silly or wrong or dumb.

"Number three is to treat Mrs. Walker—otherwise known as Queen Esther—nicely. That means you do what I ask, you think about the questions I ask you, and you participate in our discussions. You follow directions and you don't—" she glared around the room for emphasis "—make her pull you out of a fight ever again."

Essie had to admit that pretty much covered it. Those three were nothing short of inspired. Basic civil behavior summed up in a three-step program. *Thanks, God.*

"There's only three commandments, but I'm very serious about them. If we all obey these, we'll actually get to have much more fun in class. The more you behave, the more fun I'll get to have with you. The more you follow these directions, the more you'll learn. Each of you can decide how you earn your way to a bigger part in the Celebration."

The next part was downright brilliant, if she did say so herself. "Next week I'll have a letter ready for your parents explaining Queen Esther's Commandments and how they'll help us decide who gets what parts for the play. I know your parents want you to do your best, so this way they can help you remember the rules in here and remind you to follow them." All the little heads were nodding again, so Essie felt safe to open the floor up to discussion. "Now, are there any questions?"

Alex Faber's hand shot up. It was the first time Alex had ever put his hand in the air and actually waited to be called upon before speaking. She recognized him, and he asked, "Are you gonna test us on this?"

"Not on paper, Alex, but in the way you act every time you're in this classroom. Every minute of every class."

Peter's hand went up next. She pointed to him. With a sniff, he asked, "Can I have my bug back now?"

Essie and Doug sat in Ghirardelli's ice-cream parlor, sharing a large chocolate sundae. Essie had dragged Doug out to celebrate her victory over the Doom Room chaos. He'd resisted at first, claiming he was too tired and had too much to do, but Essie was undaunted. In the past few weeks, Essie had enjoyed several doses of Cece's "thirty-minute walk and a dish of Ghirardelli's" stress reduction plan. Any good wife would pass on such a secret of life to her husband.

"Queen Esther? You actually told them you were Queen Esther?" Doug shook his head as he dug into the confection.

"Well, not the biblical Queen Esther. It was more of a 'She Who Must be Obeyed' kind of thing. More supreme ruler than Bible heroine. It was rather inspired, if you ask me. And really, that was the coolest part of it—I was so frustrated with those boys, I thought I was going to scream. Then when I closed my eyes and begged God for a plan, He handed it to me. Practically immediately. The whole thing came to me in a flash of what can only be explained as divine intervention."

"And they bought it?"

"Completely. They got the whole idea—the whole concept of a classroom community. They finally understood that we can have more fun if they don't act like jungle beasts to each other. Who knew a ten-foot tree could serve as such motivation?"

"Ten-foot tree, huh? Why am I suddenly sorry I said 'yes' when Arthur Mannington asked if I'd serve on the set building committee?"

Essie stared at him. "When did you say you'd work on the sets?"

"Last month. Before my job went into overdrive and I lost every moment of my free time. Back before I saw how thick that script was."

Essie's heart sank. "I don't know anything anymore. Doug, there's all these details about your life that I used to always know and now I don't." There was a lump in her throat that had nothing to do with the ice cream. "When's the last time we even sat down and talked?"

Doug got that look on his face, the one that meant he was pretty sure his guy mentality wasn't going to comprehend whatever was coming next. "Um…aren't we talking now?"

Essie moaned. "No, not just now. I mean before now. When's the last time you and I had a conversation about something other than Joshua's baby aspirin, or whose turn it was to empty out the diaper pail? I had this great picture in my head about what our life would be like out here. I thought we'd have so much more time with me home. Instead, it feels like we're just bumping into each other between responsibilities these days."

Doug reached out and touched her hand. "Es, that's not true. Okay, we're a bit stressed, but…"

"I didn't know about your layoffs or your upgrades or you being on the set committee or…" Oh great, she was going to cry again. They were out to celebrate, and she'd turned it into a hormonal sob-fest.

"We're here. We're here right now, and we're here because you dragged me out of my stressed-out afternoon to have a little bit of fun." Doug began stroking her hand. That sensation always went straight to her toes. "It's okay," he said in a soft, warm voice that made her believe. "We've got a lot on our plates, Es, we're going to drop a few balls in the juggling act." He smiled and leaned closer to her. "Besides, I'm married to the Queen. That sort of makes me King, doesn't it? Two hours ago I was a lowly technical supervisor. That's got to be worth something."

She had to ask. "You're not feeling neglected or anything?"

"I'm feeling tired. I'm feeling stressed. I'm feeling like every new dad on the planet, I guess. But I'm not feeling neglected."

"No?" She was sure he was just sugarcoating things so she wouldn't cry in public. Again.

"Do I wish I had my wife's undivided attention again? Well, yes. I'd like to have enough energy to pounce on you on the couch and kiss you senseless." Doug yawned, as if the mere utterance of the word "couch" produced a craving for a Sunday afternoon nap. "And I think, maybe in a dozen years or so, I will." His eyes shifted to Joshua, who was happily fiddling with a plastic spoon in his stroller next to the table. "But I kinda like this new distraction, and he seems worth the chaos. Like your little royal subjects there."

"Oh, I don't know," Essie replied, finding a particularly thick vein of hot fudge deep in one side of the dish. "I'm not sure they're worth it yet."

"Oh, yes, you are." He stared at her. "You can't even see it, can you? It comes so naturally to you, you don't even realize how invested you already are in these kids. Look at you—you're hyped up about them catching on to things. You come home every Sunday full of things that happened in class—stuff kids did or things they said. I know they drive you nuts—sounds like these boys would drive anybody nuts—but you see things in them no one else does." He put his chin in his hand, as if admiring a piece of artwork or a landscape. "It's why you're such a great teacher. You care. I mean really care. Not just about the classroom stuff, but the kids themselves." He paused for a moment before adding softly, "It's why you're going to be such a great mother."

Every ounce of ice cream in the state of California could not have healed her more. And how like Doug; she brought him out for a little encouragement, and he ended up encouraging her. If he really wanted her not to cry in public, he was going about it all the wrong way—and she loved every bit of it.

"Josh has got himself one pretty amazing Daddy, you know." She was too choked up to get out any more than that.

Doug reached over into the stroller and picked up Josh. He began to make silly faces at his son, sending him into little bubbles of laughter. "Joshua Walker is one pretty lucky little boy, aren't you, sport? Are you gonna grow up and get all goofy when you're in second grade, little guy? I bet you are. I just bet you are." Josh laughed and planted his hand on Doug's nose. "Hey, by the way, have you seen the set list for this little...ouch, buddy!" Doug had to pause for a moment and pry Joshua's viselike grip from off his nose. "Extravaganza?" Your ten-foot tree has nothing on the sixth-grade Pharaoh's pyramid. We're going to need to call in a special effects team from Hollywood if this keeps up."

"Don't say anything like that around Arthur Mannington. He'll take you up on it." Essie relished the last bit of the sundae before setting down her spoon.

"Someone needs to have a talk with that man about the virtues of simplicity. Like a pastor or something. Know anyone?"

"Very funny. Mark-o doesn't seem to mind this thing." She narrowed her eyes. "I think he likes having the biggest show in town."

"Probably because he doesn't have to build the biggest show in town."

"How are you going to do this, Doug? When are you going to find the time? You've got enough unfinished projects in your own workshop—I'd hate to see you have to put those on hold to build a self-parting Red Sea or a hydraulic pearly gate."

"Well," said Doug, taking off his glasses because Josh had now completely smeared them, "I don't know yet. But even so, I think I'd rather figure that out than have to go deal with Icky Vicki. Your coffee date with her is tomorrow, isn't it?"

Essie made a face. She'd blocked that out completely. Her

first impulse was to call the whole thing off, but the church's November event, the Harvest of Witnesses, was coming up fast. As she told Dahlia, the class needed baskets for the event, and Essie did not possess the craft gene that enabled women to do things like transform paper-towel tubes into cornucopia. Like it or not, she needed Vicki's help—and no less than three women had pointed her in Vicki's direction.

Hmm, Essie thought, eyeing the empty sundae dish, *do you think I could lose twelve pounds by Monday?* Essie just knew Vicki would be tiny and slim and polished…

And clueless. Even on the phone, the woman had a voice that had "shopping mall" written all over it.

"Oh, come on," said Doug. Evidently her face had broadcast her thoughts. "She can't be all that bad. You said so yourself, she can help with the baskets you need for that harvest thing in November. You're not exactly Queen Esther of the Glue Gun, you know."

Essie rolled her eyes. "That's what I liked so much about high school. No crafts."

Doug straightened. "The craftsman in me resents that."

"I'll remember that when your life turns into an episode of *This Old Pyramid*."

"Well," said Doug, yawning, "if I want to get home anytime before nine any day next week, we'd better get back. I've got a stack of production schedules to get through this afternoon before Bible study."

Doug was working on a Sunday. Doug would never work on Sundays before. Just how much pressure was he under? As she edged the stroller out of the ice-cream parlor, Essie decided it was better not to ask.

When they got home and she saw the huge stack of papers he pulled out of his briefcase, she knew she'd made the right choice in not bringing the subject of Coach Jemmings up. Doug didn't need one more ounce of stress on this day or any other.

Chapter 12

Reluctant Coffee to Go

I am nowhere near cool enough for this place. No, I take that back. ninety percent of the entire world isn't cool enough for this place.

Icky Vicki had named the trendiest coffee bar in town as the location for their meeting. It didn't really surprise Essie that Vicki hadn't invited her to meet in their home—and Essie sure wasn't ready to have the likes of Vicki staring down her Gucci sunglasses at the humble Walker abode. Essie had done her best to look polished—tailored, burgundy turtleneck, pressed khakis, ballet flat and Josh in brand-new OshKosh B'Gosh attire from head to toe. Even as she put her hand to the door handle of the coffeehouse, however, Essie knew she was out of her league. One glance around the room told her that the shoes on most of the people here cost more than her entire outfit—even if you added in Josh's clothes and the stroller. No siree, she'd entered the land of the nanny. The au pair. The private preschool with electives in Latin and foreign policy.

One look at Vicki—or at least the woman Essie could only suppose must be Vicki—told her just how stereotypes got their start. She was a stunning blonde in—of course—a headband and twinset in the most perfect turquoise. She was young and tiny. Bangs, king-sized diamond studs, perfect nails, monstrous ring, designer everything. This was not a woman who knew the recipe for Toll House cookies by heart. Essie gulped and sucked in her postpartum abdomen.

Vicki popped up off her leather stool and stretched out a hand. "You've just got to be Essie. You found the place okay?" Essie wasn't sure if it was something in the tone of her voice, or simply her own insecurities, for she sensed the implied "because I'm sure you've never been here before." "I just…" Her cell phone went off. "Ooo, hang on a sec, will you?"

Essie settled herself at the table where three surprisingly masculine baskets were set for review. Vicki had quite the gift. Or quite the staff. Still, one had to admire the woman's ability to meet the design challenge of macho baskets for eight-year-olds.

"All right then, Fritz," said Vicki into her cell phone, scowling, "have those plants delivered by ten sharp or heads will roll. And tell Andre that I simply will not stand for ferns anywhere. If he can't bear my color scheme, then he can just close his eyes. Thanks, love." With a sigh, she flipped her phone closed and pushed back a lock of hair. She flashed a gleaming white smile in Essie's direction. "So, what do you think?"

"They're really amazing, you…"

The cell phone rang again, and Vicki shot up a single "hang on" finger as she flipped open the phone again. "Victoria Hinton-Faber here…no, Julian, I thought I made that clear—we're going with the navy blue drapes in the west bedroom. Don't talk color to me, I know exactly what I want and that isn't it…."

Essie decided now might be a good time to go get some coffee. She pushed herself up off the stool and wheeled Josh's stroller over to the counter. Lush racks of gooey pastries called to her. There were healthy ones with organic, vitamin-packed names and flours she'd never even heard of before. There were also fabulously non-nutritional treats; things that looked like they'd melt in your mouth, biscotti that simply begged for a dunk in hot coffee, muffins that looked as if you couldn't help but sigh as you ate them.

It was all wonderfully tempting until Essie caught sight of the prices on the board behind the counter. Passing up a seven-dollar muffin was suddenly feeling easier. And since when did a caramel latte run almost nine dollars? The ten-dollar bill in her pocket was supposed to cover this morning's treats and pick up a few groceries on the way home. One glance back at Vicki told her the woman had already ordered for herself and had no intention of picking up the tab for this morning. Sighing, Essie ordered a sugar cookie and a small coffee, glad to come out of the transaction with any change at all. She grabbed her little ceramic tile with a hand-painted order number on it, and headed back to her table.

Vicki had finished her color consultation, and was jotting notes down on a chic-looking leather pad. Essie tried to convince herself that Vicki's huge, Dahlia Mannington–style pen wasn't a portent. It almost worked.

"So they'll do for our little guys?" She picked up the basket decorated in a sports theme, turning it this way and that. "I think they turned out fabulous."

"They're wonderful," Essie replied. And they were. "You're very talented."

"A quick sketch here, a quick sketch there, and *poof,* my guys spring into action. You should see us go all out for Easter."

Essie picked up a basket decorated like a highway, with race cars zooming around the brim. "I can imagine. Alex is a lucky guy."

"Alex?" Vicki looked as though Essie had just said something very odd. As if she wasn't used to people connecting her to an eight-year-old boy, and she didn't much enjoy it. Maybe Alex really was picking up on something beyond the usual stress of a newly blended family.

"I can just imagine," replied Essie, suddenly feeling as though she had to explain, "what you're able to do in your house. You must have a lovely home."

"Yes, well, we're getting there. You'd think, though, that people know what you mean when you use the term 'navy blue.' Really." Vicki stared at the cell phone as if poor Julian, whomever he was, could still hear her displeasure from his end.

"Alex is a great boy. I'll bet he would really like..."

Before another word, Vicki's cell phone went off again. "Last call, I promise." She flipped the phone open again, pen poised.

Essie busied herself looking at the dinosaur-themed third basket. It soon became clear, however, that the conversation was bearing bad news. She tried hard not to eavesdrop, but when words like "doctor" and "test" and "biopsy" popped up, it became impossible.

"What do you mean, 'more tests'? There can't be anything wrong, I feel fine. Take those results back and get them read by someone who knows what he's doing. How dare you call me with scare tactics like this? What on earth do I pay you all that money for, anyway? It's not as if I enjoy having my upper extremities squished between two refrigerator doors every year. I'll give my housekeeper a piece of my mind for giving you this number—why couldn't you have left a message instead of hunting me down with this... this...obvious error?" There was a layer of fear creeping over Vicki's sharp words. Her eyes darted around the room, as if looking for an escape. "I don't care how many messages you've already left, this is uncalled for. Send those results back or I'll find someone who can."

Essie tried desperately not to look uncomfortable. *Help, Lord! What do I do now?*

"Uh...give me a minute, will you, Essie? I'm going to go outside with this." With an applied look of annoyance that didn't begin to cover the panic in her eyes, Vicki grabbed her latte and bolted out the door.

Essie caught her breath, feeling her own panic at being spectator to someone else's crisis. This was Mark-o's territory, not hers. A black-turtlenecked server arrived with her coffee and cookie. Pasting a smile on her face, Essie tried to meet his stare, to broadcast, "It's okay," but it seemed as if the entire room was either staring at Vicki's frantic pacing on the sidewalk, or at her. Essie cleared her throat. "Could I...um..."

"Get this to go, madam?" The waiter looked at her from over his artful wire glasses.

She nodded. Feeling like she'd much rather do a timeout in stinky whale guts than go near the woman out on the sidewalk, Essie plunked down the last of her funds for a tip, gathered food, baskets and baby, and headed out.

Her first impulse was to just leave. Give Vicki a little privacy to deal with whatever that phone call had thrown at her—which, given the shreds of conversation Essie had heard, wasn't hard to guess. She glanced up and down the sidewalk and found Vicki sitting on a raised planter a few doors down. She had donned sunglasses and lit up a cigarette. Her back was erect, she had her legs crossed and one foot was bobbing furiously. Everything about her screamed "Back off!"

Essie had absolutely no idea what to say. Or what to do. She wanted to turn in the other direction and get away as fast as she could. But she knew she couldn't. She shouldn't. She knew in undeniable terms that this was no time to leave Vicki to her well-armored exclusivity. "Hey," she said quietly, angling Josh's stroller as far away from the cigarette smoke as she could without looking obvious. "You okay?"

"I'm fine." The words were ice-cold and razor sharp.

"I don't think anybody would be fine after a phone call like that."

Vicki's head snapped in her direction. "Like what?"

"I wasn't eavesdropping or anything, but it was pretty clear that phone call wasn't about draperies."

"Incompetent idiots." Vicki swore softly and flicked an ash into the planter.

Essie drank her coffee to buy some thinking time. An old coach's advice came to her from out of the fog of memory—*go with what you know.* "You're awfully young to be having annual mammograms. Family history?"

It was half a cigarette before Vicki answered, "Two aunts and a grandmother." The choke in her voice squeezed Essie's heart.

"That's rough. I'm sorry."

Vicki drained her latte. "Don't be. I'll have it cleared up by noon."

"I'm not so sure that's the best way to approach this. Listen, Vicki, I…"

"I'm fine. You read about errors like this all the time. I'll have Jack find me the best docs in town and they'll…" She never finished the sentence.

Jack. That was his name. Essie had been trying to remember Alex's dad's name for the last two minutes. "You should call Jack. That'd be a good idea."

"Would be—" Vicki sighed "—if it weren't the middle of the night in Singapore."

That was Alex's dad all right, halfway around the world most of the time. Alex was always bringing in matchbooks from hotels in the most exotic places. Essie always wondered why she was the first adult to think it might be a good idea to remove the matches from them before Alex toted them around in his pants pockets any longer. "Somehow I think it'd be okay to wake up your husband in the middle of the night for this."

"Your husband, maybe. Jack's not exactly the 'Oh, honey I'll be right there for you' type." The words were dripping with far too much sarcasm for someone married less than a year.

"A friend, maybe?"

"Oh, yes, I've got tons of friends lined up to help me pick out a biopsy outfit. As long as it doesn't conflict with their hair appointments, that is."

"Look, I…"

"Hey, look, I'm fine, okay? It's a glitch, nothing more. I've got an eleven-thirty, so can we just go over the baskets and be done with it?" She fished in her tiny purse for another cigarette. "When do you need them ready?" Her voice was nearly mean.

"Well, I guess two weeks from Friday," Essie replied, unable to think of anything else to say.

"Done. And...uh...nothing to Pastor Taylor, okay? Nothing to *anybody*." As if hearing her own sharpness, she suddenly added, "I mean, um, I'd appreciate it."

"Sure. Certainly."

With a swish and a flick and an open cell phone, Vicki was off down the street.

Gripping her leather tote with white knuckles.

Vicki's eyes haunted Essie's entire walk home. Pain. Fear. Sure, Vicki was young and glossy, but she was still a person. A young woman facing a terrifying possibility just when life ought to be perfect. Vicki should be madly in love, decorating her first home married to a rich and successful man, not facing biopsies or deciding how many of her lymph nodes to keep.

Vicki should have a wise comforting friend at her side.

So what was Essie Walker doing there?

For that matter, what was Essie Walker doing in California?

A wave of homesickness, a feeling of bone-deep displacement washed over Essie with a strength that stole her breath.

I don't belong here. I'm falling short here, Lord. I can't measure up. I can't deal with all these people with all these problems. Why can't You send Pop a doctor he'll actually listen to? Why do I have to be the one to deal with Dahlia Mannington? Why are You slamming me into problems that are far too big for me to handle, Lord? Don't You know what I'm feeling? Don't You see what Vicki's feel-

ing? Aren't You smart enough to put somebody useful into that cof-
fee bar with her to get a phone call like that?

By the time she reached her own door, Essie was a mess. She was scared for Vicki, scared for her Dad, unsure of herself and her family's future. Justified or not, Essie Walker declared herself a one-woman pity extravaganza. She was just barely holding back the tears when she bumped into the shaggy boy standing in her hallway. He was knocking on her apartment door while trying to hang on to the large crate in his hands.

A fruit crate actually, from one of those gift-basket companies that are always sending pop-up messages on the Internet: 1-800-citrus or whatever.

A crate of grapefruits.

Grapefruits!

Anna had sent her a crate of grapefruits. Three dozen of them. It was the most perfect pick-me-up anyone could ever send. The delivery boy looked downright baffled at how much Essie cooed over the gift, obviously thinking no one had any right to get that excited over citrus fruit. Essie didn't care. She was in possession of three dozen perfect grapefruits and she knew just what to do with them.

For fun, she actually ate one after she tucked Josh down for his nap. With a grapefruit spoon, no less. The sheer absurdity of it all made her laugh out loud alone at her kitchen table and hoist a spoonful toast to Cece, wherever she was. The rest of the fruit? Well, she'd get to that as soon as she could.

For once, Josh's nap seemed to take too long. One hour and seventeen minutes later, Josh and Essie were headed out the door. It had taken creativity to fit all thirty-five remaining grapefruits into the stroller—they had to come out of the crate and were tucked in every basket, pouch and corner, not to mention a small shopping bag hanging off the handle. Essie hummed as she pressed the elevator button.

The eight blocks to the waterfront passed by in a whir of anticipation. Having had Josh's nap to think up the perfect spot, Essie pronounced the small beach near the pier—the spot populated this time of day with all kinds of seabirds and the chorus of lounging sea lions—the optimum location. After all, these golden goodies had to be of use to someone else after she was done with them. Positioning the stroller in a patch of shade just to her left, Essie kicked off her sandals, tightened her hair elastic and picked up a grapefruit.

A little big, far too light, but still more than suitable. She gave it a small toss with her hand, getting a feel for it. Walking toward the center of the tiny beach, she stretched out her left arm, reaching out to the ocean's green-gray horizon. *See it.* It felt as if energy surrounded her in the wind and sunlight. She pulled a full breath of Pacific breeze into her lungs and closed her eyes. Bending, she nestled the yellow globe under her chin, fingers of her right hand flexing and rearranging themselves by instinct. *Set it.* Her toes found just the right angles in the sand. The coiled, pure, perfect expectation of launch. The birth of distance, the creation of speed and momentum. The muscles in her body seemed to sing at the chance to take this familiar pose. *Shoot it.*

Turn, lift, now!

With a noise that was half grunt, half yell, Essie sent the grapefruit in a satisfying arc out and into the water. Cocking her head to one side and squinting, she guessed it at twenty-five yards. Not bad for a gal who hadn't picked up a shot in almost a year. Nowhere near her grapefruit-lobbing record, but still an admirable showing. And, as it always had, a bit of her stress flew out of her body to sail alongside the orb. How she and Anna had ever gotten the idea to do this, neither of them could remember. It hardly mattered anymore.

Essie wondered why she'd not thought of this herself. It was funny how stress could cloud a brain, so that things you knew were good solutions, help you knew had always been there, became somehow hidden.

How many times, after botched track meets, boyfriend breakups, or just plain bad days, had she and Anna piled a fistful of crumpled dollars onto the counter of the local grocer for a bag of overripe grapefruits. Mr. Norman, the friendly grocer of unknown European descent, had even taken to saving them up—knowing through experience just when squishy became *too* squishy. When they'd 'fessed up one afternoon as to the use of the grapefruits—Mr. Norman had grilled them about latching on to some dangerous fad diet—he had laughed and considered it an honor to join in the fun.

See it, set it, shoot it. Essie sent another fruit arcing into the harbor. Anna had found a way to zoom across the miles and make things better. The miles that spread from one coast to another seemed smaller now. *Zoom!* Life slid into place with each lengthening toss.

By the time fruit number thirty-four hit the water with a commendable splash, Essie's arm was sore, her audience of sea creatures was offering up loud thanks for the show and Essie began to feel as though she might be able to handle her world. The gawks of confused spectators—including one pier guard who seemed concerned at first but then tolerant—only added to the moment. Even Josh, who alternated between dozing and making happy gurgily sounds, had cheered her on.

Sitting afterwards in the shade, letting Josh bang his tiny hands on the last remaining grapefruit, Essie knew she'd found a foothold. Okay, maybe only a toehold, but it was enough. She kissed the top of Josh's head and leaned back against the tree. No problems had been solved, but for this moment, Essie felt as if she'd pulled her world slightly back into control.

To her left, her eyes caught a glimpse of the familiar red silhouette of the Golden Gate Bridge. Essie was surprised to learn it was red—somehow she'd always pictured it gold due to the name. It had seemed to her a strange joke to play on the world. The funny thing about that bridge, though, was that it never looked the same color at any given time. The bay fog, the angle of the sun, clouds, or even the dreaded California smog would play tricks on the eyes and make it appear one of any of a dozen different colors. Pink, gray, even purple and blue, depending on the weather. She'd not noticed the phenomenon until Anna had sent her a clipping from a woman's magazine last month. The clipping talked about that very color illusion—but with a highly potent lesson. Essie knew, as she recalled the brief article, that it was no coincidence she had spied the bridge in its true bright red just now. It was a reminder.

The article had said that the true color of the Golden Gate bridge is like the true nature of God—it never changes. It is only the human viewpoint that alters the color. The God who crafted the perfect life and perfect family in New Jersey had not left her. No matter how the atmosphere—geographical, social, medical, or emotional—played tricks with her eyes, Essie could count on the goodness of

God to be as constant as the color of the bridge. Trick was, she reminded herself, to remember how one given viewpoint isn't always reality.

God had neither moved nor changed.

She'd just stopped looking closely.

God wanted her here. She had felt that back in New Jersey, and it was still truth today. She should be here. Life could be here, could be this messy, and still be okay. She knew that now. God had reached down into her world and said, in terms meant just for her, "I see you. I see where you are. I know where you are and how you feel. I see you, Essie Walker, and I'm still with you."

Chapter 13

On the Verge of Pop-icide

"He's *where?*"

"The E.R. at San Francisco General. Mom called an ambulance about an hour ago when he started complaining of chest pains."

"Mom called an ambulance?"

"Would you really have wanted Mom to drive?" Essie heard Mark-o mumble something to someone and realized he was calling from the hospital.

"No, no I guess not. But I wish she'd called one of us." Essie sat up to sit in bed, her hands groping on the bedside table for the clock. "What time is it, anyway?"

"Four-thirty. It was pure providence that I was already here and the E.R. staff knew me enough to page me in the hospital."

Essie rubbed her eyes. "You were already there?"

"Mavis O'Neil died tonight. Tony O'Neil's wife. Overdose. He's pretty much a wreck right now, but we called his brother in from Sausalito."

The weary pain in his voice reminded her how much weight her brother carried on his shoulders every day. There was a truckload of pain under all those pretty clothes and perfect homes. Hadn't yesterday shown her that? She knew what her own heart felt like watching Vicki. She could only imagine how someone with Mark-o's endless compassion ached while watching someone like Tony O'Neil. "I'm sorry," she said, and meaning it more than she'd meant it in months. "That's awful. What should I do? You want me to come out?"

Mark-o yawned on the other end. "Well, they've got Pop upstairs for testing. We won't know anything for a couple of hours, near as I can guess, but they don't seem to think he's in any immediate danger. Tell you what—I'll stay here if you can pick things up at about seven. Will Josh be up by then?"

"Relax, babies are portable." Essie couldn't believe she was using the words she'd thrown back at Mark-o during their last argument over Pop. It felt like all they'd done recently was argue over Pop. "Seven would be good. How is he? What's going on?" Essie grabbed her bathrobe and padded out into the kitchen, pulling the bedroom door shut behind her, for Doug had somehow managed to stay asleep.

"Something to do with his heart."

"I thought Pop had meds for that."

"Well, he does, but this isn't an exact science. He's not the picture of health, and he's not exactly cooperative, you know."

"Oh, I know, all right." Essie yawned. "How's Mom?"

"Nervous, but she's doing okay. I'll probably just shuffle

back and forth between Pop's room and Tony for the next couple of hours until things settle down. Mom'll be able to sit with Pop in his room in about twenty minutes, so that will give her something to do."

"Does she need something? And Pop? Should I swing by their house and pick up stuff?"

"Actually…hang on a sec…" She could hear her brother cover the phone and have a quick conversation with someone. "Okay, Pop's coming out of testing right now. Swinging by the house would be a good idea. Get some pajamas, toothbrush, things like that. And go into the medicine cabinet and bring every bottle with Pop's name on it—I can't tell you how many times I've told him to carry a complete list of his meds in his wallet, but you know Pop…."

They finished up a few quick details and hung up. Somehow, it had never occurred to Essie that Mark-o got called out to these sorts of things in the middle of the night. There, in his snazzy office or shaking hands in the entrance of his big church, she always thought of him more like a CEO than a counselor. He was a powerful speaker, and a gifted leader—the kind of guy you always knew would go places, even in high school. The one-on-one of pastoring—the holding of hands in emergency rooms, the triage of grief and disaster—she'd somehow never considered that side of him. Yet, it had always been there. He would be right there with her when she was younger and facing any crisis or problem. He would enter into her situation and be there completely for her.

How had they lost that? How had they fallen into such bickering? When was the last time they just had Mark-o and Peggy over, and she had the joy of watching Mark-o down on the floor playing with Josh?

We need a family Thanksgiving this year, that's what we need. A real this-is-home-now family Thanksgiving. Got that, Lord? You can help me pull together a Thanksgiving, can't You?

Even though sleep would probably be impossible, Essie was too tired not to at least try. She lay down on the couch and pulled up the afghan her grandmother had made for her when she and Doug were first married. The crochet stitches smelled of years and use and love. *Maybe I should learn to crochet,* she thought to herself, and then laughed it off. She was lucky she had time to sit these days, much less time to do anything so…so…

She drifted off to sleep trying to think of the right word.

Hours later, Essie stood in her parents' bathroom and banged Mark-o's speed dial number into her phone. "Mark-o, I'm gonna kill him. Tell the doctors to just stop whatever they're doing because I'm coming over there right now to strangle Pop with my own two hands."

"Whoa, Es, hang on there. What's going on?"

"I'm at Mom and Pop's, and I'm going through the medicine cabinet like you said, and I found a pill splitter."

"A what?"

"A pill cutter!" Essie was pacing again, walking up and down the hallway in her parents' home, holding out the pill cutter as if it were state's evidence. "One of those plastic gadgets that cuts pills in half. Only none of dad's prescriptions call for half a pill. I checked. He's been cutting his heart pills in half. I found one in the bottle. He's been skimping on his meds because he's such a cheapskate he'd rather *save a buck than stay alive.* Well, I'll save him the trouble because I'm gonna kill him."

"You're sure?"

Essie stopped pacing. "Yes, I'm sure. I should have seen this one coming. I've read about this sort of thing. Go hide him somewhere, or pray for an earthquake, because when I get my hands on him, I'll..."

"Okay, okay, I believe you. Calm down, will you? We're not going to get anywhere if you come barreling in here like the medicine-cabinet police."

"Medicine-cabinet police? Oh, no, I'm wa-a-ay beyond that. I'm a full-fledged medicine-cabinet commando." Essie plunged a pair of her father's pajamas into a shopping bag, dumping the collection of prescription bottles in on top. "Does he want to die early? Does he not *want* to be here for Josh's first steps? His first day of school?" With an exasperated groan, she threw the pill splitter in as well.

"Come on, this isn't helping things. I'm angry, too, but we both know yelling at Pop won't get us anywhere. We've yelled before and not gotten anywhere."

Essie sat down on her parents' couch. "I know, I know. I'm just so..."

"Me, too. Just try to back down on the storm trooper attitude before you get here, okay? Pop's cardiologist is scheduled to come in and talk to him in half an hour. Can you get here by then?"

"No problem."

"Just get here when you can, and don't rush. Everything's going to be fine, no one's in any danger—except maybe Pop if you don't get a grip on yourself. Oh, I almost forgot—Mom asked if you could bring her toothbrush and some tea bags."

"Tea bags? There's no *tea* at the hospital?"

"She doesn't like their brand."

"Her husband's been skimping on his medicine, she just

took an ambulance ride and the cardiologist is on his way, and she's fussing about tea brands?"

"Essie…"

Essie merely grunted into the phone.

"He's gonna be fine, Es, really. He's had a good scare, and maybe that's just what he needed. Give that nephew a kiss for me and I'll see you soon."

Wow. Mark-o hadn't said something like that in a long time. "Sure. See ya." She snapped her phone shut and tucked Joshua back into the carrier. "Hey, kiddo, maybe your uncle isn't such a bad guy after all. Here—" she kissed him "—this is from your Uncle Mark-o. Now, let's go yell at Grandpa."

By the time Essie lugged Josh's stroller down the hospital hallway, balancing the tower of purse, diaper bag, baby and shopping bag, she had simmered down into sort of an aggravated pity. A sad resolve that her father's deranged viewpoint was decades in the making and wouldn't change soon or easily. A weary understanding that this morning wouldn't be the last of such episodes.

Dr. Einhart was already there when she entered the hospital room. Essie listened as he read Pop the riot act. He went after Mom, too, because he made her admit she knew Pop had been splitting his pills. Finally, at the end of a rather lengthy lecture on medicine and responsibility, Dr. Einhart turned to Essie with his arms stretched out.

"May I borrow your son for a moment?"

Startled, Essie scooped Josh up out of his carrier and handed him to the doctor.

"Bob, what's your grandson's name again?"

Everyone in the room seemed baffled at the sudden shift in subject from Dr. Einhart. "Joshua," Pop replied.

Dr. Einhart held Joshua up right in front of her dad's face. "What's this little cutie worth to you, Bob?" Pop didn't answer. Dr. Einhart didn't seem to expect him to, for he kept right on holding the baby in front of her father's face. "Is he worth the two-fifty each one of those little pills costs you? What's it worth, Bob, to be able to see this little guy grow up?"

Essie got a lump in her throat. She was exhausted, and Dr. Einhart was pushing all the right buttons.

"Next time you're tempted to cut corners with your medicine, Bob, you remember Joshua here. He's not going to remember one thing about you if you don't shape up and do what it takes to keep you alive. What you did was foolish and irresponsible. Lots of things aren't worth the price we pay for them, but those pills are worth every single penny you shell out, you hear me? And they're worth it because your life is worth it. If you won't do it for yourself, then do it for Joshua. I sure won't do it for you. Make no mistake, though—" Dr. Einhart looked Pop straight in the eye, his voice sharp and serious "—if you pull another stunt like this I'll stick you with the meanest, pushiest, most obnoxious home nurse I can find to stuff your pills down your throat. Do we understand each other?"

No one in the room said anything. Except for Joshua, who added a gurgle that Essie interpreted to mean, "Yeah, Grandpa, what *he* said!"

Essie blinked back tears as she took Josh back from Dr. Einhart, who winked at her as he handed back the baby. "Medicine-cabinet commando, hmm?" he quipped softly.

Essie's eyes popped open, and she shot Mark-o a look. Her brother simply grinned and shrugged his shoulders.

Oh, yes, it'd be a swell Thanksgiving. *Swell*.

Chapter 14

The Family History of Airborne Produce

At Bayside Christian Church, the first day of November rivaled any holiday the calendar could dish out. Bayside had considerable resources, all of which were trained on throwing the biggest bash Essie had ever seen. How Mark-o and his colleagues had ever come up with the idea of celebrating the great heroes of the Christian faith with a sort of carnival/trick-or-treat style extravaganza, she'd never know. This was the fifth year of Bayside's Harvest of Witnesses, and by now the press—and most of San Francisco, it seemed—had caught on that this was the place to be. The church was swarming with hundreds of children this Friday evening, many of whom she didn't recognize.

The church drama team staffed each of the classrooms—and any nook or cranny they could fit a body and a pile of goodies—with actors in various costumes spouting various fact-laden, but downright entertaining monologues about saints, apostles, Bible figures, martyrs, evangelists and missionaries. Sunday school teachers like Essie, along with a small army of other volunteers, accompanied the roving packs of children. Each room had its own presentation, and its own small souvenir. Some rooms gave bookmarks, others small toys, others edible goodies; and the children went from room to room with baskets "harvesting" information and trinkets.

Essie worried that her boys' baskets would seem overdone but one good glance down the bustling hallways put that fear to rest. The fifth-grade girls couldn't have looked more turned out than if they were carrying Prada handbags. Each young lady had a hand-beaded basket of a different harvest theme. It was hard to even call them baskets; Essie thought they could have easily passed for evening bags. Not to be outdone, the fifth-grade boys had baskets made of actual bread. Someone wise enough to know they were dealing with ten-year-old appetites had shellacked the baskets, but Essie had to wonder who had been drafted—or more likely paid—to spend the countless hours required to weave and bake bread baskets.

She could barely contain her astonished laughter when one of the first-grade classes came down the hall pulling wicker cornucopia on wheels. Someone had fashioned little wagons out of the wicker horns, complete with leaf-embellished grapevine pulling ropes. Of course, one of the little darlings decided it might be fun to see if he could ride his little vehicle down the wheelchair ramp. It collapsed right under his little bottom halfway down the incline. It was something her guys would have done.

Watching all the classes go by—when she could catch a moment to look around and not be pulling Justin's fingers out of Decker's ribs or stopping Alex from bashing Steven over the head with his basket—was rather like watching the Rose Bowl Parade. The number of man-hours dedicated to creating baskets must have been staggering. One-upsmanship filled the halls as parents scoped out the competition for most creative, most expensive, most-likely-to-end-up-on-the-cover-of-*Better-Homes-&-Churches-Magazine* baskets.

When Mark-o came around the corner a moment later, Essie's jaw dropped open. It took a second or two for her to even realize that the man in front of her was her own brother. He was decked out, down to the last detail, as Moses from *The Ten Commandments.* As if someone had raided Cecil B. DeMille's wardrobe department. The red striped robe, the long hair and beard with gray streaks, the staff, the sandals, the works. Seemingly compelled to do so, the "sea" of small bodies parted itself in front of his path. Awestruck children stared at him, while their parents admired the cast-of-thousands-worthy costume.

"Pastor Taylor!" came one tiny voice registering complete disbelief. "Is that really *you?*"

Mark-o knelt down to the preschool girl. He took her hand and let her tug on the fake beard enough to let his own cheeks show through. She squealed in delight. "It's me, Abby," he whispered as if revealing a fantastic secret. "I get to play Moses today."

You might as well have told the girl Mark-o got to be President of the United States. She looked absolutely starstruck. Hearing her own boys' admiring "wows," Essie realized another of Mark-o's great gifts. He had achieved the most treasured prize of all youth attitudes: he was cool. Mark Taylor, cool dude of God. As she looked at the faces of not only her own class, but the fifth-grade boys who had plenty of other devious places to focus their admiration, she realized what Mark-o had accomplished. And she admired him.

And right there in that chaotic hallway, she thanked God for using him so mightily.

At least until Stanton Mannington threw an apple at him, knocking his wig sideways and probably giving Pastor Moses Mark-o a shiner.

Somehow, Essie was certain "good aim" was not a spiritual gift.

After the melee ended, Essie went in search of Cece to confirm a lunch date. She found her in the church kitchen, handing Mark-o an ice pack for the bruise now fully blossomed over his left eye. "Dahlia's absolutely mortified." Cece giggled as she helped Mark-o out of the wig he was wearing. "She's upstairs groveling to your wife right now."

Essie was feeling bad enough for not having sufficient control over her pack of harvest-hyper boys; she could only imagine how Dahlia was feeling. Essie couldn't stop herself from chuckling at the image of Dahlia, apologizing to crowds of staring parishioners over how her son had injured the Senior Pastor. She pictured Dahlia like a slug in salt— writhing in mortification over such a public display of bad behavior. Okay, a well-dressed slug in imported sea salt.

Which was unkind, but nevertheless extremely funny.

"If we start a church baseball team," Mark-o said while laughing with Cece as he shrugged out of the red-striped cloak, "I think we've found our pitcher."

"I don't know," replied Cece, waving to Essie as she caught her eye. "I feel much safer if I don't think of Stanton as actually aiming for you. Do you really want to think of your portrayal of Moses as inspiring that kind of be-havior?"

Mark-o laughed. "Hadn't thought of that. You may be right there. Or, perhaps I'd better opt to play the Roman Centurion next year. You know, someone with armor on."

"Oh, no," said Essie, coming up to help Mark-o with the rest of the costume. "Moses was fabulous. You looked ter-rific. My guys were awestruck."

"No, I'm the one who was struck, remember?"

"Yeah, sorry about that. You okay?"

"I'll be fine." Mark-o removed the ice pack and gingerly poked at his swollen eye. "As a matter of fact, I think there may be a sermon lurking in all of this."

"You might start with going upstairs and finding your wife," replied Cece. "Dahlia's probably drowning Peggy in apologies as we speak." Mark-o tried to hand her back the ice pack. "Oh, no, Pastor, I think you'd better hang on to that for a while."

Mark-o nodded, reapplied the pack, and then headed upstairs. Cece, who evidently had been holding it in dur-ing her administration of first aid, burst out laughing the minute the kitchen door swung shut behind him.

"Oh, Essie, couldn't you just fall over laughing?" Cece was laughing so hard that tears were slipping from the corners of her eyes. "Stanton, of all people, to whack Pastor Tay-lor." She folded the red robe, still chuckling. "Well, you can be sure no one will be giving out apples next year, hmm?"

"Nerf balls, maybe?"

That image sent Cece into new fits of laughter. "Who'd have thought Pastor Taylor needed bodyguards? For *flying fruit?*"

Essie thought of herself sending grapefruit soaring out

into the bay. *Lady, you have no idea of my family's history with airborne produce.*

They both laughed for a few minutes more, and Essie decided it might not be the end of the world that she'd not prevented Stanton's lousy behavior. This little episode would surely produce a note from Dahlia—most likely with a list of "suggestions" for better supervising her little prodigy. Maybe even a phone call from the ever-concerned Mrs. Bendenfogle.

"Years from now," said Cece, as if reading Essie's furrowed brow, "when Stanton Mannington is CEO of something and serving his seventh term on the Board of Elders, we'll all laugh about the day he beaned Pastor Taylor with an apple."

"Promise?"

Cece sighed. "No, but it's better to think of it that way. We still on for lunch Thursday?"

"Absolutely." They began to work together folding up Mark-o's costume. After a moment, Essie asked, "By the way, did you run into Vicki Faber at all today?"

"As a matter of fact, I did. I saw her outside picking up Alex. I went over to tell her how great I thought her baskets turned out. She barely said two words to me. Come to think of it, she looked awful."

Essie's heart sank. That could only mean that a call to one of Jack's high-priced doctors hadn't turned up any errors at all. Vicki seemed to have taken up residence in Essie's brain. Despite her best intentions to keep a distance, Essie hosted a reluctant, constant concern for the woman. It was clear Vicki didn't want any kind of involvement from her, but Essie could not stop thinking about her. Worrying about her. Wondering just how thick a wall Vicki had thrown up by now. "I just wanted to thank her, that's all."

"Well, she looked as though she could use a 'thank you,' that's for sure."

"I'll call her later."

"Hey, how's your dad? That was quite a scare he gave you the other day."

"I've never been so angry at Pop. Cutting his pills in half to save money." Essie blew out an exasperated breath. "He may be the first man to actually die of cheapness."

"Oh, no," countered Cece, "he'd be far from the first. I've known husbands in this congregation who've shelled out six figures for a sports car, or thousands of dollars for golf clubs, but gripe about how much their cholesterol medication is costing them."

Essie stared at her. "Why is that? I just don't get it. Why do such things happen?"

"Near as I can tell," said Cece, smoothing out the wrinkles on Moses' cloak, "once we reach adulthood—or especially parenthood—we figure out that our parents aren't the idiots we thought they were in high school. We realize they were pretty smart people all along. If we're lucky, we spend some of that adulthood in a genuine friendship with our parents. We have more things in common, we see the world in more similar ways. For a while things seem great. Then…"

"Then?"

"Then they get old. *Old* old. And the nifty creative grandma we thought we had for our kids slowly slips into this cranky old lady complaining about the price of bread or how things break down too much anymore. The grandpa who swore he'd teach our kids to build things now just sits in his recliner and watches *Jeopardy* with the volume turned way up high. Pretty soon they're doing things that seem ridiculous to us, or even downright stupid. Then downright stupid becomes downright dangerous, until suddenly we wake up one morning and realize we're parenting them."

"No kidding. Oh, I'm there all right."

"Then comes the kids. Your adorable, perfect babies become obnoxious toddlers or obnoxious teenagers, and your parents start telling you they're undisciplined or they dress awful or—I don't know, take your pick. Samantha got a third ear piercing for her birthday this year, and you'd think I'd have gotten her a tattoo to hear my parents' reaction." Cece stared at Essie. "Do you know my dad actually called Sam a 'Jezebel'? While she was in the room?"

"Sam? Your Samantha? The head-on-straight, good-grades Sam?" Essie huffed. "Obviously, your dad hasn't seen the inside of a high school in a decade or so."

"I don't think it would help if he did. I love the guy, but the truth is that my father is a grumpy old man."

Essie was silent for a long moment. "I want Pop to live long enough to complain about Josh's clothes. I want him to stay alive, Cece. This week was too scary. I don't like to think about what might happen next time."

"Sometimes, all we get is now. Look at Mavis and Tony O'Neil. Who'd have thought Tony would be standing at her grave with their children? You've got to go with what's in front of you."

"Thanksgiving."

"Hmm?"

"Thanksgiving," Essie repeated. "That's what's in front of me. I mentioned to my mom that it'd be nice to have Thanksgiving with everyone this year, and she got so excited. She said she wants to go all out hosting Thanksgiving this year. A big old-fashioned holiday. I'm really glad. I think we need it."

Cece looked at her. It was that slanted, analytical look. As if she was deciding how much of a secret to reveal. The same look she had before letting Essie in on the fantastic grapefruit-spoon trick.

"What?" said Essie, not liking her expression. "I think Mom hosting a big Thanksgiving is a great idea." The look persisted. "What?"

"I'm going to let you in on a little secret."

"I gathered as much."

"That big Thanksgiving your mom has in mind? Well, as far as my own experience goes, when old ladies say 'big Thanksgiving,' it really means 'you make the big Thanksgiving, and I pretend to host it.'"

"Meaning…"

"Meaning a few days before the holiday, your mother's going to suddenly come up with a huge list of things *you* have to do, food *you* have to cook, errands *you* have to run. And, if she's anything like my mother was, she'll hand you a grocery list sixty items long and a twenty-dollar bill to cover the costs."

"No, she loves this kind of…"

"Oh, you just watch. She'll tell you how she's taking care of everything. How now that the whole family's together, she's going to make a holiday like she used to…whatever. She'll tell you to leave it all up to her." Cece shook her head. "Come the week before Thanksgiving, I guarantee it, she'll dump the whole load on you. I could hand you a list of two or three dozen women who've had the same thing happen to them." She waved her hands in the air. "It happens, and I tell you, you're better off just knowing. Clear your schedule, tweak your budget, and no matter what…"

Essie's heart was sinking fast. "No matter what…"

"Call me the minute she dumps it on you. We'll have you fixed up in no time."

Essie slumped against the kitchen counter. All her Norman Rockwell happy holiday illusions were going up in smoke. She stared off into space until Cece handed a scrap of paper to her. "What's this?" she asked as she stared at the phone number.

"Guswell's Meat Market. I'd go ahead and preorder the turkey now."

Chapter 15

*Just When You Thought it Was Safe
To Go Back in the Kitchen...*

Josh and Doug had stayed for the first part of the Harvest
of Witnesses extravaganza, heading for home halfway
through the Friday night event. Essie was grateful Doug
could carve even that small chunk of time out of his schedule this week. Things were supposed to be "letting up" at
work, but only very slightly. Doug rarely made it home for
dinner, often missing a wide-awake Joshua all together. Essie
was doing her best to put up a good front, but she was getting tired of hearing "it'll lighten up next week," only to
have some new crisis fall onto Doug's shoulders.

Occasionally, though, there were adorable light spots.
Such as the scene that greeted her as she walked through her
front door tonight. Doug was in the kitchen, making a complete idiot of himself in an effort to convince Josh that rice
cereal was interesting and tasty. Josh wasn't buying any of it,
preferring instead to discover the many fascinating ways one
can spit out rice cereal. Or wear it. Or smear Daddy with it.

"Oh, this is good stuff, Josh, my boy. Filled with delicious nutrients and yummy vitamins. Jam-packed with…ugh, not in Daddy's eyes, okay?" Doug turned just in time to dodge a second glob of cereal, which soared past him to land with a distinct "plop" on the kitchen floor in front of Essie's left foot.

"Oh, good one. The boy's got shot-put genes in him for sure."

"One thing's for sure," sighed Doug, "he doesn't have much rice cereal in him."

"Not exactly gobbling it down, is he?" Essie had been through several shooting matches of her own trying to get a nutritionally appropriate fraction of Josh's meal into his actual mouth. It usually turned into an aggravating episode of "dodge the spoon."

"I'm not even sure this qualifies as eating. Come on, Josh, will you just…" Josh cut him off by whacking the full spoon out of Doug's hand and sending it splattering to the floor. It was clear Doug was near the end of his patience.

"Well, would it help to know you're not the only man to be the target of flying food this evening?"

That got a laugh from Doug. "You mean your brother? So I heard."

"Word got out, huh?"

"Well, not exactly. Let's just say I have a new appreciation for what it's like to be on the receiving end of a lecture from Dahlia Mannington."

"She called? Already?"

"Oh, yes. Followed almost immediately by Alice Bendenfogle, who is e-mailing you a list of more nutritionally appropriate goodies for next year's event. She was distinctly unhappy with the sugar content of this year's selections."

"Do these women have nothing better to do?"

"You know," said Doug, calling it quits and extracting a gooey Joshua from the high chair, "I think we should just take the phone off the hook after the drama thing."

"Not a bad idea." Essie grabbed a washcloth and started going after the sticky spots on the floor.

"Your mom called, too." There was an edge in Doug's voice that hadn't been there a moment ago.

"And…"

"And I hadn't realized we'd decided on Thanksgiving with your family already."

Essie winced. She'd been so absorbed by the chaos in her own family that she'd gone off and assumed they'd be spending Thanksgiving here in San Francisco. Assumed. Without even talking to Doug.

Well, he wasn't around to talk to, was he?

That was no excuse, and she knew it.

I've botched it again. Essie wanted to crawl under a rock and disappear.

"It would have been a good idea to *discuss* it, Es."

"Well, with everything that was going on…" Even though she knew that didn't hold water as an argument, even though she knew this was mostly her fault, Essie got defensive. Why did everything have to turn on her? Why was she the one who had to pull all the frazzled ends together? Why couldn't it just be someone else's job for a change?

"It's been 'going on' since we got here. It's never going to stop 'going on' with your family. We're finally within driving distance of my parents, and we spent last Thanksgiving with your parents. Bob and Dorothy see Josh almost every week. My parents haven't seen him since we moved here."

"Your parents are in perfect health and they own a car.

Three of them, if I remember right. They could come up and see Josh anytime they wanted to."

Doug wheeled around. "And just *where* do you think we would put them? In sleeping bags under the kitchen table? Do you have any idea how expensive hotel rooms are in San Francisco?"

Essie merely glared at him. Part of her knew he was right, but her patience was worn so thin right now she'd have picked a fight with the Angel Gabriel. "I'm hanging on by a thread here, and you want me to travel? Besides, just how are you going to get off work to visit your folks when you haven't been able to visit with your own son?"

Doug glared. "That's a low blow. We need that year-end bonus, in case you haven't noticed."

"The only thing I've noticed around here lately is how much you're not around." Essie threw the towel in the sink, not caring that it knocked a trio of clean bottles back into the dirty dishwater. "I feel like a single parent, Doug. You're never around, and even when you are you're either working from home or sleeping. How can you blame me for spending time with my family when there's no one ever home?"

He jabbed finger at her. "Hey, you *wanted* to be home, remember?"

"Now who's not being fair? Do you have any idea what it's like to be with Josh 24/7 these days? What it's like to get up for the fourth time in a night? No, you don't. This is no picnic, Doug. I'm not exactly sitting at home watching soaps and doing my nails. I'm happy if I get to *shower* these days." Her anger twisted itself into knots in her throat. She started to cry, which made her even angrier. She turned to Doug, who was trying to keep a lid on his own anger and keep Josh from bursting into tears at the same time. Essie fisted her hands, almost punching the air. "I hate this. I hate *hating* it. I hate the way I feel. I hate the way you look at me like I'm some sort of grumpy old lady who used to be your wife. I hate the way I feel about Josh some nights. I hate all of it." She stared at him, suddenly burning to say the one thing she'd swore she'd never say to his face. It spilled out of her, hot and dangerous like a volcanic eruption. *"I wish we'd stayed in New Jersey!"*

She started, shocked by her own statement, stung by the look in Doug's eyes. There she was, standing in her kitchen holding the verbal smoking gun, unable to look away from the hole she'd just shot in her husband's heart. Fully aware of everything that statement held, of the damage it did, how she would never be able to take it back, and almost ready not to care.

There was a long, awful pause.

Doug started to say something, then stopped himself. He was the angriest she'd ever seen him. Without another word, Doug handed Josh to her, being acutely careful he never touched her in the handoff. Then he snatched his jacket off the coatrack and left, slamming the door shut behind him.

Josh broke into open wails on her shoulder.

Essie stood there, holding her screaming son, staring at the door that seemed to still be vibrating from the force of Doug's slam. Half of her was glad she'd said it. Glad she'd finally admitted to someone how far all of this was from what she'd thought it'd be. The other half of her worried that she'd regret her outburst forever. Half of her knew Doug would come back after he'd burned off some steam. The other half of her wondered if he'd ever come back at all.

It was hard to say who cried more in the next thirty minutes; she or Josh. The world felt horrible and awful. Her home felt dark and lonesome. Her lungs felt as if they were filled with broken glass while her heart felt gaping and empty.

She felt so alone.

Something had to be done. She could only think of one thing.

So, after an hour's brooding, Essie e-mailed her resume to Coach Jemmings.

She fell asleep on the couch with Josh nestled in the crook of her arm. Even her grandmother's afghan couldn't keep out the cold that seemed to creep in from the dark corners of the apartment.

Doug sat on the recliner, watching his wife sleep. It was late. The apartment was dark and brittle-feeling. Essie looked like he felt—eyes swollen, hands fisted even in sleep, knees pulled up in a posture of pain.

How had they gotten here?

How had the initial certainty of their move dissolved into this muddle of anger and doubt? How had the joy of Joshua's birth fallen into this abrasive life of tension and sleeplessness? He was stretched tight from the strain of work and the pressure of knowing their financial future lay on his shoulders alone now. He was weary from continually tamping down the ache to go home and play with his son. His new family needed the overtime pay, they needed his success. He needed his success. Work needed him, home needed him. His parents' recent e-mail, thick with indignation, had been the last straw. *Lord,* Doug moaned into the darkness, *help me fix this. How do I fix this?*

No answer came to him.

Nothing came to him except an overwhelming regret. He spent the next hour just staring at his wife, his son and their frazzled home. Taking in every detail of this dark, desperate hole they were in, completely at a loss for how to dig out. Doug Walker, the man who unraveled technology's thorniest knots for a living, couldn't fix this.

He sat there, turning the dilemma over and over in his mind the way he did with a computer bug. In every problem, there was always one small place to start. One equation to tweak, one command to rewrite. That small solution usually led to another equation, then another and then another. It was like carpentry: start with one piece, then attach it to another, then another, and keep going until you had what you needed.

Trouble was, Doug had no idea what he needed.

No, that was wrong. He knew exactly what it was he needed.

His wife.

The look in her eyes when she'd snapped out her regret at coming here, the full scope of not wanting to care and yet caring too much; it had all been there. He knew she'd held it back as long as she could. He knew she'd been thinking it for weeks—he'd been thinking it himself. He knew she was frustrated. Hadn't he spent the last half hour before she came home wondering how she put up with Josh's cranky behavior all day long? The pair of phone calls from those boys' parents had gotten his own dander up, and he didn't even have anything to do with them. And Essie's parents—well, there simply weren't words for them.

Still, she was in the wrong.

Then again, so was he.

How do you win an argument when everyone's wrong?

You don't, was the answer that floated to him on the darkness. No one wins. Everyone loses.

So what do I do now, Lord?

Find the one thing you can fix, then fix it. The words of his old college computer prof rung in his ears. But what could he fix?

When Essie shifted position and opened her eyes, he knew.

"I'm sorry."

She stared at him, drained from a fitful sleep. "Me, too," was her quiet reply.

He leaned his head back on the chair. "I don't know what to do here, Es."

She didn't move, but wrapped one hand tenderly around Josh, who was sleeping peacefully against her chest. "Me, neither."

For a while neither of them said anything. This wasn't a "kiss and make up" kind of situation—it was complicated and uncomfortable and it wasn't going away anytime soon. Part of him felt as though he should cross the dark room, go to her and say something more romantic than "I'm sorry." But no words came to mind. Essie sat up, nestled Josh into the crook of her arm, but made no move to cross the room, either. It was comforting, in an odd way, for them to both admit that an easy answer was not in the making. The honesty of it seemed a good place to start. More sad than angry.

Finally, almost before he realized he'd said the thought out loud, Doug sighed, "I need a manual."

"A what?" Essie brushed the hair out of her eyes and looked at him. Their eyes met for the first time since she'd talked about wishing they'd never left New Jersey.

"A manual." He shifted the recliner upright. "What we're dealing with here is essentially an upgrade. A new version of an old program that now doesn't work. All the old pieces are still here, but the new ones we've added have messed things up. It's an upgrade glitch."

"Funny," Essie, said smirking, "it doesn't feel like an upgrade. Upgrades are supposed to be improvements, right? I'm not feeling very improved."

Doug sat forward on his chair now. He'd found his first equation, and his brain was already solving and searching. "No, no, that's just it. Upgrades never feel like upgrades at first. It always feels like everything's been ruined until you work the bugs out."

"It's not that simple, Doug." Her voice was thick with resignation.

"No," he said on a sigh, "this is life, not binary math. But that's why I wish we had a manual."

Essie's face told him she wasn't following his thinking. Which was okay, because he wasn't exactly sure where his own thinking went himself. "I still don't get it." She yawned.

"When I'm stuck in an upgrade, I read the manual. Okay, I think it might just give me something to do that looks like I'm working, but nine times out of ten, I'll come across something in the manual that gives me an inkling of where to go."

She didn't say anything. She just stared at him. He was glad to see, however, that it was just a stare, not the sharp glare he'd seen in the kitchen. She was simply watching him think.

"I need a life manual," he said more to himself than to her.

Finally, Essie gave out a sort of half-hearted giggle. It was more of a snort, actually, but he chose not to point that out at this particular time. "You don't see it, do you?"

"See what?"

"You really don't see where this is heading? Not at all?" She was genuinely amused now.

Which was rather annoying. "No, Mrs. Walker, if there's something important going on here I wish you'd clue me in."

"Life manual. You're looking for a life manual." Her eyes were wide, as if cueing him in some sinister interpersonal game of charades.

"I said that already."

"Life manual. Wake up, Doug—life manual."

He was getting ready to get angry again when something came flying across the room at him. For a split second he debated if catching it or ducking was the better option. He caught it.

It was a Bible.

Chapter 16

Endless Opportunities for Bad Behavior

"How many bars this time, sweetie?" Lenora, the owl-eyed lady behind the pharmacy counter, smiled as Essie filled this year's ten-thousandth prescription for amoxicillin. Well, really it was only something like the sixth, but it certainly felt like she'd hit the five-digit range. "You've had quite a run," she said, affixing the label to the bottle. "I'm thinkin' I oughta buy stock in whoever makes this stuff."

"Josh Walker," said Essie, nodding her head toward her son, who was dozing in the stroller to her left. "Single handedly holding up the pharmaceutical industry at the tender age of eight months. No candy, Lenora. I'm on my way to a meeting and they always have more than enough gooey sweets there anyway."

Lenora smiled. "Howzabout I throw one in anyway? For the road."

"Howzabout I fit into my pre-baby jeans sometime next year?"

That made Lenora laugh. She had a funny, hiccupy laugh, too. The kind that made anyone around her laugh just because her laugh was so funny. She was wearing an exceedingly festive sweatshirt boasting a velvet turkey with his tail spread in a full arc of sequined splendor. Each earring was a tiny plastic cornucopia. That was Lenora; God's little sparkle of light behind the pharmacy counter. If anyone could make Kaopectate amusing, it'd be Lenora. Essie hoped she never had to test that particular theory.

Having read through the script, Essie didn't know what to expect at the pre-production meeting of the Celebration of Bible Heroes. The whole thing seemed so ridiculously overblown that she wasn't sure she could attend the meeting with a straight face. In fact, she'd seriously considered skipping all together until Cece called and asked if she wanted to go to lunch afterward.

As she walked in the room after depositing the sleeping Josh in the nursery with a volunteer sitter, it struck Essie just how far she'd come in her few months at Bayside. The table was filled with familiar faces. Sure, they were still faces that looked like they belonged on a magazine cover, but there were now personalities behind each face. They weren't mindless rows of twinsets anymore, they were people.

Not that "being people" was an improvement in all cases. Some of them were still loonies, and no amount of familiarity would change that. Essie yearned to face Dahlia and howl, "It's not my fault your son behaves badly, lady!" Even though Essie had twice pointed out to Dahlia that Stanton's ongoing disregard for Queen Esther's Commandments was making it very difficult to cast him as Jesus, it wasn't sinking in. Dahlia's response was always the same: a long look which seemed to broadcast that the achievement of Jesus-worthy behavior rested entirely on Essie's shoulders. Essie had no doubt that Stanton's failure to be cast as Jesus would be viewed as a personal failure on her part. And, based on the most recent episode of Stanton using Moses for target practice, failure was looming large indeed.

Beyond Stanton's talent for mischief, the entire production was evolving into endless opportunities for bad behavior. "Are we sure," Essie actually found herself saying, "that real sand is a good idea?" Could no one else imagine what several dozen rowdy children could do if they got their hands on that? The group stared at her as if she were calling the authenticity of the show's six desert scenes into question. Thankfully, the Doom Room's scene took place on the "Temple Square" set in Act Two, with only a ten foot ficus tree to worry about.

When Dahlia distributed a practice schedule worthy of the San Francisco Giants' training camp, Essie barely hid her sigh. If she'd taken on this class as a way to understand boys, she was going to get her wish. According to the schedule, she'd practically be living with these boys by January. What was that about being careful what you prayed for?

"I can't stand it anymore!" Essie burst out as she and Cece were walking down the front steps toward a nearby deli after the meeting. "Can no one see how extravagant this is? Does anyone else find this all a bit too much?"

"It is kind of complicated, isn't it?" Cece laughed. Nothing ever seemed to get under that woman's skin.

"'Kind of complicated'? Perhaps like brain surgery is 'kind of complicated.'"

"It always seems like too much work at the beginning. At the end, though, the kids are so proud of what they've done that it all seems worth it."

Essie shot her a look. "The kids don't have to clean up fifty bags of real sand or build a self-separating pyramid."

"That pyramid will be fabulous, won't it?"

Essie stopped pushing the stroller and squared off at Cece. "None of this bothers you?"

"Oh, I didn't say that. I've got a thing or two to say about quite a bit that goes on with this."

"But…"

"But kids and parents get obsessed with things. Either it's soccer or music or sneakers or clothes or any number of things. Why is it bad that they've become obsessed with church? With learning far too many details about Bible heroes? I just don't see how all that time and energy directed at the word of God can be a bad thing, even if it feels—what'd you say?—'extravagant.' My husband knows way too much about baseball. What's so bad if he knows way too much about first-century temple structure?"

"Because I hardly see my husband now, and if he has to build that first-century temple and I have to herd eight boys through it, I'll never see him." Where'd that come from? How was it that Cece made things pop out of her mouth before she could stop them?

"Oh, now I see."

Essie didn't like the tone of that. Not a bit. "Now you see what?"

"I thought you were looking a little ragged around the edges today. You and Doug hit the wall, didn't you?"

Essie arched her eyebrows. "The wall?"

Cece motioned to continue walking. "Of course, it's not really a wall, but I've always called it the wall. It's a place, a spot that everyone hits just about—how old is Josh?"

"Eight months."

That seemed to be just the answer Cece was looking for. "Yep, always somewhere between six and nine months. Suddenly all the pressures of being a parent collide and Mom and Dad have a colossal blow out. The holidays are especially good at bringing this on."

"Is this supposed to make me feel better? It's not working."

Cece laughed. "If I guess the nature of the spat, will you let me buy lunch?"

"I'll let you buy lunch if you're wrong, too, you know."

"Good." Cece crossed her hands over her chest as she walked. "I'm guessing it went something like 'This baby is hard work and you don't realize it' followed by 'Well, now that I have to do all the breadwinning around here' with a dash of 'Why are we spending Thanksgiving with your family?' and a pinch of 'We never talk anymore.'"

Essie could only stare and try to keep her mouth from falling open.

"Am I close?"

"Close? You're beyond close. You're creepy."

"Not creepy, just experienced. Let's just say I've had that particular go-round enough times to know it when I see it." Cece put a hand on Essie's shoulder. "So where did you leave off?"

Essie could only smile. "I threw The Book at him."

"What?"

"I threw The Book at him."

"I thought you said that. This isn't some kind of shot-put ritual, is it? Which book did you throw?"

"*The* Book."

"The…" She looked alarmed as it dawned on her. "You threw a Bible at your husband?"

"It was a lot more clever-sounding at the time. He was talking about needing a life manual. It's complicated."

Cece smiled. "No, it's creepy, to use your word. Oh, I can just imagine how that called the argument to a complete halt."

"No, actually, it did." She pulled open the deli door for Cece. "I'll tell you the whole thing over that lunch you're going to buy me."

Just as she had done many times before, Cece was the perfect listener. She laughed in all the right places, sighed in all the others, commiserated at points and chided at others. And even unflappable Cece raised an eyebrow at the phone calls from Dahlia and Alice. "You really are under the microscope in there. Try not to worry—I think you're doing just fine. You might want to follow Doug's advice, though, and turn off the phone for a day or two after the production. Come to think of it, you might want to leave town after you put up the cast list."

"I'm worried about how vicious stage mothers can be when they discover their son didn't make the cut to be Jesus. There aren't any lawyers among our class parents, are there?"

Cece laughed. "Three. And Jack Faber could probably sic his public relations department on you, too, if provoked."

Ah, the Fabers. Try as she might, Essie still could not get Vicki Faber out of her mind. Vicki—or reminders of Vicki—plagued her constantly. She couldn't shake the disturbing notion that Vicki's troubles went far deeper than a bad mammogram. Finally, after another ten minutes of conversation still failed to distract her, Essie set down her soda and said, "Cece, I need some advice."

"Sure."

"I've stumbled onto some information about someone.

Someone who needs some help. I'm worried they won't get it. At least I don't think they will…well, I don't know them well enough to be sure. I don't know how to convince them to get help. They don't seem to want it. I'm worried about them, but I'm not really close and so…"

"Es…" Cece put her hands on Essie's arm to stop the flow of babble. "It would be easier if we just came out and talked about who."

"I can't. I promised not to say anything. To anyone."

Cece sat back in her chair. "That's not always a wise promise to keep."

"I know, but I think I need to try. For now."

Cece sighed. "Okay, so how can I help?"

"I need to find some breast cancer survivors. This person… they've found a lump…she's had tests but I don't know much more. She…um…needs someone to talk to."

Cece grew very serious. "Essie, if you've gotten some scary news, don't think for a moment that…"

"No, no really, it's not me. I promise, it's not me. But this person is really frightened—I think. I mean I really don't know her that well at all. It's an accident that I know at all."

"An accident?"

"Yes. I just happened to be there when she…just one of those fluke-y things. An accident."

"Well I doubt that."

"Huh?"

"I don't think it's an accident that you know, Essie. Those kinds of things aren't accidents, they're God. You were there because you were supposed to be there. You know for a reason."

Essie pulled back. "Oh, no, you don't. This isn't God's idea of a rescue mission. I'm botching my own life quite nicely here, it'd be poor planning to add anyone else's to the mix."

"So you're sitting here, picking my brains for help for someone you don't want to help?"

"Yes. No! Well…ugh, do you have any idea how aggravating you are?"

Cece spread her arms. "Yes, it's a gift."

"We're not friends. We could never be friends. I'm…I'm not her type."

"Says who?"

"Look around here, Cece. I'm out of my league with most of these people. Our church is filled with people who make more money in one week that Doug does in a month. People who've picked out their preschooler's Ivy League college careers already. People who have more exes than they do cars. I can't exactly strike up a close friendship with this woman—who, by the way, I didn't like even before this—simply because I got in earshot of an unfortunate cell phone call."

She'd done it again. Shot off her mouth before she thought better of it. From the looks of it, Cece didn't much care for that last little speech. *Way to go, Walker. Care to offend anyone else in the room while you're on a roll?*

"Do you really want to know what I think?"

"Look, I'm sorry, Cece, I wasn't talking about you, but I…"

"No, I think you really ought to know what I think." Cece cut her off. "I think you need to take a good hard look around this church. Look good and hard until you see human beings, not just stereotypes. Yes, they seem different than what you knew in New Jersey. Seem. Some of them come in some very pretty packages. Some of them have gotten very caught up in things they thought would lead to success. But they're human beings. People that hurt and seek and botch life up just the same as you do. You have everything in common with these people if you have faith. No, sir, I think God has a big lesson for you in all this. I'll help you find some women to talk to this new friend—" she used the word with emphasis "—of yours, but that doesn't knock you out of the picture."

Essie was quiet for a long moment, not really having any ammunition against that kind of speech. Finally, almost in a surrender, she sighed. "Cece, I don't think she wants my help."

"Which is precisely why you should help her."

"But…"

Cece cut her off again. "It's no fluke that you know. It's no fluke you were there. It's no fluke that you obviously can't get her out of your mind. You're in this, Esther Walker. God's not in the fluke business. Don't you dare walk away now just because it's uncomfortable."

"I don't…"

"Want to see how well I can throw The Book at you?"

Essie gulped. "No, ma'am."

"All right then, it's settled. Tell me all you can tell me without breaking any promises. And I'm going back for cheesecake—do you want some?"

Essie resigned herself to the fact that this lunch was going to cost her a whole lot more than no money. "None for me, thanks. My pre-baby jeans are calling to me."

"I wouldn't listen to them. But suit yourself."

You don't have to listen. Your present jeans look to be about a size six. Go ahead, eat your cheesecake, plan my life, throw me into the pit with Icky Vicki and her designer cell phone. I'm on earache number six and I don't have the energy to argue with you.

"Headbands, Josh." Essie sank her chin into her hand as Cece walked across the room to order a slice of delicious-looking cheesecake. "You gotta stay away from the head-bands."

Chapter 17

Something Bigger To Think About

Essie pointed to the clipboard hanging beside the doorway. The one with the running tally of good-behavior points that would decide who got to be Jesus. "Today, gentlemen, I will announce the cast for the Celebration. Decker, you might want to remember that before you pull out whatever it was you just reached into your pocket for…"

Decker froze. He pasted a "Who me?" smirk on his face, then sauntered back to his chair to finish pasting together his Coat of Many Colors.

Essie continued talking as she walked among the boys supervising their artwork. The cast list was already typed up and waiting in her notebook, but she wasn't about to lose one second of the leverage she'd gladly held over these boys for the past few weeks. "At the end of class today, you'll find out which parts you have in the Celebration. That way you'll have time to look them over with your families during the Thanksgiving break and be ready when rehearsals start up in December." Cece had come up with the brilliant idea of having all the Sunday school teachers announce their casts the Sunday before Thanksgiving. While Essie was sure it wouldn't altogether stop the tirade of angry parents, the looming prospect of holiday preparations might at least keep protests down to a dull roar. "Now, who can tell me how Joseph's brothers planned to get rid of Joseph?" Sure as the sunrise, Stanton Mannington's hand shot up. That boy liked to show off that he knew his Bible, but he liked to be first even more. "Stanton?"

"First, they were gonna kill 'im. Cut him up into tiny pieces. Then, they decided they might get in trouble so they stuck him in a hole so he'd die all on his own. Then, some rich squishy kite guys came and they sold Joseph to them instead."

Essie laughed. "The 'squishy kite' guys were the Ishma-lites. And you're exactly right—they sold Joseph to them to be a slave."

"That was dumb," interjected Peter. "There were all kinds of cool bugs that could have eaten him alive in that hole."

"Nah," said David, "it would have been better to stake him out on the ground or something so the lions could eat him. You know, rip his arms off his body and stuff." David ripped one arm off his paper Joseph figure just to illustrate his theory. Then he made screaming noises, making his figure jump around the desk as if in agony. The other boys, of course, found this highly entertaining. It was all Essie could do to keep several paper Josephs from being mutilated on the spot.

"He lost his leg. Augh! Now his arm is gone! He's bleeding all over the place! He's loosing body parts everywhere!" Decker was getting ready to behead his Joseph.

"My mom's lost body parts," offered Stanton, to the surprise of everyone in the room. The boy simply had to come out on top, no matter what the issue.

"Stanton, I've seen your mother," countered Essie, ready to nip this little bit of one-upsmanship in the bud. "She has all her body parts. She's not even missing a pinky finger."

"No she doesn't. I found some the other day." He looked around the room, making sure he had everyone's full attention before he pronounced, "I pulled open her drawer the other day and found her *boobs* lying in there. Cut off. Both of 'em. They were all…"

"That's *enough!*" Essie gasped. Just when she thought she'd reached the pinnacle of inappropriate behavior in this class… "Stanton, that's the *last* I ever want to hear about that." It was a full ten minutes before she could wrench the class back to some kind of order. Leave it to Stanton to pull something *that* atrocious. Essie could just imagine the phone calls she'd get from Dahlia and Alice tonight. No, they wouldn't wait one hour. Her answering-machine light would probably be blinking by the time she and Doug walked in their apartment door.

There was one bright side; even Dahlia would agree that talking about his mother's private body parts in class was definitely *not* Jesus-worthy behavior. And Dahlia certainly couldn't blame the teacher for this outburst.

Could she?

Essie fumbled through the rest of class, nearly forgetting to hand out the cast list. It was hard to tell who was more surprised: Stanton at not getting cast as Jesus, or Justin at getting the part. Decker seemed almost indifferent to getting the part of Zacchaeus, until he remembered that it meant he got to climb the tree. Then he was thrilled. David and

Alex got a few speaking lines, and the rest of the Doom Room made up the crowd of onlookers.

Stanton had no lines. Essie had a long list of Stanton's bad behavior to back up her casting, but she didn't fool herself into thinking that would placate Dahlia Mannington. Essie had her heels dug in, ready for battle—even before today's episode.

With a quick excuse that Josh had been wailing up in the nursery, Essie wished everyone a happy Thanksgiving and got herself out of there before the melee hit. She, Josh and Doug were out the door and halfway down the sidewalk before it hit her.

Dahlia. Two "boobs" in her drawer.

Prostheses.

Dahlia had had a mastectomy. Maybe even a double mastectomy.

Dahlia was a breast cancer survivor.

Oh, no, Lord, you can't mean I have to deal with both of them! Don't do this! Essie could barely put one foot in front of the other as they made their way home. If she could have picked the two people in this world she last wanted to get up close and personal with, these ladies would have topped the list. What a choice: picking between breaking her word with Vicki and telling Dahlia about Vicki's problem, or attempting to jump-start a friendship between these ladies and somehow prodding them to share it themselves. If ever there was a time for "send someone else, Lord," this was it. Essie could just picture the phone conversation now: *Dahlia, dear, I know I just dashed your hopes of Stanton's stage career, but we really must face up to the fact that obedience and discernment do not top Stanton's list of spiritual gifts lately. And no, I'm quite sure it's not something I've done. Having said that, would you mind very much if I*

shared your deep dark secrets with Icky Vicki? Come on, it'll be fun.
Just us girls and a few life-threatening medical issues. Denial's so
much more fun in groups, don't you think?

Essie must have been sending her anxiety out through her
feet, for a few seconds later she heard Doug panting, "Slow
down, hon. Where's the fire?"

"Oh, Doug, this is bad. Really bad. We've got to get
home so I can tell you about it." She froze. "I mean, I…can't
tell you." Essie's spirits sunk. There was no way to talk about
this without breaking her promise to Vicki. No, God seemed
to be up there in His universe, orchestrating events so that
Essie had no way to weasel out of this. No way to pass it
on to someone with better interpersonal skills. Someone
with a better wardrobe, at least, to level the playing field.

With a laugh, Essie remembered that she'd asked God earlier this week to give her something bigger to think about
than the Doom Room cast list.

Thanks, Lord. You didn't need to go quite this far.

"Es!"

Essie shook her head to clear her thoughts, only to find
Doug standing in front of her, waiving his hands to get her
attention.

"Come back to me, Esther."

"I'm sorry. I was off thinking about this problem."

"No kidding. I was trying to ask you if you brought Josh's
medicine home from the nursery."

Essie rolled her eyes. "Oh, no. I left it in the little refrigerator in the nursery. I swear, if I have to see…"

Doug held up his hands. "Josh and I will go back for the
bottle, you head on home. You look like you'd rather die
than go back there right now."

"You're sure?"

"Maybe they won't hurt me when I'm holding an infant. Maybe they'll just make me carry back a message of doom."

It came to Essie's mind like the big, slanted title of a fifties Sci–Fi B–movie. *Queen Esther and the Second Graders of Doom. Mayhem! Chaos! Interpersonal Conflict! Coming soon to a theater near you!*

"Pass the popcorn." Essie whimpered as she watched Doug and Josh head back up the street toward Bayside. She could hardly wait to see what would be on her answering machine.

Sure enough, there were three messages on the machine. From her mother.

Each one adding to a list of things Essie "could just lend a hand with" for the holiday: Things like 1) get and thaw the turkey (which would have to be done in the next twenty-four hours if they had any chance at all of getting it stuffed), 2) come get the china out of storage and wash it up (which could only mean polishing the silver wouldn't be far behind), and 3) a grocery list larger than Essie's regular weekly grocery list (complete with brand names from the New Jersey stores Essie was somehow sure she'd be reprimanded for not finding). Not to mention the seventeen—*seventeen*—other "oh, and could you…"'s over the three messages.

"What did these people do before I got here?" snapped Essie at the blinking light that seemed to be laughing at her and the long list she'd taken down from the phone messages. "Didn't they *have* Thanksgiving before I got to California?"

Essie spun in slow circles in the center of the room, looking for something to yell at, somewhere to release the H-bomb of frustration going off inside her. Something to throw that wouldn't cause damage. Okay, not too much damage.

There was nothing. No one to yell at, nothing to throw, nothing.

For lack of a better option, Essie grabbed a pillow off the couch, punched it a few times, then held it to her mouth and screamed. "Everyone in my life is just plain *nuts!*" she yelled into the chenille. "This is *crazy.* They're all *looney toons* out here!" and several other versions before she caught her breath and pulled the pillow away from her face.

She didn't know what to do. There seemed to be nowhere to turn, no escape from the ever-mounting pile of demands. It stung that Cece had been so right. About her mother. About her own judgmental nature. About how she was going to deal with this situation into which God had thrown her. And He had thrown her. She'd spent the last few days trying desperately to deny it, but it was true. She knew it the moment Cece said it. The woman was undeniably right. About everything, annoyingly enough.

Life had officially spun out of control. Everything seemed to be falling apart at the seams. She wasn't the only woman coping with the demands of family, extended family and community. Why wasn't everyone else falling apart like she was? What was she missing?

Pacing like a caged lion, Essie could find no solutions. Her parents would continue to be draining and crises-laden, her husband would continue to work long hours because they needed the money, Mark-o would probably never wake up and do his share, she'd still be staring Dahlia and Vicki in the face every Sunday, and Josh was going to need her for about the next eighteen years.

There simply wasn't enough Essie to go around.

It felt like she was being eaten alive by some savage species of South American ant—thousands of tiny needy bites taken out of her from every direction until all that would be left was her skeleton picked clean on the kitchen floor.

Oh, come on, Essie, that's a bit dramatic, isn't it?

But her own efforts to calm herself down proved useless. This was too much. Everybody needed too much. There was nothing to be done. In the middle of her kitchen floor, hugging one of the pillows that had landed there and crying into a paper towel, Essie quit.

Essie, who never quit, and swore she'd never quit, simply quit.

It started out quiet, like a surrender. It didn't stay that way for long. Within minutes Essie's surrender had boiled into a full-blown declaration of war. Essie Walker versus The World. And no one declares war on the world from the confines of their tiny kitchen. Essie was heading right back out there onto the field of battle.

Scrawling out a quick note in case she missed Doug in transit, Essie headed back to Bayside. The way she was fuming, it took her half the normal time to make the trip. Without even so much as a "hello" to anyone, she stormed into Mark-o's office.

He was chatting with someone from the missions committee. Her silent glare was so foreboding that he ended the conversation in a flash and shut his office door once Essie was inside. Good. She wanted him to know she'd reached her boiling point.

Trying to stay reasonable, she held up the papers bearing her mother's demands. "Do *you* have a list?"

He had the nerve to look at her with an expression that said, "Is that all this is about?" but the smarts not to say it out loud. "As a matter of fact, I do." He said it wearily, but the piece of paper he held up looked like a fraction of her own list.

"What's on *your* list?" She plunked down in one of his nice, cushy office chairs. She waited, arms crossed, foot tapping.

"Well, I don't know where she thinks I'll find the time to get all this done before Thursday."

Essie was undiverted. "What's on the list, Mark-o?"

"Get not one, but three different kinds of coffee." He leaned against his large, shiny desk, doing a fine job of sounding "put out." "Find a centerpiece—c'mon, a centerpiece?—and bring Peggy's chafing dish. She'll have to polish it or something, I don't think we've used it since last Thanksgiving."

Essie paused a long, dangerous moment before responding, "That's all?"

"That's more than enough, I think. Hey, listen, I need to talk to you about something I just heard. Please tell me there wasn't a discussion about women's anatomy in your class today."

Now it was Esther Walker versus The Entire Known Universe.

She fired up out of her chair. "You know, Mark-o, that's it. I've had it, I'm tired of it, and that's it. That's *it!*"

He looked at her blankly. That only made it worse.

"I quit!" She thrust her hand up to her chin, glaring at him. "I've had it up to *here* with those boys and their mothers! With Mom! With everything!" She poked a finger in the air at him, stopping just short of saying, "With *you!*" Instead, she began pacing around his conference table, pointing at him with every other word. "Find someone *else* to herd those precious *darlings* through Bible lessons, find someone *else* to make Thanksgiving happen for Mom, *you* be the one to go keep Pop from killing himself, because *I have had it!*"

"Now, Es…"

"Don't you 'now Es' me. Don't you *dare* put on your smooth pastor voice with me. I am done with it. With all of it. Go herd your flock through the world without my help. As a matter of fact, go have a lovely little holiday without me, because…because I'm…I'm not doing Thanksgiving this year." She threw the list on his conference table and yanked open his office door. "I'm not helping. You know what? I'm not even *coming,*" she barked as she walked through the doorway. "I quit. I resign. I'm done." She said the last three sentences without even looking back. And not caring who heard.

The first volley of Essie Walker versus The World had been fired. Now it was time to finish it off. And that meant Mom and Pop. She shot out the church door and stood on the sidewalk for a moment, debating her path. Go home first? No, the time to do this was right now, while she was good and angry. In a surge of self-indulgence, she hailed a cab rather than walk—no sense burning off needed energy. In minutes she'd reached her parents' doorstep.

Essie went straight to it the moment the door opened. "Doug, Josh and I won't be here for Thanksgiving, Mom. There's been a change of plans. I gave your list to Mark-o." She wouldn't even allow herself to step into the living room.

Her mother responded with a look that made it seem as

though Essie had just thrust a meat cleaver through her mother's heart. "Honey, no," she whimpered.

"Yes, Mom." *Stay strong, Essie. This is war.*

She heard the creaking of her father's chair as he struggled to get up out of it. "What's going on? What'd she say?"

"I said," Essie repeated, forcing strength into her voice. Suddenly she was seven years old, a little girl stamping her feet and refusing to take one more stupid ballet lesson. "We won't be here for Thanksgiving, Pop. Our plans have changed."

"What kind of talk is that?"

"Mom…"

Her mother put her hand to her chest in maternal agony. "Who talks like that to their mother? Bob, who talks like that to their mother?"

It would have been smarter to do this on the phone. It's much harder to hang up in person.

Where's a screaming baby when you need one?

Essie wasn't sure if it took minutes or hours to walk home.

"Whoa, boy, this looks bad," Doug pronounced when she shuffled into the kitchen. "Hey, Josh, it's a good thing we stopped for pizza on the way home, isn't it? How many times in life do you ask God for a way to help your wife and He tells you to go get pizza?"

"Huh?" Josh was exploring a bowl of peaches in his high chair while Doug sat in front of a fabulously large pizza box on the table. Essie realized, with the odd detachment catharsis brings, that Doug's disposition is what made him so good at what he did. Computer crises also turned sane people into lunatics. Doug's software was meant to expedite one of the most stressful events in any office's life: the switch to a new

computer system. When she thought about it, Doug probably spent most of his day talking formerly sane people off
cyber-ledges. Great. So now he gets World War Essie. It
made her feel even worse for giving him more of the same
at home when he was getting enough of it at work.

"Es," he said, looking so much more calm than she felt,
"I've been married to you long enough to know the 'I'm
gonna explode' look. And this one looked like a biggie.
And…truth be told…I heard enough at church to put the
pieces together that class hadn't exactly gone well today. Did
Stanton really talk about his mother's *breasts?*"

"Great. Gotten around already, has it?"

"Well, Alice Bendenfogle…"

Essie put her hand up. "I don't want to know. Actually,
the sick part of it is, that's not even the half of it. I can't tell
you the rest, except for the part about Mom. And Mark-o.
And Thanksgiving. That, I can fill you in on."

Doug poked Josh in the nose. "Yes, we heard the answering-machine messages. Grandma's making Mommy
crazy. Now there's a surprise." Doug kicked out a chair with
his foot, motioning for her to sit down. "Pepperoni."

"I just quit."

"Quit what? Sunday school?"

"And Mom and Thanksgiving and I think pretty much
the whole world."

She opened the pizza box, suddenly aware of how hungry she was. It was foolish to skip breakfast today in order
to get to church early. Any athlete would have known that
a day like today needed serious protein, if not marathon-style
carbo-loading. No one wages war on an empty stomach.

"Okay," he said slowly in his technical-support voice,

"but there's an entire Thanksgiving meal ordered on our answering machine. What's *Dorothy* doing?"

"Hosting." Essie nearly spit the word out.

"And Mark-o and Peggy?"

Essie really tried to take the whiny third-grade tone out of her voice, but it wouldn't budge. "Getting three pounds of coffee, some flowers and digging their chafing dish out of storage. Honestly, between the church calendar and Peggy's sales convention, Mark-o's not sure where they'll find the time to get it all done."

"And you got to do the rest?"

"You know, since I'm…"

"Not working," they said simultaneously.

Doug sighed and leaned his head back against the wall. "You really just quit Thanksgiving?"

"In person. Mark-o first, then Mom and Pop."

Doug looked downright amazed. "How'd they take it?"

Essie glared at him. "How do you think?"

Doug chuckled and shook his head, imagining the drama. There was a long silence before he said on a sigh, "How long are you going to let this go on, Es?"

"It's not going on. I just quit Thanksgiving."

"You know what I mean."

"I don't know. They're my parents, Doug."

"So that gives them license to be unreasonable? To dump on you like this? This Thanksgiving thing is ridiculous, but Essie, they've been eating you alive since you got here."

"Tell them to get in line. I seem to be California's 'special of the day.'"

Doug didn't get the joke.

She didn't care.

Chapter 18

The Thanksgiving That Wasn't...

Guilt had awakened Essie early Wednesday morning. She could count on the fingers of one hand the number of mornings she'd awakened before Josh, but this morning her eyes had popped open, tense and unrested. Wearily, she pulled the bedroom door shut behind her and padded to the kitchen. It wasn't until the coffeemaker was halfway done brewing that the thought struck her: this was a day to start in prayer. Not only because she wanted to be very sure that she was doing the right thing, but because she needed to tell Doug about Dahlia and Vicki. She felt like she'd already received God's permission to step away from her family for the holiday, even though pangs of doubt showed up here and there. What she still needed was God's blessing to "bend" her promise to Vicki and bring Doug's sound judgment into the situation. Essie still wasn't sure that was a good idea. Was she just looking to get some of this weight off her shoulders? Caving on the conviction that she alone must do this?

She sat on her Adirondack chair for an hour, huddled inside a blanket with a coffee cup steaming up into the chilly morning air. Slowly, peace and clarity came to her. She had made the right move. She did need to draw a border around her parents endless demands. There would be lots of bumps in the road to making *her* family—she, Doug and Joshua—her new priority. She just needed to find the middle ground between "honor thy mother and father" and "go insane."

And then there was Vicki. She knew she needed to do something, only didn't know what it was she should be doing. Wasn't shouldering a heavy weight alone exactly what she was trying to prevent Vicki from doing? In her own insistence on telling no one, wasn't she isolating herself in the same way Vicki was? And wasn't that just as dangerous? She mulled it over for a while, sending up sighs and prayers and running back once for the nursery room monitor—because surely Josh was sick if he was sleeping so late—until she came away with the clear sense that telling Doug was the right thing to do.

She should tell Doug about Vicki.

For that matter, she should have told Doug about Coach Jemmings weeks ago. Still, she kept it secret. Even though she knew better. It was a defensive reaction, an escape hatch to her old world. I'll find a way to tell him later, Essie thought to herself.

She returned to the kitchen to begin packing the cooler.

Essie rang her mother's doorbell that afternoon with an astounding sense of calm. Once she'd simmered down from her epic fit on Sunday, the decision to opt out of Thanksgiving settled around her like a soft quilt. It was a quiet, solid sense of self-preservation that fueled her actions.

The diplomatic coup of delivering—but not cooking—the turkey, cleverly pre-ordered from Guswell's Meat Market thanks to Cece, had been Doug's idea. The man was brilliant. When he'd called it "a poultriotic gesture," she'd laughed until tears streamed down her cheeks.

Essie Walker had quit Thanksgiving and lived.

Well, at least so far. Mom hadn't opened the door yet.

It was Peggy, actually, who pulled open the door. Mark-o was what they called a "second career pastor," as he and Peggy both had high-powered jobs before his call to ministry. Peggy still was a high-level sales executive, and she looked every inch of it this morning. Her brown hair was cut in one of those sleek bobs that never looks mussed. Dressed in beige from top to bottom, even her cooking apron looked elegant. Essie felt disheveled and disobedient next to her, but resolved to hold her ground. Peggy's expression was an odd combination of annoyance and admiration.

Her mother came up behind Peggy, looking supremely hurt. Essie took a deep breath before entering.

"Did you get the right kind of cranberries?" Mom's tone barely hid her "it's the least you could do" attitude.

"No, I didn't. I told you that on the phone. Twice. I got the turkey for you and that's all I did." Talk about selective hearing—her mother had a Ph.D. in denial.

Mom continued as if Essie's defiant lack of grocery purchases didn't exist. "I don't like those cranberries without the actual berries in them. It's like eating thick Jell-O. Cranberry relish ought to have berries, that's what I say. A&P makes the best, and the most reasonable, too. Who needs to pay more for someone else's gourmet—she pronounced it "gore-mett"—label? Not me, that's for sure."

"Here's the turkey, Mom. Have a good holiday."

Mom poked at the bird as if it had come from Mars. "Looks funny. Who knows what kind of bird they give you out here."

Peggy still said nothing. "Save yourself!" Essie wanted to cry, knowing what awaited Peggy over the next twenty-four hours.

Mark-o came around the corner into the kitchen. They hadn't talked since Sunday. Essie kept her eyes on the task of getting the turkey out of its grocery bag and into the fridge. Mark-o finally spoke from behind her. "So," he said slowly, "do I need to get a sub for Sunday school next session?" His tone was quiet, almost timid, as if he didn't know how to handle the situation. More brotherly than pastorish, which caught her off guard.

She sighed, still on her haunches in front of the fridge. "I don't know. I want to think about it for a few days."

"Would it help if I told you how thrilled Justin Baker's parents are that Justin will be playing Jesus?"

Well, that did help. A little. "Justin's a good kid. Well, good by Doom Room standards."

"That's just it, Es. Justin's a quiet kid—okay, quiet for second grade—who tries to do good. Those kind of boys disappear in a place as big and flashy as Bayside. But he didn't disappear to you." Mark-o finished the soda he was holding, and set the can down carefully.

It was the first time she'd seen him uncomfortable in a long time.

"Justin's so excited at getting to be a hero by being... well, by being exactly who he is, not by beating out the raving band of extroverts that usually get those parts." He laughed a little—a nervous laugh. "Your little system of

'Queen Esther's Commandments' made that happen." He stared at Essie. "Don't think I don't see that kind of stuff. I do."

Essie stood up, wiping her hands on a kitchen towel she'd pulled from the fridge handle. "You know, you *do* see the important details. You get it, most of the time." She busied herself refolding the towel, only because it felt better to say this without looking at him. "But you have blinders on when it comes to your own family. Do you have any idea how many balls I'm keeping in the air here, Mark-o? How many things are pulling on me—how many people want stuff from me?" She'd built up enough courage to look at him. "Can you *just for a moment* remember that I've just uprooted my family, left my friends, have a husband in a high-stress job and that I haven't had a decent night's sleep in months?"

He didn't answer. She'd waded into this water, she wasn't going to turn back now.

"Did you *think*—" Catching her rising voice, she softened her tone and repeated, "Did you think I *offered* to run around to six different stores on Mom's menu marching orders? No, Mark-o, she *dumped* it on me. On *me,* because she doesn't dump it on you. I feel like all I do anymore is pick up your slack with this family."

"Now, wait a minute…"

"No, *you* wait a minute.."

"No, *you* wait a minute. You never asked me to help. You only stormed out of my office. If you'd have asked…"

Essie grabbed her jacket. She should have sent Doug to deliver the bird. "Oh, yeah, like you'd have cleared your schedule." She started toward the living room to wish her parents happy Thanksgiving and get out of there.

"I can't help if you don't ask me."

She turned back toward him. "Oh, I think I've learned how useful *asking* is with you. Let's talk about Dad's doctor appointments, shall we?"

"I can't control that."

"Don't give me that. You *won't* control that."

"That's out of…" Mark-o raised his voice.

"Oh, no, it's not…" Essie raised hers.

Until Peggy jutted her head around the door. "Could you two knock it off, please? Things are bad enough as it is."

Essie's glare shot back and forth between Peggy and Mark-o. Why on earth had she ever thought Thanksgiving would be the answer to her problems? It was all her problems wrapped up in one.

"Happy Thanksgiving, Mom! Happy Thanksgiving, Pop! I'll see you Monday!" she called in the perkiest voice she could manage while still tamping down the urge to throttle her brother.

She would be leaving for her in-laws in Nevada within the hour. The North Pole wouldn't have put enough distance between her and this crazy family.

Essie, Doug and Josh drove to Nevada that afternoon, their first official road trip since crossing the country to re-settle in San Francisco. Her sense of exhilaration bloomed as they sped down the highway. It didn't even matter to her that they had to stop twice in the first hour to change a succession of diapers from Josh. She'd ditched her family on Thanksgiving. It felt wild and rebellious and very, very healthy. Five days away from Bayside stage-mom phone calls was highly appealing. Five days away from the Mom-and-Pop circus was downright invigorating.

Doug seemed to relax as well as they drove. In an unexpected but welcome gesture, Nytex was closed through the end of the week. Since it was business software they produced, even the help lines were on a skeleton staff during the holiday weekend. It was, without a doubt, a breath of fresh air for the entire family.

She told Doug of the coffeehouse phone call, the "infamous body part incident" as Mark-o now called it, and how she'd put the facts together and come to her conclusion. She told Doug why she'd not felt free to tell him before, and why she needed his help now.

When she'd finished the whole long story, Doug shot her a look out of the corner of his eye. "I can see why you're so antsy. This isn't exactly your thing. Cheering on—you can do that. But hand-holding? You're out of your league on this one. Isn't this really your brother's territory?"

Essie leaned her head against the window, fiddling with a toy from Josh's diaper bag. "Don't you think I know that? I'd give anything to pass this one off to Mark-o. But somehow I know I'm not supposed to. I overheard that phone call for a reason. Stanton made that comment…"

"And what a winner *that* was," Doug interjected, laughing.

"That ridiculous comment in my classroom because I was supposed to hear it. God threw this in my lap. I can't get over that feeling. But you're right—I'm not at all the person who should be doing this sort of thing. The thought of bringing those two women together just makes me cringe. I'm scared. I admit it. Openly. I'm a complete coward on this one."

They rode along in silence for a minute or two. "I just don't know what to do," she offered, still stumped despite having brought Doug into the picture. "You have any ideas?"

Doug sighed. "Well, only that this is complicated. There isn't going to be a one-step solution to this. It sounds like it will be a process—something done in a dozen tiny steps."

"As in not quick and painless?" Essie winced.

"Well, I don't know about the pain part, but it doesn't strike me as a quick-fix thing." He caught Essie's eye for a moment as he glanced over his shoulder to change lanes. "You didn't expect to be able to just introduce them and send them off on their merry way to expose their deepest fears and secrets to one another, did you?"

"Well…"

"Look we've got a couple of days to ponder this while we're at my mom's. Why don't we let it rest for a while and talk about it again on the way home? Besides, the guy in the backseat is just about awake and looking hungry. I'd say a stop for lunch is in order for all the Walker men and their Queen."

Essie's own stomach rumbled as if on cue. "Sounds fine."

Doug's parents were outstanding grandparents. That may have had something to do with the fact that Josh was grandchild number six, but Essie guessed it was far more in the attitude than the multitude. She and Doug had planned to come the day after Thanksgiving, but Doug's parents had welcomed the last-minute change in plans with open arms. Watching Jason Walker down on the floor, holding Josh upright and laughing as tiny baby feet stomped on his considerable belly, Essie sent up a silent thanks that God had brought her here. There were bits of tension here and there—Doug's mother was one of those people who equated food with love, thereby "loving" everyone into near obesity over the weekend—but it was mostly a joyous, comforting time. Even the two phone calls from her mother, despite clear, or so Essie thought, guidelines on what constituted "an emergency worthy of calling me in Nevada," couldn't dent the sense of peace that washed over Essie out there in the desert.

Dianne, Doug's mother, excelled at quilting. The two lovely hangings in Essie's living room had been Dianne's wedding present. She had already crafted Josh a stunning baby blanket when he was born. She outdid herself, though, by presenting Josh with the most beautiful velour Christmas suit Essie had ever seen. She had guessed the correct size with masterful accuracy—just a bit big now, so that it would be perfect in a month or so. The rich burgundy color of the overalls, booties and matching hat were trimmed with just enough dark green ribbon to look festive but not fussy. Tiny Christmas trees and reindeer were appliquéd on each piece. And, best of all, the whole ensemble was completely machine washable. When Dianne produced a Josh-sized velour teddy bear—decked out in an identical miniature outfit—Essie lost all hope of not crying. Surely, no child was ever so loved. How could she have thought the near-constant frustration of days with her parents would be a better choice than these loving, laughing days with Doug's folks?

How could she convince the Walkers to move to San Francisco? Tomorrow?

"Douglas Walker," Essie pronounced as they drove to the Walkers' church that Sunday morning, "I'd have married you for your parents even if you weren't such a handsome guy."

"Yeah, well I'll try to remember that when I'm bald and bulging."

"Your dad's not bulging, he's just…cuddly."

"I'll tell him you said that. 'Course, even he would tell

you he's about thirty pounds too cuddly, but forty years of Mom's cheesecake can do that to a guy."

Essie smiled. "Four days of your mother's cooking has already done it to me."

"The woman raised four boys. That's like feeding a small country for twenty years. I just think she never learned to downsize."

While Essie wouldn't have thought the weekend could get any better, the church service was outstanding. And only a small portion of that had to do with the fact that none of the Doom Room inhabitants were present. It had everything to do with the sermon.

Which was, by some extraordinary show of divine intervention, about Queen Esther.

Essie tried not to gape as the pastor talked about how Esther had been flung into a situation far beyond her abilities. He recounted the story of how a young girl named Esther had been chosen to become Queen to powerful King Xerxes. How Mordecai, her uncle, revealed a plot by the royal official Haman to kill Esther's people, the Jews. Suddenly Esther found herself as the only person with the power to sway the King's judgment against the plot. This girl was asked to risk her life in order to gain the King's ear. She had to muster the courage to deal with powerful and intimidating people who could just as easily have humiliated her, or worse, as help her accomplish what God seemed to be asking of her.

Hmm.

Esther had read the story of her namesake dozens of times, but it had never come alive for her as it did this morning. Faced with the do-or-die challenge of saving her people from the evil plot against them, what had Esther done? Had she attacked it in a single blow? No. Esther had tread slowly, carefully. Queen Esther rallied the power of relationship. Simply put, she took the two people involved in her problem and had them over to dinner.

Repeatedly. She'd taken the scary step of initiating a closer relationship with the people God had put in front of her.

Hmm.

The message was coming through loud and clear: take the risk and build the relationship first, then solve the problem.

Wasn't that exactly what Doug had said? That it wouldn't be as simple as introducing Dahlia and Vicki to each other and commanding they buddy-up? No, she was going to have to get to know each of them, to create a friendship that would facilitate the bond God was asking her to forge. Befriend Dahlia and Vicki. That sounded frightening, but if Queen Esther could do it in the face of death and genocide, surely Queen Essie could do it in the face of a little social discomfort.

Befriend Dahlia and Vicki.

Cope with her parents.

Accept the challenges of being Queen Esther to the Second Graders of Doom.

Be where God had placed her. Here. Now. With these people.

Never had the familiar words of "for such a time as this," rung more true for Esther Walker. Just as the Bible's Esther had been brought to power to save her people, Essie had been brought to San Francisco.

To deal with her parents, these outrageous boys, and two women who didn't realize how much they needed each other.

Oh, boy.

Chapter 19

And the Victory Goes to...Whom?

Esther paused, and drew in a deep cleansing breath. *See it.* She reached out and palmed her weapon, tucking it firmly to her chin. She checked around her, adjusting her stance, catching Doug's eyes for a moment, closing her eyes while she focused. *Set it.*

Two more breaths, accompanied by a clear visualization of success. She was ready. *Shoot it.*

Essie dialed Dahlia Mannington's phone number.

A familiar voice answered the phone. "Mannington residence. This is Stanton speaking." He clipped the words out with such precision that Essie half expected him to say, "How may I direct your call?"

"Hi, Stanton. This is Mrs. Walker calling. Did you have a good Thanksgiving?"

"It was okay. My baby cousin's kind of a pain."

"Oh, do you have family staying at your house? Maybe

I should call back later if you've still got company." Essie felt guilty for taking advantage of a possible out.

"Oh, no," Stanton replied, "they live nearby. They just came for the day. But it was a really long day. Babies cry a lot and they smell funny."

Figures. Essie rolled her shoulders back and grabbed her notes. Her *notes.* When was the last time she was nervous enough about a phone call to have to use notes? "I know how hard cranky babies can be to live with—even just for a day. Is this a good time to talk to your mom?"

"Sure," the boy replied. Then, in the seemingly universal habit of children on the phone everywhere, Stanton yelled, "Mo-oommm! Pho-oon-nneee!" directly into the Essie's ear. She imagined the man who invented the phone mute button was rolling over in his grave these days.

"Hello," came Dahlia's smooth voice as she picked up another extension. "Thank you, Stanton, you can hang up now."

"I'll see you next week in Sunday school," Essie got in before Stanton slammed down the receiver.

"Essie? Oh, I've been meaning to call you, but Pastor Mark told me you were out of town."

Oh, I'll bet you have, Dahlia. At that moment, Essie realized the advantage she had in being the one to call. It was nice to be prepared for conversations with Dahlia Mannington rather than having them sprung on her like pop quizzes. "I thought it might be good for us to have a conversation with so much going on. It's really too bad Stanton's behavior didn't allow me to give him a larger part in the Celebration—I'm sure he'd have been wonderful." It had taken her four drafts to come up with that opening.

"Yes, well…" Dahlia paused, probably giving herself a moment to compose a properly evaluative response.

Essie took that pause to continue her momentum. "I thought it might be nice to get together. I could use your thoughts on some things. The Celebration feels a little overwhelming right now. I don't exactly have your gift for hospitality, and I know it's short notice, but would you come over for coffee next Tuesday? We could cover some things before Thursday's committee meeting." Essie made sure to hit all the right buttons—complimenting Dahlia's hosting skills, requesting her guidance—even though she knew Dahlia would probably heap it on whether she asked for it or not—and efficiency for the upcoming meeting. It was Essie's version of Esther's famous, and effective, line, "If it pleases the King."

"Well, if you like, you can always come over here and Carmen will whip something up for us."

She expected that response and was ready for it. "Oh, that sounds tempting, but I've already invited Vicki Faber to come, too, so we're all set." *Shame on you, Essie Walker, that is an out-and-out lie. I'm sure Queen Esther never fibbed.* Essie was planning on inviting Vicki in the next phone call, but she wanted a victory with Dahlia under her belt before moving on to the far greater challenge of getting Vicki Faber to come for coffee. Before Dahlia could come up with another suggestion, Essie kept going. "So, will you come? I'd really appreciate it."

After a moment's pause, Dahlia's consummate graciousness kicked into gear. "Why, *certainly* I'll come. It's lovely of you to have me."

"It's not much, but…"

"Well now, how about I help you out and have Carmen make me up a box of goodies to bring over? Surely that darling baby of yours can't give you much time to bake."

Lady, I don't have time to breathe, much less bake. I'd be a fool to say no. "Oh, I can't turn that offer down. Not once I've tasted Carmen's baking. That'd be wonderful, and a big help. Thanks."

"Well, then, Tuesday it is."

"Great. See you then. Say hello again to Stanton for me."

Essie hung up and thrust her hands in the air as if she'd just kicked the Super Bowl's winning field goal. "And Round One goes to Queen Esther...." Doug and Joshua did a tiny, one-and-a half-person "wave" from the couch.

So much for the preliminaries. Now it was time for the big one.

Even though it was Sunday evening, Essie dialed Vicki's cell phone number. Somehow, she was sure Vicki would answer that line faster than the house number. She was halfway through the digits before she stopped and put the phone down. She closed her eyes. *Lord, this woman has absolutely no reason to say yes. I have nothing to offer her, except the uncomfortable fact that You've thrown us together. This is beyond me. Ball's in Your court, Lord. If she's going to come, You're going to have to make that happen.*

Doug had watched her pause. "Es?"

She opened one eye. "Just praying for success. Or guidance. Or a miracle. Or whatever it's gonna take."

She squeezed her eyes shut as if shot-putting the prayer to heaven. *Amen, Lord.*

Essie opened her eyes, pulled in a deep breath and redialed. Sure enough, Vicki's effervescent, efficient voice chimed, "Victoria Hinton-Faber," on the line.

"Vicki, I'm so glad to have caught you. This is Essie. Essie Walker, Alex's Sunday school teacher?" Essie couldn't shake the notion that Vicki Faber didn't spend a lot of time keeping up on Alex's activities.

"Hello," Vicki replied, a touch of discomfort in her voice.

Essie chose to ignore it. She knew this conversation would be an uphill battle, so she dug her heels in and kept going. "I have a favor I'd like to ask of you. I need your assistance with some of the early plans for the Spring Celebration. If I could just grab a few minutes with you next week, it would save the whole class a lot of hassle later on in the production. Plus," Essie added, trying to put the sound of a smile into her voice, "it's my turn to buy the coffee. I know you're busy, but do you think you could spare an hour Tuesday morning at ten-thirty? Dahlia Mannington's coming over, and between the three of us I'm sure we can nail down the plans for the class in a way that should make it easier on all the parents." Essie was finished with her monologue before she realized she'd said it all in one breath.

There was a long, awful silence. Essie bit her lip twice to keep from babbling to fill it, but something told her to stay quiet and let Vicki ponder the offer.

"Ten-thirty?" Vicki finally asked.

Essie let out the breath she was holding. "If that's okay with you."

"Well…"

Again, Essie fought the urge to say something else that might persuade the woman. She felt like something was telling her to hold her tongue.

"All right, but I've only got an hour. That'll have to do."

Breaking into a wide grin, Essie gave Doug a silent "thumbs-up." He, in return, silently clapped Joshua's hands together and mouthed, "Yea, Mom!"

"That'll do just fine. I really appreciate it. You have no idea how much this will help me." After a few more bits of small talk, Essie gave Vicki her address, apologized in advance for the less-than-designer state of her apartment and said goodbye.

No one was more shocked than Essie that her plans had succeeded.

Okay, God's plans had succeeded.

But God didn't have to figure out how to clean this living room before these two stylish ladies descended upon the humble Walker household.

As she folded a load of laundry that night, marveling how tiny socks that went into the dryer as pairs always seemed to return solo, Essie considered the past week. Wasn't last Sunday afternoon the time when she slammed the phone down on her brother? Had she really survived the pinnacle of bad-boy behavior, ditched a Thanksgiving dinner, visited her in-laws, had a major spiritual breakthrough and conquered the Ladies Who Lunch all in one week?

Well, now, she hadn't really conquered the ladies, had she? No, she'd merely invited them over, and that was a long way from conquest. In fact, it felt far more like an invasion. A vision burst into her head of Queen Esther, running around the palace in a royal panic about the banquet she was throwing for the King Xerxes and Haman. Queen Esther wasn't just spiffing up for a coffee with a pair of women who might slander her decorating scheme; she was preparing for a set of actions that might very well get her killed. All you're trying to do, Essie kept reminding herself, is bring two women together who don't know how much they need each other yet. You don't have to expose any evil plots, just soften up a few hearts. A few judgmental, toughened hearts, but hearts just the same.

It's just three women having coffee. It's just three women

having coffee. It's just three women having coffee in my shabby kitchen…

"It'll be fine," came Doug's voice from behind her, kneading her knotted shoulders. Had her tension been that obvious? "You've already done the hardest part—you got them to say 'yes.' I have to admit I thought it couldn't be done." When Essie turned to shoot him a look he added, "Ah, but I married a woman who spent years defying gravity." Doug smiled. "So I knew you could do it all along."

"Okay, so *you* stay for coffee," Essie kidded, handing a stack of clean baby pajamas to her husband.

"Oh, no, you don't. Nytex is launching the accounting software this week. I've got my own battles to wage."

Essie tried not to whine. "*Another* upgrade? Didn't you just launch the database upgrade? How many products is Nytex upgrading these days?" Once again, she'd manage to miss major information about Doug's work life. What was it going to take for her to keep better track of this stuff?

"This is the third of five."

Essie moaned and rolled her eyes. "*Two more* after this?"

After a long night with a cranky baby, Essie stifled yet another yawn as she pulled the string off Dahlia's bakery-style box Tuesday morning. *Lord, You know it would have been much nicer to do this on more sleep.* Who kept bakery boxes in their house? People like Dahlia Mannington, she answered herself and she poured the coffee from the coffeemaker into a charming little carafe she'd borrowed from Peggy. People who have Carmens. People like those ladies in your living room.

Cece's voice invaded her head. "Those ladies in your liv-

ing room are *people*. And God's given you something to do
with those people. So get in there and do it!'"

Essie walked into the living room, coffee and Carmen's
scones arranged as stylishly as she could manage on a painted
wooden tray, again on loan from Peggy. Josh sat enjoying his
electric swing, the *whosh-whosh* of the mechanism puffing
a soft rhythm to his happy babbles.

The room did look nice. And she had Peggy to thank
for it. It'd been a huge slice of humble pie to ask her
sister-in-law for decorating assistance. Especially after
dumping Thanksgiving in Mark-o's lap—which she knew
very well would be dumping it in Peggy's lap. She'd had a
tight throat as she asked Peggy's forgiveness for the holiday
chaos and blurted out her need for "home makeover" help.

All she really needed was a carafe and a tray. After
Thanksgiving, she didn't expect much more than access to
Peggy's serving dishes—if she got that.

She got much more. Peggy surprised her by responding like the Home Decorating SWAT Team. The evening
of Essie's Monday afternoon call, Peggy arrived with a
large laundry basket full of afghans, pillows, scarfy things
she called valances, dried-plant things and all sorts of ob-
jets d'art. She was as warm and friendly as she'd ever
been. Often cool and efficient, evidently this kind of help
was the kind Peggy loved to give. Essie and Josh simply
sat back and watched as Peggy moved this, borrowed that
from another room, put one item together with another
and created cozy style where there had once been messy
chaos. The whole deal *did* come with an ongoing tuto-
rial about organization and the virtues of home decorating, but Essie hushed up and took her lumps. She deserved

this, and was grateful to get any help at all after her holiday hissy fit.

So Dahlia and Vicki were now standing in a somewhat stylish living room. The pair was standing in front of the two quilted wall hangings Doug's mother had done. The hangings were exquisite—the most lovely thing she and Doug owned as far as Essie was concerned—and they were beautifully complemented by the violet afghan Peggy had draped over the couch. Two more pillows and a ceramic vase with pussy willows artfully arranged inside, and the colorful little tableau in the living room was downright appealing.

"You say your mother-in-law did these?" asked Vicki, eyeing them with her head cocked to one side and sounding impressed.

"Yes, Dianne's quite an artist, isn't she?"

"I'd say," agreed Dahlia.

Vicki tapped her finger against her chin, gears spinning. "I could get her a dozen commissions for pieces within weeks." Vicki was always doing business.

"Oh, she's been asked. Lots of times as far as I can tell. She's turned every one of them down. Dianne holds to the notion that she'd rather do it for love than for money."

Both women responded with "isn't that quaint?" expressions. Essie decided not to let that get to her. "Speaking of true art, make sure you give Carmen our thanks for these great scones, Dahlia. Talk about someone who could line up customers!" The resulting looks had Essie instantly regretting that last remark. Good one, Es. Let's start things off by implying that someone's hired help could be raking in the bucks elsewhere.

"Yes, well…" Essie had come to recognize that those two words were Dahlia's standard reply to something she did not like.

Willing herself not to wince, Essie pressed on. She carefully nudged the women into conversation. Getting Dahlia to talk about Stanton was effortless. Getting Vicki to talk about Alex was closer to pulling teeth. In fact, if Essie had kept score, Dahlia might have actually said more about Alex than Vicki had. Twenty excruciating minutes passed before the two women finally hit on a mutual friend and a few mutual topics. At last, the conversation was off and running.

Sort of. "Loping or shuffling" might have been a better description.

It was Vicki, sadly enough, who stepped on the first conversational land mine. "So," Vicki said brightly, thinking she'd landed on a pleasant topic of conversation, "what part does Stanton have in the Spring Celebration?"

Oh, yes, let's talk to the Education Chairwoman, the driving force behind the Celebration, about how her son landed only a walk-on. Let's open up a dialogue on Stanton's lack of decent behavior. That's a great way to foster a relationship, ladies! Lord! Essie yelled in her head, *do something!*

"Yes, well…" Dahlia straightened in her chair.

"Stanton is my secret weapon in the crowd of onlookers," interjected Essie, suddenly—and thankfully—struck with inspiration. "He's probably the only one who can keep that crowd of boys who have no lines from doing something onstage we'd all regret, so he agreed to be my leader of the extras."

Dahlia, who had been taking a breath to answer, actually broke into a smile. She raised her eyebrows at Vicki in a "you know how boys will be boys" expression. Essie could swear she look relieved. She even smiled right at Essie.

Essie made a mental note to make sure the program read:

Leader of the Extras...........*Stanton Mannington*

"Alex seems to be tying himself in knots over the few lines he does have," offered Vicki. She sounded rather annoyed, as if this exposed a character flaw in her stepson. "Really. It's *how* many months away? And already he's nervous."

Get in line, thought Essie.

Dahlia, sensing an opportunity for parental superiority, jumped on the case. "You know, this is a tricky age for boys. A very challenging time for even the most experienced of mothers."

Essie would have liked to have done without the dig about Vicki's age and spanking-new-parent status. This wasn't exactly going smoothly.

"The oddest things throw them," continued Dahlia. "Things I thought would send Stanton into fits have just glided by, and then the things that I can't imagine being any trouble are suddenly blowing up in my face. Stanton's voice coach tells me such things happen to boys Stanton's age all the time."

Stanton has a voice coach? For what?

"Really? Where do you take him?" Vicki suddenly showed great interest, and reached into her handbag for pen and paper.

Lots of second graders have voice coaches? No wonder I can't get these kids to hush up—their parents are spending thousands of dollars on *talking lessons.* The two women went off on a ten-minute tangent comparing the credentials of four different voice coaches. Essie just sat there, thinking *what planet have I landed on?*

Until, that was, she remembered that the whole point of this meeting was to get Dahlia and Vicki talking to each other. Who cares if it was about expensive private vocal tutoring?

They were segueing into the best summer camps when Vicki suddenly looked at her watch. "Oh, I've got a noon meeting across town. I can't stay more than a few more minutes. Essie, we've not even gotten to whatever it was you needed. Can you just e-mail me?"

Essie, who had quite a lot of time to think as the women were chatting, was on it instantly. "You know, could we just meet back here next week? I'm sure I can last until then— but I still need help from both of you."

Come on, Lord, we've gotten this far, Essie prayed as both women simultaneously flipped open their respective calendars and PalmPilots.

"I've got another appointment," said Vicki, and Essie's heart sank. "But I'll have my assistant move it."

Victory! Queen Esther…um…God wins again!

Chapter 20

*World War Three and the
Base-Level Bailout*

The following Sunday marked the Celebration's first rehearsal. Actually, it was more of an assembly than a rehearsal, as all the classes did was sit and listen to grown-ups talking to them from the auditorium stage. Sitting with the squirming boys, Essie realized that this would be the last time she saw these boys only once a week. From here on in she would be graced with their rambunctious presence two times a week.

Yippee.

Decker had figured out how to flip up his theater-style auditorium seat in such a way as to wedge his body inside and show the world how easily he could hook his ankles behind his head. When this failed to garner enough attention, Decker decided that wailing as if he had been trapped accidentally in the seat rather than intentionally would get him better noticed. When a first-grade girl noticed his wailing contortions and screamed, it took Essie and the first-grade girls' teacher some time to calm both classes down.

"Well, then…" Essie heard Dahlia's voice chirping out over the sound system as she tried to broadcast instructions from the stage. She was reading a carefully prepared but completely lifeless "pep talk" about the production and its important role in the life of Bayside Christian Church. The Doom Room wasn't buying it. Stanton and Steven had tuned her out in the first ninety seconds, opting to ball up and play catch with the church bulletin they'd found under their seats.

Inspired, three or four other second-grade heads immediately bobbed down under their own seats to look for more bulletins. When they found none, Stanton and Steven's game of two-way catch turned to six-way keep-away.

Essie implemented the Queen Esther Glare. To no avail.

Finally, she vaulted out of her seat in time to catch the airborne bulletin ball with her right hand while simultaneously shoving Alex Faber back down into his seat with her left. As quietly as she could, which wasn't quietly at all, she began bodily moving the boys to seats with vacant seats between them—sort of a boy-chair-boy-chair seating plan.

When even that failed to keep chaos at bay, Essie sunk to the lowest of all teacher tactics.

The Tootsie Roll.

Yummy, wrapped in a non-noisy wrapper, and requiring considerable time and energy to chew, the Tootsie Roll was the last resort of frazzled teachers everywhere. Three of them could buy you as much as twenty minutes of near-silence.

And she had seventy-two of them in her tote bag.

Sure, Alice Bendenfogle was going to go out of her sugar-free-organic little mind. But Alice Bendenfogle wasn't here, and Alice Bendenfogle wasn't trying to prevent World

War Three on Day One of play rehearsal. *Hey lady,* Essie thought, defending herself in her imagination, *drastic times called for drastic measures.*

As she handed them out, Essie tried to think of it as a victory. Yes, she'd sunk this far.

But at least she'd lasted until December to do it.

A dozen Tootsie Rolls and four requests to go to the bathroom later, Essie finally heard Dahlia dismiss the classes back to their respective rooms.

Essie was finishing up things when Justin's mom appeared in the doorway to pick him up. She flashed a sheepish grin and tapped Essie on the elbow as Justin shuffled out the door. "He's thrilled, Mrs. Walker. Nervous, but thrilled. Thank you." It wasn't hard to see the source of Justin's mild nature; that was the most Mrs. Baker had spoken to Essie all year.

Essie touched the woman's arm lightly, as if too much of a grip might frighten her. "You're welcome. Justin's a wonderful boy." And Justin was wonderful. A little too easily lead astray by the dastardly minds of the Doom Room, but if that was his worst quality he was way ahead of the game for this group. She watched mother and son walk down the hallway together, Mrs. Baker's hand brushing the top of Justin's head in maternal love and pride.

It was a warm and tender moment—until Stanton's loafer flew by her face so close she could feel the air rush past her cheek. It landed with a thunk—and a sizable black mark—on the hallway wall.

"Stanton, what is it with you and throwing things?" Essie returned her gaze to the room to find that the eight seconds she'd taken her attention away to speak with Mrs. Baker had been seven seconds too long. The boys were once again in a pile of writhing limbs, giggling and shouting. At least this time it seemed like innocent play, not minor warfare. Still, this wasn't exactly the way a teacher wants parents to find their offspring when they're supposed to be studying the Bible. Sighing, Essie found the first available limb and began to pull. Essie had her hands on Stanton's wrist and Alex's elbow when both respective mothers appeared in the doorway. Together.

That in itself was amazing, but the fact that Vicki Faber had *actually appeared* to gather Alex from class—for the first time ever—was nothing short of fantastical.

Essie was unable to stop the pleasant surprise from sparking her sense of humor. Even though Dahlia was holding Stanton's wayward loafer with a decidedly "yes, well" look on her face, she grinned and hoisted both boys upright. "Ladies, I believe these belong to you?"

"I knew it." Essie glared at the answering-machine message light when she, Doug and Josh got home. "Alice Bendenfogle versus the Tootsie Roll."

"What?" said Doug, looking confused.

"I'll tell you later. Let me get this over with first." Essie closed her eyes and hit Play.

"Es, it's Pop. Your mother's feeling sick, and I don't like the look of her. It's Sunday so I know I can't get ahold of Mark-o. I want you to come over here and take a look at her when you get home."

An optimistic woman would have though "well, at least it's not Alice Bendenfogle." Today was not a good day for optimism.

Doug came up behind her. "Doesn't he know you have a cell phone?"

Essie groaned. "He won't call it. Says he doesn't want other people listening in on his phone conversations."

Now Doug groaned. "It's a cell phone, not a speaker phone. Can't he…"

"Don't." Essie held up her hand. Now matter how many times she had tried to reason with Pop about the advantages of the wireless world, there was only so far you could get with a man who still couldn't even master his own answering machine. She closed her eyes and held out both hands, as if to ward off one more shred of bad news. "I'm going over there. He's never asked me to do this before—either she's really bad or *he's* really bad and unwilling to tell me."

Essie walked to the freezer to count the stored up bottles of milk—who knew how long this episode would last? "Mom's been wound up like a clock ever since that night Pop earned himself a round of chest pains by being a tightwad with his medicine." She closed the freezer door and walked to the hallway, where she rummaged through the piles of stuff on the closet floor until she found a tote bag. "I suppose I even saw this coming—it'd only be a matter of time before something got to her."

Essie trotted around the house, keeping up a running monologue as Doug and Josh followed her. "You hear about it all the time—caregiver trauma, burnout, that sort of thing." Into the bag went two packages of graham crackers and a bottle of spring water. "Dr. Einhart even told me to watch for it. Says it's usually just one thing after another when they get to this age." It was only after the words had left her mouth that she realized the quote was not Dr. Einhart's, regarding elderly parents, but Lenora's from the pharmacy. Regarding *babies*.

Great. What could be more fun that being sandwiched between two generations of never-ending crises?

For such a time as this. The Bible verse echoed on her thoughts, smoothing the panic. *I'm here because I'm needed.*

Essie stuffed a clean sweatshirt, a hairbrush and elastic and package of gum into the bag. As she squished things to one side to put in the Celebration script and a pen, she turned to look at Doug and Josh. "Misters Walker and Walker, welcome to my new life. Try not to come down with anything serious before I get back, will you?"

Doug got that "you're getting all weird on me again" look on his face and simply said, "Yeah. Well, take care, Mrs. Walker."

"Care?" Essie called over her shoulder, fumbling in a dish on the hall table where they kept the keys until she located the ones for Pop's apartment and his car. She should just give up and keep them permanently on her key ring. "Care. Yep, that's exactly what it will take."

Mom *did* look awful. As a matter of fact, Essie was sure that only Pop's cheapskate instincts kept him from calling an ambulance instead of calling his daughter. She did her best not to be angry at her Pop for not resorting to a cell phone—why on earth did he sit there and wait for Essie to get home when Mom looked so bad? Her skin had a scary, flushed tint to it, and she was showing signs of mild confusion. As if her thoughts and words couldn't quite get themselves to the right places in her brain. She was spiking a fever, complained of a backache, and according to Pop she hadn't eaten well in a day or so.

Dr. Einhart answered his page quickly. He was only Pop's cardiologist, but Mom, of course, had neglected to find a physician of her own while tending to Pop's health. Dr. Einhart wasn't surprised to hear that, and quickly set up an internist from his group to meet Essie and her mother at the hospital.

Essie and her mother. *Without* her father. It was an odd request, but Dr. Einhart seemed to know what he was doing, and Essie trusted his suggestion.

Getting Pop to go along with that was another story. Ah, thought Essie as she stuffed Mom's things into a bag she'd found in her parents' hall closet, here is just the job for Mark-o.

Essie punched in Mark-o's speed dial and cradled the phone against her shoulder as she stuffed. Toothbrush, nightgown, slippers.

"Mark Taylor."

"Mark-o, you need to get over here and sit with Pop while I take Mom to the hospital." Underwear, medicines, sweater.

"I *what?*"

"Mom's looking bad, Dr. Einhart's setting up an exam at the hospital but he wants Pop to stay home. Pop's not buying it, and I need you here to deal with him." Essie walked to the kitchen and tossed a handful of tea bags into the bag, remembering last time.

She heard Mark-o cover the phone and talk to someone. "Can you give me an hour?"

"Nope. This one is a 'right now' kind of thing. I'm telling Pop you're on your way and I'll call you from the E.R." She gave herself a split second to be proud of her assertiveness.

Then she heard Mark-o sigh on the other end. She was taking a breath to launch into a "don't you do this to me" speech when he said, "Okay, I'll be there."

Thanks, Lord. Essie zipped up the bag and pulled her mother's coat out of the closet.

"I don't see why..." Pop was grousing from the recliner. She knew he'd acquiesced, though, because despite making lots of noise about leaving, he'd not gotten up off his chair.

"Mark-o's on his way, Pop. I'll call you when I can. It'll all be okay. I'm glad you called me to help you with this." Mom wasn't putting up a fight at all, but she was mumbling quietly to herself as she let Essie slip the coat over her sagging shoulders. She'd lost weight, Essie noticed. Her hair was thinning out. How had she been too focused on her own aggravation to notice such things?

"I should be..."

"You should be hearing from Mark-o any minute. You just sit tight, okay? I'm going to take care of everything. Dr. Einhart's got someone meeting us at the hospital to check Mom out." Essie turned to look at her father.

He looked frightened.

In all the traumas they'd been through with him, his face always broadcast frustration or annoyance. Now that they were worrying about his bride, the woman who'd seen him though all those traumas, he looked genuinely afraid.

A wave of pity washed over her. She saw the face of the man who'd scooped her up from bicycle falls, who'd held her hand while they stitched her knee, who kept an all-night vigil over her when she fell from the high jump and suffered a bad concussion. Essie felt a lump rise in her throat.

She walked over to Pop and kissed him gently on the forehead. "It's gonna be okay, Pop. We'll get Mom checked out. Mark-o will bring you if you need to come, but for now you stay here and I'll take care of Mom." She buttoned up her own coat, blinking back the threat of tears. "It's gonna be fine, you'll see. You did the right thing in calling."

She kept repeating it to herself as she helped her mother down the hall to the car. *It's gonna be fine. It's gonna be fine. It's gonna be fine.*

Fighting the Undertow

It was nearly 11:00 p.m. by the time Essie returned to her apartment. Being at the hospital was, as Doug was fond of saying, *déjà vu* all over again. It was amazing, she thought to herself as she headed home, what someone could come to view as normal. Maybe that's what helped Mark-o do what he did, being roused in the middle of the night—or the middle of his life—to deal with the *crises du jour*. Once she'd gotten over the initial shock and fear of getting Pop to the E.R., she was astounded at how calm she was taking Mom there.

Dr. Einhart, who was approaching hero status in Essie's point of view, had been dead-on in suggesting Mom come without Pop. Without Pop in the room, without her constant consideration of his health, Mom opened up. Granted, it might have been that her defenses were worn down by symptoms, but Mom finally began to talk about the stress of dealing with her husband. The insurance papers, which were frustrating enough to send Mother Teresa into road rage, were getting to her. Pop's nagging was getting to her. The city atmosphere was getting to her. Age was getting to her.

Dr. Gupta was a serene Indian man who possessed the kindest voice Essie thought she'd ever heard. He knew how to ask just the right questions. Essie could practically watch her mom's fingers unclench as he spoke with her. Thanks to his calming bedside manner and Dr. Einhart's heads-up, within in thirty minutes they'd identified the problem. Mom had ignored symptoms of a urinary tract infection for weeks; long enough for it to become a full-blown kidney infection. She was fatigued from not sleeping, running a fever from the infection and in enough pain to make her foggy.

This had been brewing for weeks. And she'd missed it completely. Essie began doubting if she could really monitor her parents' health well at all. Old people ached all the time. How on earth does one distinguish between ordinary geriatric crankiness and true signs of trouble?

Two prescriptions and three tests later, Dr. Gupta had ordered Dorothy be admitted overnight for IV antibiotics and observation. Essie had an appointment at 1:00 p.m. the next afternoon to come back and take her home.

Shutting her apartment door softly, Essie laid down her keys as quietly as she could. She paused, listening. Telltale whimpering came from Josh's room. Her hopes that everyone was happily asleep hadn't come true.

With a sense of dread, she pushed open the door to Josh's room. Her gaze met a red-faced, sniffling child, held by a pale-faced, drawn-out-looking husband. On the side table beside the rocker were the portents of doom: a thermometer and a bottle of baby Tylenol.

Oh, no.

"We tried not to come down with anything while you were gone," said Doug, his attempt to make humor falling miserably short, "but...um...we failed."

Essie expected the usual surge of frustration to overtake her. Instead, a dig-your-heels-in-'cause-this-is-how-it-goes-from-here sort of feeling came over her. A settling, somewhere between resolve and resignation. A steadiness of sorts. The kind attributed to someone described as "unflappable."

She sighed, motioned for Doug to come up out of the chair, and began unbuttoning her shirt for a fussing Josh to nurse. "Hand me the cordless phone," she heard her steady voice saying. "I think I'm going to order some Chinese food."

The next morning, Essie called Mark-o and gave him a choice: fussy baby or fussy mother. Since Josh's fever, which heralded yet another ear infection, wouldn't allow him to go inside the hospital, Mark-o would either have to pick up their mother or babysit while Essie fetched Mom. Before he could utter one word of dissent, Essie reminded him that according to the church calendar, Mondays were Pastor's day off.

It came as no surprise that Mark-o opted to pick up Mom. Even after a night in the hospital, Essie guessed her mother was the lesser of two fussies. Essie wondered, as she stretched out on the couch for a nap once a now-medicated Josh finally dozed off, if her life would ever cease to be punctuated with ear infections. When life would ever become more than that thing she got to do in between doctor and pharmacy visits. Actually, Lenora had taken pity on

Esther and personally delivered the amoxicillin on her way home from her morning shift at the pharmacy. "You're a regular, so I thought it'd be nice" she had said, her jingle-bell earrings chiming as she spoke. "There's a chocolate Santa in there, too. On me. Consider it an early Christmas present." Lenora gave Essie a wink and a nudge, and trotted off down the hall to press the elevator button before Essie could get a syllable of thanks out of her mouth.

Essie thought she just might live through the week, until she remembered that today was Monday.

Which meant tomorrow was Tuesday.

Which meant Dahlia and Vicki were descending on her house in less than twenty-four hours.

A debate sprung up in Essie's mind. Surely, she couldn't hope to manage the diplomatic negotiations required by a Vicki-Dahlia visit on the few hours sleep she'd get tonight. Then again, when would ever be the right time?

This was not just anything, either; this was Vicki and Dahlia. And even if Coffee #1 had gone well, there was no telling what mayhem Coffee #2 would bring. Hadn't Dr. Einhart warned her about healthy boundaries? Protecting her own health? Hadn't she just given the same speech to her mom?

I can't do this.

I'm supposed to do this.

There was still time to call it off.

There was still time to pull it off.

Lord, Essie prayed as she pulled the afghan up to her chin protectively, *I have absolutely no idea what to do. Are You asking me to lean into Your provision, to trust that You'll pull these details together? Or are You showing me I've got too much on my plate? I need a little more clarity here. I need direction. I need giant, flash-*

ing neon road signs, thunderbolts, unignorably pertinent passages of scripture, those kinds of things. This is no time for subtlety, Lord, I need a whack over the head here.

Essie fell asleep waiting for a lightning bolt to strike her living room.

She dreamed of the wide, flat, playground of a beach from her childhood in New Jersey. The salt spray stuck to her ankles as she played a game of tag with the waves. A big one would come barreling into the shore, covering the plane of flat sand and pushing the tide farther into the dry sand. Essie loved when the tide was rising—it brought a sense of delightful urgency, a "ready or not here I come" atmosphere to the beach. In her dream, she was running back and forth, claiming every inch of beach she could as the wave receded, getting as far out as she could before a new wave took back the sand.

Some kids were afraid of the rising tide. Tanned clusters of beach moms would always tell stories of the dangerous undertow to their children. Every child who grew up on the coast learned a healthy respect for the power of the sea.

Some kids let those stories rule them. Those kids would never challenge the waves. "Tide pool kids" Essie would call them—and it wasn't a compliment. Essie was no "tide pool kid." Her competitive nature adored the duel of sand and sea. That place, that glossy flat stretch of sand where the waves washed over, was the most fun place on earth. Sure, the waves took it back every few seconds, but in between those advances Essie would have the time of her life skipping in the shallows.

She woke with an unearthly sense of peace, knowing just what to do. Yes, the tide was rising, but in her life right now, the tide would always be rising. Esther was Queen of the

Waves, and knew just how to master the undertow. Of the Atlantic, or of life.

There was even a hint of a smile on her face as Essie dialed Cece to ask for 1) prayer (no details, just a request for general prayer support), 2) her coffee grinder and some beans that didn't come from a can, and 3) a trip to the bakery for coffee cake.

Josh slept fine that night, the amoxicillin once again proving its incredible powers.

It was Essie who was up all night.

Coach Jemmings had e-mailed her asking her if she was ready to come in for an interview. She hadn't managed to tell Doug. If she told him now, she'd have to admit to him that she hadn't told him before. If she said "no," to the interview request Doug would never really need to know anything, right? She knew that was a lie. Besides, how could she add employment to the circus her life was quickly becoming? The checkbook, however, was quickly becoming a circus of its own. Doug's stress had a lot to do with how hard it was for them to make ends meet. A little extra income would go a long way. What was she supposed to do?

As if that wasn't enough, Essie's imagination kept brewing up scenario after excruciating scenario of the upcoming coffee date. Vicki, yelling at her to keep her nose out of other people's business. Dahlia, scowling at her for ever allowing the subject of breasts to come up in grade-school conversation. Both women furious at the invasion of their privacy. Dahlia asking the education committee to remove Essie from her teaching position. Mark-o lecturing her on the virtue of confidentiality. Cece, staring at her with a hand on one hip, asking, "What were you thinking?"

Morning found Essie grinding coffee in a bleary-eyed fog. She put her hands on the phone receiver three times to dial the women and call it off, but couldn't bring herself to do it. When the doorbell rang, Essie answered it with the desperate resignation of a woman walking to the gallows.

Vicki looked as bad as she did. It was a glossed over, polished sort of bad, but Essie recognized the same sleep-starved look in Vicki's eyes that she felt in her own. Essie chose not to say anything—it was clear Vicki was trying to cover up whatever was bothering her. *Oh, Lord,* Essie prayed as she took Vicki's coat, *I sure hope You know what You're doing.*

"Sorry, things are a bit messy," Essie blurted out, motioning toward the hastily tidied living room. "I hardly got a wink of sleep last night, even though Josh slept like a…well, like a baby." She wasn't sure why she said that. It sounded rather stupid to her, and she was sure Vicki regarded it the same way. "I was going to make the coffee on the strong side this morning, if that's okay with you."

"I'd like that." Not the usual, clipped, "fine" that was Vicki's response to most questions. There was a weariness to her voice. What was going on?

Essie made small talk as she prepared the coffee and cake. Vicki seemed far off and distracted. She didn't look the high-powered professional today. She looked young and fragile and very scared. As if God had peeled away the veneer to expose the frail girl who hid underneath.

The phone rang. It was Carmen, sputtering out in her broken English that "ma'am is going to be late porqué Stanton had forgot his ¿Cómosedice?…ah…sword," she pronounced the "w" in sword which made it almost funny, "for the fencing and ma'am had to bring to school." *Fencing.*

Handing any second-grader—much less Stanton—a weapon seemed just plain insane. No wonder he was always poking people. Or was that Decker?

"Dahlia's running a bit late."

"Um." Vicki hardly even registered the information.

"Vicki, are you all right?"

Vicki snapped back into composure. "Sure, I'm fine. Fine."

Suddenly, Essie needed to reach out to Vicki more than she needed to care what Vicki thought of her in the aftermath. "I don't think that's true. You're no more fine than I am, and I don't know about you, but I don't have the energy to keep up a front today. What's going on?"

"Nothing. I'm fine."

Essie was never more sure of a lie in her life. It dared her, like the big waves, to go out as far as she could into the current. She sat down on the chair across from Vicki. "No, I don't think you're anything close to fine. So while Dahlia's running late, I'm going to tell you something you need to hear. You can do whatever you want with this information, including hate me, but *you* need to know it and *I* need to tell you."

Vicki stared at her, shocked. She made no reply whatsoever.

"Stanton told me in class a few weeks ago that he came across something in Dahlia's dresser drawer. He came across her prostheses, Vicki. Her breast forms. I think Dahlia's had a mastectomy. I think Dahlia is a breast cancer survivor. I haven't asked her yet and she sure hasn't offered the information, but I'm pretty sure she's been through what you're facing."

Vicki's eyes widened. Still, she remained silent.

"I can't even begin to imagine what it's like for you, but

I'm pretty sure that I'd really want to talk to someone if I were you. Someone who's been through this and come out okay. I know it seems like no one wants to talk about it, but I think you're long past want here—you *need* to talk to someone. You said so yourself, your friends aren't exactly lining up in support on this one—and that's if you've told them at all."

Vicki's only response was to lower her eyes. No movement, no sound, no argument, no confirmation. Nothing. She'd been right: Vicki was going down this road completely alone.

"You can do what you like with that information. I've done what I needed to do, I've let you know there's a woman out there who can help you. *Help,* Vicki, there's help out there. Where it goes from here is up to you. But I really think…"

At that moment the doorbell rang. Essie felt as if she were left to twist in the wind. She didn't know whether Vicki would get up and leave, start talking, start yelling, or simply yank that veneer back up and pretend nothing happened. It felt awful. Exposed. She couldn't even bring herself to say something like "please think about this." The doorbell rang a second time. The room filled with uncomfortable silence as Essie rose to get the door.

In swept the social tidal wave that was Dahlia Mannington. From the moment Essie opened the door, Dahlia began a monologue of Celebration issues dotted with an occasional jab at Stanton's teachers who obviously forgot to check his schedule and remind him of which equipment was needed at school. It was a good three minutes before she settled herself onto a chair with her coffee and pronounced, "So, Essie, dear, what can we do for you?"

Be human? Show compassion? Go beneath the surface for just one morning?

Pulling out her notebook after a long pause, Essie resigned herself to defeat. She'd done all she could, but the likelihood of these two women ever getting to the real messes of life was near impossible. Vicki might never forgive her outburst, and Essie felt like she'd never be able to muster up enough courage to ask Dahlia to make the first move.

Dahlia seemed downright oblivious to Vicki's demeanor. Vicki looked as if she was going to slip right off the edge of the couch and Dahlia chatted away, offering suggestions and tips and the occasional cutting remark as to someone's ability to do this or that.

Essie groped her way through the tasks she'd invented for the meeting. Each one seemed more silly and unnecessary than the last, and Essie's sense of failure grew with every minute.

She wasn't master of the undertow at all. She was adrift. She'd stuck her nose in where it didn't belong, and now held the distinction of adding to a scared young woman's misery.

"And I think we can surely pull that together," continued Dahlia, her pen bobbing. She continued to tick off ideas for each of Essie's tasks when Vicki silently got up off the couch. She's going to walk out, thought Essie, just leave without a word. Instead, Vicki walked over to the side table where Essie had left Josh's Christmas outfit alongside some other clean laundry. *Ugh,* she'd meant to put that away but never got to it. Essie watched as she fingered the little appliquéd reindeer on one leg, then the matching overalls on the tiny bear. Something in the set of her shoulders was heartbreaking. Essie wanted to shake Dahlia's shoulders and yell, "Can't you see? Don't you see how much pain she's in?"

"So I think it'd be marvelous for you to come to tomorrow's meeting, if you can squeeze it in," Dahlia was going on. "You'd have that sort of thing done in a flash, Vicki, with your eye for it. Can you make it at eleven?"

Vicki's fingers stilled. Essie couldn't see her face, just the way her hand stilled on the fabric. "I can't make that, I have an…appointment." She choked on the word. Essie's heart squeezed tight at the sound of it.

"I have a…a…doctor's appointment then."

Vicki was crying.

"Actually, it's not a doctor's appointment at all," she continued, straightening herself but not yet turning around. "It's with the radiologist. I start radiation tomorrow. I won't be able to come to the meeting because I start radiation tomorrow." She said it with the shaky declaration of an alcoholic at her first AA meeting.

The room fell completely silent.

"What did you say, dear?" Dahlia spoke very slowly.

Essie wanted to scream. Was Dahlia made of stone? Was she really going to make Vicki repeat herself when the woman was hanging on by a thread?

"I said," said Vicki turning around to show a face streaked with tears, "I have breast cancer and I start radiation tomorrow."

Dahlia made a complete transformation in seconds. She shot out of her chair and walked toward Vicki. "I heard you, honey," she said, pulling Vicki into her arms even though Vicki resisted. "I heard you. Shh. I heard you."

"You mean there's a whole network of you?" Vicki sniffed.

"Twenty-nine to be exact. By tomorrow afternoon, we'll have you set up for meals and rides for weeks."

"How come no one knows about this?"

Dahlia looked as though the answer were perfectly obvious. "Well, it's not the sort of thing one wants to get around now, is it?"

Only Dahlia Mannington and Bayside Church could pull off an entire secret society of breast cancer survivors. They'd even made Essie promise secrecy. Dahlia refused to name names while Essie was in the room. Who knew compassion and denial could be such effective bedfellows? It drove Essie nuts—so much pain could be avoided if these women would just open up to each other.

Then again, they were who they were. "Warts and all," Mark-o would say. Essie couldn't change Dahlia Mannington any more than she could make Pop pay retail. Or take his expensive medicine gratefully.

As Essie watched these women in utter amazement—both in the best and the worse sense of that word—she thought of the undertow. Every coastal child knew the two cardinal rules of beach life: 1) never swim alone, and 2) don't try to fight the current. As soon as kids could swim, they were taught that if the current took you out, you couldn't fight your way straight back. You had to angle your way down the beach, fighting the current a little bit at a time, until you hit shore.

Essie closed the door an hour later, realizing she had not had a single cup of coffee. Still, the energy of what she'd just achieved—or, she reminded herself, what God had just achieved through her—was beyond caffeine.

She called Doug at work, only to get his voice mail.

She went to call Cece, but realized she couldn't.

She thought to call Anna, but even though she was miles away and knew none of the parties involved, it would still be a breech of confidentiality.

Strapped for someone to celebrate with, Essie told Josh the entire story when he woke up a few minutes later. She recounted the details in energized, dramatic fashion as she fed and changed him. She asked him what he thought of the bizarre existence of this secret network so many needed but so few knew about. Of why they had to hide it at all.

Josh's inability to answer didn't matter. This felt better than any record-breaking throw, any medal, any professional accomplishment Essie could name. The Queens Esther—biblical and contemporary—had taken on their foes and won the day.

Chapter 22

Deck the Halls

Second-grade boys, thought Essie as she turned the lock on the classroom door, should be illegal. They should be locked up somewhere until they reach the Age of Reason, which tonight Essie guessed to be somewhere around twenty-three.

The last five rehearsals had exceeded all bounds of civility, decency and dignity. The looming prospect of Christmas, with its vacations, presents and dramas, both family and stage—Bayside's Christmas pageant was the sole property of the drama team, the adult drama team, thankfully—had whipped these boys into a frenzy of monumental proportions. Add too much sugar, and *ka-pow! Run for cover, people!*

Vicki disappeared off the radar in the dozen days following that meeting, but a wink from Dahlia as she dropped off Alex for each rehearsal and class told her Vicki was in good hands. Essie theorized that Dahlia did all the dropping off so that Essie, who evidently was a serious breach in security for this clandestine task force, would never know its other members. Essie would ask careful questions of Alex every couple of days. Essie's queries were designed to get information without giving away how much she knew. So far, it sounded like Vicki was holding her own, and Alex seemed to have a healthy oblivion for the nature of his step-mom's "medicine stuff."

Essie's mom, knee-deep in her own "medicine stuff," was back on her feet. Essie had grilled her for a solid week about her health, getting shamelessly nosy until Mom finally held up her hands and promised to tell anyone if she was feeling badly from now on in. "I'll tell you my temperature every day if you'll just stop asking me about my kidneys!" she'd pleaded.

Josh had managed to stave off further illnesses, and Essie harbored a cautious, careful optimism for the holidays ahead. Cautious, because she remembered that the really big waves often sneaked up without warning. Careful, because it was hard to be awash in jubilation with the grinch-worthy Christmas budget Doug had given her.

More frugal than festive. Which, in this corner of the world, was decidedly hard. Dahlia seemed just astounded that Essie had not hired someone to decorate their house for the holidays. Essie didn't even know people did that sort of thing. In New Jersey, every year someone's dad on the block broke something or other falling off the roof while hanging lights. Wasn't "Deck the Halls" sort of a *hands-on* command? In this city the carol seemed to have been revised to "Have some-one in to deck the halls, fa–la–la–la–la, etc." There was even a "Fa-La-La, Inc." company advertised in the paper, promising "magazine-worthy splendor for all your holiday decorating needs."

Still, as she cut frugal-but-festive red-and-green con-
struction paper chains for their tree, Essie nurtured a spark
of holiday glow. Last Christmas she'd been pregnant, just
showing, and feeling the magic of Handel's "unto us a
child is born—unto us, a son is given" in fantastic new
ways. This Christmas she watched her son widen his eyes
at the lights and sounds that filled the air. "It's so different
with children," Anna had said in their last phone call.
"Christmas is a whole new thing with kids. It's just marvelous."

And it was.

If only Doug were home and awake to enjoy it.

Essie tried not to be resentful. She reminded herself that
Doug held a lot of weight on his shoulders, that providing
for a young family was a big burden. She'd lecture herself
every time she prickled at Doug's hastily eaten dinners—
when he was home to eat dinner at all—before heading out
again. Three nights last week he'd either returned to work
or went to a church set-construction meeting. That despi-
cable self-separating pyramid was really getting to her. Who
really needed a revolving Mount Sinai anyway? And what
idiot had continued to insist on real sand? Was every man
in Bayside shirking off their holidays in the name of set con-
struction? Or just hers?

"How does he have so much free time?" Essie had de-
manded of Mark-o one day, noting that Mike, the chairman
of the set committee was one man who seemed to have
countless hours to devote to dreaming up complicated set
ideas.

"Mike has so much *free time*—" Mark-o emphasized the
words with a sharp edge "—because he was laid off from
his job three months ago."

So be thankful your husband still has his job, those edgy words seemed to imply.

She ripped the paper link she was working on and had to start over.

Merry Christmas, Charlie Brown came on the television, and Essie blew out an exasperated breath. Here she was, about to partake in her very favorite Christmas special, enjoying it for the first time with a child of her own…and on her own.

And yes, I'm mad. Rip.

By the time Linus had launched into his famous recitation of Luke's Gospel, she'd ripped a dozen paper links. The evening lay in ruins like the paper shreds before her. "Merry Christmas to you, too, Douglas Walker!" Essie called at the unopened front door. She gathered up the papers and set about putting Josh to bed.

By nine o'clock, there was still no sign of Doug. Essie decided she'd better fire up the computer and begin drafting the letter she'd yet to send out with their Christmas cards. She'd already gone through two rolls of film capturing the absolute perfect shot of Josh to enclose, his bright eyes gleaming from within those spectacular overalls Doug's mom had created. He looked like a catalogue baby. Adorable, glowing, full of innocence.

She'd barely been able to get Doug's attention long enough to approve her photo choice. As she opened the word-processing program, she decided it wasn't worth waiting any longer for Doug to approve this letter if they were going to have them arrive before Christmas. No, Essie'd quickly realized that one of the by-products of being home is that all domestic projects fall squarely on your lap— whether you want them to or not.

I'm a housewife.

When did I become a housewife? I don't even own an apron. I've never made a pot roast.

Suddenly I'm Mrs. Walker, Josh's mom.

Where'd Essie go?

The flashing blue envelope on her screen told her that Mrs. Walker The Housewife at least had some e-mail waiting. There was an e-mail from Doug's parents confirming all their travel plans for Christmas—even they had started sending their stuff to *her,* rather than try and catch Doug's attention. There were two short, annoyingly cheerful holiday greetings from friends home in New Jersey, and then there was the last one.

From Coach Jemmings.

She'd replied a few weeks ago, hedging, saying she was still interested but wanted to wait until after the holidays to think about it.

Jemmings informed her that if she wanted to stay in the running—he added a nice bit about wanting her to, which made her feel very good—she'd need to at least begin the application and interview process. "To help entice you," he'd written, "I've attached information on the college's childcare program. Our child development students run an on-site center that will be available to you at a subsidized cost. I'd be happy to forward a few references from parent employees who use the center if you're interested."

Essie grabbed her purse from the side table and flipped open the checkbook. Oh man, she thought, if only *I* were this lean. She looked at the clock: it was just before ten and still Doug was off building pyramids. She looked at herself in the hallway mirror, just catching a corner of it from her chair: who was that woman staring back? She looked so tired, so…frumpy.

As the clock struck ten, Essie downloaded the attachments and sent a reply message with three dates and times she was available to come in and interview.

She'd tell Doug.

Next time they had more than fifteen minutes together.

Which, as it turned out, wasn't until Christmas Eve.

Once unshackled from the harrows of his office cubicle, Doug seemed to finally unwind at the prospect of three whole days off. Essie could tell that he'd had to work hard to extricate himself from Nytex. He was wound up like a clock when he finally walked through the door at 6:00 p.m. on the 23rd. Yet, as his parents arrived from Nevada the next day bearing a nearly obscene amount of gifts, the Doug she knew and loved seemed to return.

None of Thanksgiving's tension was present at Christmas Eve dinner, where both sets of grandparents and even Mark-o and Peggy, although they only stayed for an hour, shoe-horned themselves into Essie's tiny apartment. Josh giggled at being passed from adoring grandparent to adoring grandparent. Essie managed to find a pair of pants with an actual waistband that didn't feel as if they were slowly sawing her in half. Doug made his famous mulled cider recipe—a trademark of his in New Jersey—and the house smelled like Christmas ought to smell.

Christmas Day was right out of a storybook. They met Doug's parents at their hotel, taking a moment to show Josh the beautifully decorated lobby. Doug's parents took Josh to Bayside while Essie and Doug went to pick up Essie's parents to bring them to the church service. Three times on the way to the town house, Essie thought to bring up the subject of Coach Jemmings's offer. Each time the magic feeling of the day defied any such sticky issue. It had been so long since things had felt so "in place." She didn't want to make waves, not today.

The Spirit of Christmas Present had evidently visited Pop—and knocked him over the head, Essie mused—for he was ready, dressed and cheerfully cooperative when they arrived at the town house. Mom had a wonderfully familiar fussiness, fluttering around adjusting this, that, fixing ties, finding lint on lapels, and other such motherly fidgeting. Essie was thankful to have her old Mom back. It had frightened her to see her mother ill—even temporarily. If anyone could have told Essie she would come to cherish her mother's fussing, she'd never have believed them. Today, she couldn't help but smile as Mom reknotted Essie's scarf and straightened her Christmas pin.

As the church choir swelled in chorus of "Joy to the World," Josh snuggled sleepily in her arms. His perfect little face calm, unaware of the tidal wave of presents about to come his way once church and brunch were done. It was just plain perfect. Essie felt as if her heart would burst with the grace and glory of Christmas.

"A *what!?*"

"A health-club membership. Doug gave me a health-club membership for Christmas."

"No, not Doug." Cece shook her head over the salads they were sharing at her kitchen table the following Monday.

"Yes, he did. He had all kinds of sensible, logical reasons why it made such a great gift. But…"

"But he still didn't get the fact that women do not want exercise—in any form whatsoever—for Christmas."

Essie put down her fork. "Where do they get these ideas? Did I ever give him a tin of protein powder and hint that I might like him to bulk up for Valentine's Day?"

Cece looked as though she thought that a rather creative comeback. "Well, you've got time before February."

Essie laughed. Cece then recited a list of appliances, self-help products, and other man-conceived-and-highly-inappropriate Yuletide tidings Tom had given her over the years. "I only really yelled when he gave me the scale. It didn't matter that I had admired it in the store two weeks earlier. There simply is never a time when giving a woman a bathroom scale is ever, *ever* acceptable."

"Amen." Essie agreed. It was almost amusing how Doug could not understand that this highly useful, thoughtful gift of a club membership might really get under the skin of a postpartum, Christmas-cookie-bloated female. Truly, he could not get his mind around the idea that this wasn't just the perfect gift for his once-athletic wife. "So you can watch Josh next Tuesday?"

Cece tickled Josh's toes, now shod in the adorable tiny sneakers Anna had sent from New Jersey. "I insist. Where'd you say you were going, anyway? Going to use up that Ghirardelli's gift card I gave you?"

"Funny. I'm…" Essie had a ten-second internal debate as to whether to tell Cece before continuing. "I'm going to talk to the coach at Bay Area Community College. They have a coaching position open there, and they've invited me to apply."

Cece seemed surprised. "That is big news. Are you seriously considering it?"

"I don't know yet. Parts of it seem tailormade for me. I can't help thinking that God has opened a door to the perfect job for me out here."

"But…" Cece cued, reading Essie's expression.

"But I don't know. Doug might hate the idea. I might hate the idea."

"What do you mean, 'might hate'? Don't tell me you haven't talked this over with him."

"Well…"

"Essie, you have to know what a bad idea that is. What were you thinking?"

"This isn't the kind of conversation we can have in ten minutes. I want time to talk this over with him. And I haven't seen him for more than ten minutes in weeks, between work and Bayside. He's never home. And when he's home, he's tired and grumpy or he's wolfing down dinner so he can go back out to work or church. When do I have time to discuss it with him?"

Cece got that look again. That look that meant Essie wasn't going to like whatever she said next. "Is this really about you working, or is this about Doug's schedule? You two had better talk this over before you go to that meeting. I'd feel much better watching Josh so you two can hash this out than watching him so you can go look into a job."

"What? So now I need his approval to look into work?" "Housewife, housewife," echoed in Essie's ears.

"This isn't about permission. This is about making decisions as a couple. Has Doug ever said how he feels about you returning to work?"

"He doesn't need to say a word. The checkbook is yelling loud and clear."

"So it's just yelling at *you,* is it? This isn't a problem for you and Doug to solve *together?*"

"I don't even know if I'm going to get serious about this. What's the point of getting into a fight about something I don't even know about yet?" Essie speared a cherry tomato with javelinlike accuracy.

Cece was quiet for a time before she said, "Why are you afraid to talk to Doug about this?"

"I am not afraid," Essie shot back, but, of course, the minute the words left her mouth she knew Cece was right. That woman was just plain annoying in her ability to read people. Cece let the silence hang there between them. "Afraid's not the right word. I can't really put my finger on what it feels like. But mostly, it feels like, well, caving in. Am I supposed to go back to who I was in New Jersey? Or is there some new version of me in the works out here? I love coaching. I'm good at it. I know how to coach." Essie put down her fork and looked up at Cece, needing to see her eyes when she truly admitted what she was feeling. "I don't know how to do what I'm doing now. This whole mom thing. Mom and Pop. Doug. We're all the same people we were in New Jersey, but nothing's the same. It's like someone changed all the rules on me. I wanted this. If you asked me back in New Jersey if we were supposed to move, I'd have been nervous, but I'd have been sure. I'd have given you a dozen reasons why God wanted us here. Now…"

There just wasn't any way to finish that sentence. The "now whats?" of her life had been thumping in her head for days, beating down her sense of self. Suddenly, a gut-level urge came over Essie. An urge to say the deep-down truth of what she was feeling, even if it made Cece think badly of her. "I don't want to be an invisible housewife."

Essie expected Cece to be insulted. To take her blurted comment as a judgment on the fact that Cece lovingly tended to home and hearth with grace and style Essie could never hope to achieve. Instead, a look of complete sympathy poured over Cece's features, much like the transformation Essie had seen come over Dahlia with Vicki. "Oh, don't I know that feeling." Cece sighed as she reached across the table to grab Essie's hand. "It does feel invisible, doesn't it? Like nobody anywhere on earth gives a hoot about what you do anymore. Like the human race has just passed you by."

Essie could only nod.

"And talking to this 'coach whomever' is like admitting that, isn't it? Like saying to yourself that taking care of Josh isn't enough—and that isn't even about the checkbook, is it?"

Essie wondered why it was that God went so overboard in giving Cece the ability to see right through people. The woman was an emotional X-ray machine.

"Josh is almost ten months old and I still feel like I don't know what I'm doing. I'm tired of never being clean and never being done and never having enough money or enough time." Essie, struck by a wildly clear thought, stared at Cece. "Everybody around here looks so...so...together. So pleased with themselves. Like their lives are so—" she searched for a suitably irritating word "—so gratifying." Essie planted both hands on the table. "Isn't anyone else out there as frustrated as I am?"

"They all are," Cece agreed. "You're just the only one with enough backbone to show it."

Chapter 23

Athletic Intuition

Essie cut the gauze bandage to the right length and tied it off. "You're lucky you didn't get seriously hurt, Pop. What made you think it'd be a good idea to carry all that? They deliver groceries in this city, you know."

"I'm not paying some teenager five bucks to do what I can do myself." Her Pop had stumbled on the town house steps and scraped his hand up good as he caught his fall.

Essie didn't know whether to hit him or hug him. On the one hand, he'd actually voluntarily walked someplace. On the other hand, he'd gone for groceries and way overdid it. He was huffing and puffing so hard by the time he got home that he'd missed a stair. "You're sure you're okay?"

"Fine," he grumbled.

"No, 'fine' generally does not include blood and gauze bandages, Pop. Be careful, okay?" Every cell in her body cried out its objection to her next comment of "If you need something, call. I want to help."

I want to do it myself, Pop's glare said loud and clear.

"Just try and be realistic. Don't overdo stuff."

"Don't lecture me."

"I can't lecture you any longer, I've got to be somewhere in twenty minutes. Take an aspirin if it still bugs you in an hour." It's happened, Essie thought as she pulled on her coat. I've started mothering my parents. Next thing you know I'll be doing that thing where moms lick their fingers and rub things off people's faces.

Where she had to be in twenty minutes was Bay Area Community College. For the interview. The one she still hadn't told Doug about.

Essie's brain was a tangle of thoughts as she rode the bus out to the campus. She was worried about her parents. Little details—nothing major, more like a nagging inkling— were telling her they might not be able to make it living alone much longer. Near misses like this morning made her aware of the same frightening conclusion: one day soon one of them was going to need major care. Mom would never admit to it, Pop would never stand for it. It'd be a battle no matter how it happened. Would they bring someone in? Move to one of those "assisted living" facilities advertised in the magazines where healthy, spiffy seniors "made the most of their golden years"? Who'd pay for all that? What if her parents didn't have enough?

And then there was her own generation. She'd made a nasty comment to Doug last night about the hours he was still keeping. Would it always be this way?

It felt like they were these people who used to be Doug and Essie bumping their way through Doug and Essie's busy lives. Groping their way through Doug and Essie's packed calendars, staggering under Doug and Essie's whopping to-do lists. But not Doug and Essie.

As she got off the bus, checking her cell phone to make sure Cece hadn't called with Josh trouble, Essie came to the realization that, right now, coaching seemed to be the only way to find herself again. The only foothold to the life she once had, the person she used to be. God must know that need in her, or He'd not have cleared such an amazing path to this job.

Lord, Essie prayed as she walked up the sidewalk to the Athletic Center, *show me loud and clear. I need to get this right.*

Essie pulled open the doors to the center's entrance. Instantly, scents and sounds pulled her into a familiar world. Off to her right, squeaking sneakers and echoed voices told her a large gymnasium was behind a set of double doors. To her left, the mist and shouts punctuated by metallic door slams told Essie where the locker rooms were. Bulletin boards fluttered their papers joyfully in the breeze of the open doors. Bins of towels and equipment stood ready down each side of the wide hallway. Her ear caught the chirp of whistles, and it sounded like a beautiful birdsong to her. She knew this world. She knew what to do in this world, how to make things happen in this world.

She loved this world.

In two deep breaths her entire body felt like it snapped back into place.

Coach Jemmings must have been waiting for her; he popped his buzz-cut head out of a door just down the hall and waved. "Welcome!" he said, with a wide smile.

Oh Lord, Essie's heart cried, *I'm home.*

★ ★ ★

"So that's the program." Coach Jemmings sat back in his chair, folding his hands behind his head. "I don't know what you were used to in New Jersey, but I think we do a fine job with what we've got here. If you're all Kevin says you are, I think you'll be a great addition to our staff."

Essie could only nod. Kevin had obviously gushed to Jemmings about her abilities. Essie hadn't heard this many compliments since…since who knew when? At least she hoped it came out as a nod, she was so overwhelmed, it probably made her look more like a bobble-head doll than a prospective assistant coach.

Jemmings leaned in, pushing several sheets of paper toward her. "We're small, Essie, but we get it right."

Somehow, in the way he looked at her, Essie knew that they did. This was a dream setup—all of the best basics of coaching without all the red tape and politics of a big program. The salary was just enough to really make a difference in the family budget—even after she factored in the child-care fees. The child-care center had cinched the deal—as if the deal needed cinching at all. Small, squeaky clean and staffed by students who looked like they would go nuts over Josh.

Scanning the papers for the fourth time on the bus ride home, Essie knew the time had come to talk to Doug. She had all the information she needed. She knew what she wanted to do. She thought out how to pose the question to Doug, which questions he might ask, how they should go about deciding what to do. God had sent this job just like He'd sent Doug's. Things had lined up perfectly, just like they had for Doug at Nytex.

When Doug said he'd be home for dinner and didn't have to go to Bayside until after eight, Essie had her confirmation. Things were going to be just fine.

"And you thought I'd be just fine with this?" Doug could hardly believe his ears.

"Well, yes," Essie replied. "Really, I don't see how you can't be fine with this."

Essie pushed the papers to Doug. She'd completely broadsided him with this. Without a shred of discussion, she'd gone on a job interview? Practically accepted the guy's offer without even talking about the concept of her going back to work? Since when is *this* how you run a marriage? "We've never even talked about you going back to work. You've never mentioned it—not once. You've got to see this is a little out of the blue here."

"Well, I've wanted to talk to you about it." Essie started pacing the room like she always did when she felt defensive. She turned to him, pointing. "Trouble is, you're never home to have a conversation beyond 'pass the salt' or 'whose turn is it to change Josh?'"

Why did he just know she was going to pull his schedule into this? "That's not fair, Es."

"What's fair? Is it fair that I hardly ever see you anymore? Is it fair that you've been gone four nights a week since Thanksgiving? Is it fair that you're not even really here when you are home? You took a whopping three days off for your son's first Christmas. You're turning into one of them, Doug. One of those corporate husbands who just… just checks in between business trips."

That was *way* off base. "I haven't ever left town, I'm home every night. What on earth are you talking about?"

"I never see you! Josh never sees you. You have no idea how well he's crawling now, do you. Do you?"

There she goes again. Every time he turned around these days, Essie was going off about something. Once, she was always energetic, always a dynamo, but now she was more dynamite than dynamo. Volatile. He was running out of the energy to deal with it.

"It's a tight time," he explained for what felt like the thousandth time. "We're in a squeeze. You know things won't always be like this."

"You've been saying that for three months."

"These things don't change in a week. We had crunches in New Jersey and you never acted this way. This is way off base and you know it."

"This is not way off base."

Things were getting out of hand. Doug tried to take his emotions down a notch, to lower his voice and inject some calm into this as fast as he could. "Okay," he said as he sat down, "let's take it for just a moment that I'm working a lot and that's hard for you. That still has nothing to do with the fact that you interviewed for a job without us talking about it first. Come on, Es, you know that's not the way we used to do things. I feel broadsided, here. You didn't expect me to jump up and down, did you?"

Essie's look told him she'd expected just that. "We did talk about how I might need to get a job in the new year. You know how tight things have gotten." Essie sat down. Good. At least they were both sitting now, not standing in some sort of Mexican standoff over the coffee table.

"We've only been here six months. Josh isn't even a year yet. I think the jury's still out."

"But it's harder than we thought. You *know* it's harder than we thought."

She was right there. "Okay, yes, it's been tougher than I thought it'd be. And, we did talk about it, but just in general terms. Not in 'I'm going on an interview' terms. Besides, I'm not sure you working is the answer. Things are complicated enough as it is, don't you think? What about all the stuff you're doing at Bayside? And your parents?"

"*You're* still doing lots of stuff at Bayside, aren't you?" Her voice had an ice-cold edge to it.

He had been spending a lot of time there, but it was just a crunch. Just a work crunch and a church crunch that happened to hit at the same time. "Will you stop that? Let's try to have one argument at a time, okay? This isn't about my schedule, this is about your working."

"You don't want me to work, do you?" It was an accusation, not a question.

Doug fisted his hands. "That's not what I said. I don't know how I feel about you working. It's not like I've had time to think about it, thanks to you."

"Well, I've got a pretty incredible offer on the table, so let's take an hour and talk about it, if you can spare the time."

Annoying as she was at the moment, his hot-headed wife did have a point. If he was arguing that they'd not talked about this, then he had better be good and willing to take the time to talk about this. Sure, right now seemed demanding, but there really wouldn't be a better time to tackle the issue, would there? He asked the obvious question— "Do you think we can talk about this calmly right now?"

"I'm not sure." Her voice softened a bit. "I'm willing to try."

Doug took in a long breath. "Me, too. Let's start over. Tell me about this thing from the beginning. You got an e-mail from Kevin…."

Chapter 24

The Problem with Queen Esther's Realm

No one was happier than Essie when Vicki appeared to pick Alex up from rehearsal that Sunday. She looked thin, a little pale, but generally well for someone a month into radiation. She had all her hair, for one thing. Essie knew enough to recognize this as a sign that massive radiation and chemo hadn't been necessary—they must have caught it very early. *Thanks, God,* Essie sent up a quick surge of gratitude for how well things seemed to be going.

The boys were at the first of several rehearsals that allowed them to practice on the church stage. And the actual tree. The really cool, really tall tree. It had been utter chaos until Essie suggested that each of them could get to climb the tree just once, just to get it out of their systems. That seemed to keep the coveting of the Zacchaeus role to a low boil, and give the boys sufficient focus to fumble their way through the dialogue in this new setting. They were standing in a line along the edge of the stage now, being measured for their costumes. Vicki had come up to Essie as she was watching the rehearsal from the auditorium aisle.

"Hi." It was a slightly awkward moment, their last meeting having been so emotional. Essie had longed to know how Vicki was doing, but chose to let Vicki share contact when she was ready.

"Hello, you," Essie replied, grabbing Vicki's hand because she wasn't sure if a hug would hurt. "How are you doing?"

"Okay. Not great, but okay. It's like having the world's worst sunburn right where you'd never want it, but I'm doing okay." Vicki laughed nervously. "I didn't have much holiday energy, but at least my Christmas shopping didn't have to include wigs."

"That is a good sign, isn't it?"

Vicki pulled out a tin of mints. "I had to quit smoking, though. Talk about hard…"

"I can imagine." They stood in silence for a minute, watching the boys fidget on stage. Vicki made a small, self-conscious wave to Alex when he caught sight of her.

"He's doing great," she assured Vicki. "You're right, he was really nervous about his lines, but Stanton's been helping him a lot and he's going to be just fine."

"Yep." There was a long pause before she added quietly, "Hey, thanks."

Essie smiled, even though they didn't look at each other. "Sure."

"No…no really. Thanks. I…pretty much…shut everyone out and that didn't stop you from…well, you know."

"Yeah, I know. I'm like that. Pushy broad, that sort of thing."

"I'm…um…glad you did."

At that point Essie could no longer simply stare ahead. She turned to Vicki. "Me, too."

Vicki gave a small laugh. "Hey, did you know they give you a tattoo? You know, to line up the machines and everything?"

"A *tattoo?*"

"I asked if they'd do my company logo—I mean, tiny, but as long as they had to, why not?"

Essie's eyes popped wide. "No. You didn't. Did they?"

"No, it's just a dot. But maybe when I'm all done…"

"You wouldn't!"

Vicki raised her eyebrows. "I might." The both laughed. It seemed such a far cry from the posturing and defensiveness of that first meeting in the coffee bar. "Hey, listen," continued Vicki, leaning a bit closer, "I'm thinking of taking on the ninja ladies."

Essie burst out laughing. "The what?"

"Oh, that's what I call Dahlia and her cohorts. You know, the secret force we're not supposed to know about but we know about anyway?"

Essie folded her arms. "*You* know about. Dahlia won't breathe one word to me—I swear it's like I'm a security risk or something. She always looks at me like I know too much."

"I want to take them on." Vicki's sharp-as-a-tack game face came back over her features.

"Meaning what?" This was a turn Essie hadn't expected.

"Meaning this secret stuff has to end. I've been thinking a lot about this. Nobody should have to feel like I did. Alone. It shouldn't take what you had to do to help me. Women at Bayside need to know there are people who can help you through this kind of thing." She shook her head and busied her fingers fumbling with her key chain. "I don't know, maybe it's the facing down cancer or whatever, but it seems a colossal waste of time to have felt so alone at the beginning. I wouldn't have been such a wreck if I'd have known there were twenty-nine other women who'd survived this right around me. I mean, some of them have survived far worse. Seems stupid to make another woman go through that." She narrowed her eyes. "So I've decided I'm going to take them on. Make them let the secret out."

"Really?"

"I'm not talking about publishing a directory or anything, I'm not even sure how to do it yet. Maybe just a referral through the church office, or a hotline, I'm not sure." Vicki looked at Essie. "You game?"

"Me? What do I have to do with it?"

Vicki smiled. "Well, right now you're the only security leak I've got."

Essie smiled right back. "Bring on the ninja ladies."

Before they could set a date for coffee, the sound of lumber splitting echoed through the hall. Within seconds, five boys—who had somehow all piled themselves into the stage tree without being noticed—came crashing to the ground. Parents cried out. Children cried.

Essie sprinted toward the stage, her brain reciting the timeless parental gripe, *I turn my back for one second…*

Doug was trying not to laugh, Essie could tell. It shouldn't have been funny at all, but no one involved could help but chuckle at the thought of how five boys had managed to shove themselves into the small safety harness installed in that tree without any of the surrounding adults noticing. Scrapes and bruises—and one badly mangled piece of scenery—

aside, no one had been seriously injured. That was a blessing. Especially, as Doug pointed out, three of the five boys were sons of lawyers.

It had been three hours since the incident, and Essie and Doug had simply stopped answering the phone. "Honestly," sighed Essie, "did it have to happen two minutes before the parents came to pick everyone up? If it had happened ten minutes earlier, we would have had the whole thing taken care of before the parents came. You know kids—they're fine until they see their mother, then suddenly even the smallest scrape sends them into wailing."

"I don't know," countered Doug, even though he was still chuckling at Essie's play-by-play of the disaster. "I sort of side with the parents on this one. You'd like to think five small boys shouldn't be able to get into that kind of trouble with a dozen adults around."

"You'd *think,*" replied Essie, staring at the blinking light on their answering machine. Somehow, she just knew a draft "release and hold harmless" agreement was going to come zipping though Doug's office fax machine tomorrow. This sort of thing was right up Dahlia's alley. "How many more weeks until this little escapade is over?" She sighed.

"Three. You'll make it."

"Three weeks. That's three Sunday school lessons, six rehearsals, one set of vaccinations for Josh, two doctors visits—one for Mom and one for Pop—" She looked at Doug. "And an interview."

"That's Wednesday, isn't it? Essie, are you sure about this?"

"I think so. Look, we ran the numbers again the other night—we need the money."

"No, we don't need the money. It'd be nice to have the money, but we don't need the money. Remember that."

Essie let her head fall back on the couch. "I am so tired of pinching pennies." Josh grunted as he bobbed up and down with his hand clutching the coffee table. "Cruising," as the baby book called this walking-while-holding-on-to-things routine, was his new trick, and he'd realized that if chose the right route, he could actually travel good distances—until, that is, he ran out of furniture to hold. Josh's development, not to mention the calculations that showed all over his tiny sweet face, was so amazingly amusing. She and Doug would just watch him for hours, laughing at his antics. The first time he'd done it—he'd been coming close for days before he actually did it the first time—she had jumped up and down as if Josh had just won an Olympic gold medal.

"What if you miss stuff?" Doug said quietly.

"What do you mean?"

"What if he says a whole bunch of new words while you're working, or starts walking, or any of that stuff. What if he does that while you're at work?"

Essie looked at him. He'd never talked like that before. They'd hashed out the argument that first night, but it was mostly about the fact that she'd not discussed it with him. They'd come to an agreement that Essie would go through the second round of interviews, they'd composed a list of questions for Essie to ask, then they would talk it out together after she learned the answers. It had been a long night where each of them had realized the size of the rift that had grown between them.

Still, in all the conversation, Doug had never expressed regret at the thought of her being away from Josh before. It surprised her. "Well, what if he does that while *you're* at work?"

He was quiet for a moment. "I'd hate it. But it'd be a little bit better because I'd know you were there." He spoke softly, as if it was embarrassing to admit.

"But we leave Josh in the church nursery all the time. He loves it there. What's the difference?"

She could tell Doug didn't really have an answer for that. "I don't know. In any case, I'm not sure that we're just not trading one set of stresses for another. The money won't be as tight, but there'll be all the working parent stuff to deal with. Sick days and scheduling and all that stuff."

"I know, and I'm a little worried about that, but people do it all the time. Stuff seemed scary when we first moved out here, but we found ways to make it work. We know God led you to that job at Nytex. I think he may be leading me to this one at BACC. It's such a great program, and Josh would just be in the next building."

"You couldn't do all that and still teach Sunday school though, could you?"

Essie sighed and started folding the little pile of laundry that sat in a basket by her feet. Josh began a chorus of "babababa" while he stomped his left foot. "I've been thinking about that. I don't know. Maybe right after the Celebration would be a good time to leave. It's still another three more months after that to finish out the year. This was only supposed to be a half-year commitment when we started, so it's not like I'm backing out or anything." Even as she said the words, though, they felt false in her mouth. It would feel like backing out.

Sometimes in life, though, you have to go to Plan B.

At that moment, Doug asked the very question her heart did. "What do you think God wants us to do?"

"Well, now, there's the question of the hour, isn't it?"

"Maybe we'd better ask Him again."

As Doug grabbed her hand to pray, the phone rang. "Don't you dare answer that," Essie whispered.

The answering machine kicked in. "Essie, honey," came her mother's voice over the speaker, "we're out of toilet paper over here, and I don't want your father to go traipsing off again and fall down. I don't like to bother Mark on Sundays, so could you run out and get us some? Your father uses way too much…you'd think he'd realize how expensive it is. Oh, and pick up some of that orange soda I like so much while you're there. What's the name of it again? I can never remember. I found some more magazine articles on ear infections, too. You can look at them when you come over. It seems they've discovered…well, you can see for yourself so just come on…" The machine cut her off. Mom seemed incapable of leaving a thirty-second message—the machine was always cutting her off.

"And then there is the tiny issue of toilet paper fetching," said Doug, holding his hands far apart as if to say just how "tiny" that issue really was.

"If you say 'the issue of tissue,' I'll have to throw something at you."

Doug affected a lisp as he grabbed Essie's other hand as well. "If the ith-ue of tith-ue thends you away, I'll mith-you."

Essie groaned. "Just when I didn't think it could get worse…."

"Now, see, there's the problem with Queen Esther's realm. Things can always get worse."

Doug was correct: it did get worse. *Toilet paper!* thought Essie as she headed over to her parents' house. *My own parents can't keep themselves in toilet paper? I'd crawl out in an ice storm before I'd make someone else go get me toilet paper!* Ah, but toilet paper turned into "could you go down to the storage locker and get the slow cooker?"—*did it have to be the thing under six boxes way in the back?*—to "that ridiculous television remote won't change the channels anymore" ("Well, yes, Pop, it won't if you don't change the batteries inside.") to Essie's personal favorite, "Look at this thing on my back. Your mother says I need to tell the doctor about it but I say if it ain't hurt don't grouse about it." *Ick! Just plain ick!*

By the sixth "Mom, I really have to be going now," Essie had already missed the first half hour of couples' Bible study. In an unprecedented and highly welcome show of gallantry, Doug had called her cell phone to say he'd fed Josh and would take him to church, and suggested she just go home and take a long hot bath.

"I'll gather any reports from disgruntled parents about how their child nearly fell to their death this afternoon. You just stay out of the fray and soak."

"Is it Valentine's Day?" a stunned Essie replied.

"Nope, this is still January."

"Are you Douglas Walker?"

"Last time I checked. Very funny. I'm not that insensitive a husband, am I?"

"This is the part where I just hush up and say thank-you, isn't it?"

"You always were quick on the uptake, Your Majesty."

"Okay. See you later tonight." Essie was still a little shellshocked at Doug's offer as she headed home, but not enough to turn it down. Two and a half hours of solitude in her own home. That was pretty near perfect by Essie's estimations.

As she slipped into the tub, lighting a candle and pretending that there wasn't a plastic container of two dozen rubber bath toys to her left, she let her mind pore over the chaos that had become her life.

She'd been wrong to judge Vicki Faber the way she did.

There, hiding under that flashy exterior, was a woman of resolve and courage. A smart woman who could see a problem and set her will to fixing it. A woman who, in the course of a few weeks, had decided to take on Dahlia Mannington in a way Essie wouldn't dream. And not just Dahlia, but the whole collection of—she just had to laugh at Vicki's term—ninja ladies.

Cece had been absolutely correct. Essie had been slapping labels on people from the moment she walked into Bayside. And had been wrong about most of them. In fact, when she was honest with herself, she was probably wrong about all of them. Queen Esther had proclaimed herself judge and jury, and seen the stereotypical worst in everyone. It wasn't a comforting thought. Essie's take on the world was sharp, occasionally witty, but mostly downright mean.

The human race didn't require a competitive spirit. She'd spent so much of her life measuring, ranking and competing that she'd forgotten life was a team sport. She thought of how she'd lectured Stanton on his "I must be first/best/winner" attitude. Stanton was only eight, only learning his way through the world. Here she was four times his age, and how much better had her attitude been? Hadn't she been just as judgmental? Sure, she'd made huge strides in teaching the boys to work together, to play to each other's strengths. She'd made no progress in such thinking in her own life.

Oh, Lord, I'm sorry. You see every one of these people on the in-

side, You know how they're hiding hurts and fears. And yet You've watched me cut them down with a quick glance and a snap judgment. I thought I came out here for Mom and Pop, but you brought me here for me, didn't You? What a chump I've been. A first-class idiot.

So what do I do about the coaching job? Is this something new You're going to teach me? Or just a distraction? I don't know, Lord. You've got to show me.

Usually, Essie's brain would bang with echoes of "I need to know! I need to know now!" when clear answers were nowhere to be found.

Tonight, in the gentle patter of popping bath bubbles, a new echo took shape—you'll know when you're ready.

Chapter 25

Heroics

Wednesday was a whopper of a day. This afternoon was her interview with Coach Jemmings. That alone was enough to fill her day.

The morning, however, would be taken up with an education committee meeting. A meeting which would surely contain an agenda item something like "the problem of the dangerous tree." A five-point memo and a draft of a parent's release agreement had already come whooshing through Doug's fax machine Monday morning. Fortunately—or unfortunately, depending on how you saw it—Dahlia had cc'd about six other people within the church administration, so that hot potato hopped right off Essie's lap and into the lap of her brother. No release had been distributed at the Tuesday night rehearsal, so whether Mark-o had talked Dahlia out of her release-and-hold-harmless clause, Essie couldn't guess. It was sure to be a meeting full of "Yes, well..."

Essie's big agenda item for this meeting was to pull off

yet another Queen Esther command performance. She and Vicki had decided to get Dahlia to come over for coffee one more time. Essie had uncovered that overloading the tree had been Stanton's idea in the first place, but she chose to keep that little piece of information to herself. Still, Essie wasn't sure how a coffee invitation would go over. If Dahlia said yes, Vicki and Essie would do their best to convince her and her crew to go public with "the ninjas." Well, not completely public, but at least public enough to give frightened women a contact point. Vicki had actually drawn up a proposal with four options—just the way Dahlia would like it.

Dahlia's pen was bobbing at lightning speed as she barked the meeting to order. "Yes…well, we've a lot on our plate, so let's get right to it."

Essie tried not to cringe.

"We've got a few safety issues to iron out regarding the Celebration. I'm sure you all know about the recent rehearsal incident."

I've been reliving it hourly, thought Essie.

"I've been in conference with several of the Board of Elders and Pastor Taylor over the last few days…."

I just knew you had.

"I believe we have the situation under control. In all honesty, Essie, I'm baffled as to why we haven't acted on this earlier."

I'm going to be Bayside's first fired Sunday school teacher.

"You simply cannot teach that class…"

I knew it!

"…alone. Even if your co-teacher moved at the last minute, it was irresponsible of us not to replace her as quickly as possible."

Huh? Wait a minute, haven't I been saying that to Mark-o

for months? As glad as she was to have someone else realize this class was too wild for one person, Essie got the sense that Dahlia's proclamation was somehow more of a put-down than an offer of assistance.

"In fact, we all should know that there are policies about such matters in place already at Bayside. We were remiss in taking Essie's enthusiasm for the class, and her—" Essie thought she heard a microscopic pause before Dahlia continued "—abilities for granted when a co-teacher should have been assigned immediately."

Great, but shouldn't someone be talking about this to me? Hello? Dahlia wasn't even looking in Essie's direction. Essie fought the urge to raise her hand, or interrupt, or something, but Dahlia's commanding tone of voice sounded as if even an earthquake wouldn't get her off track right now.

"A task force," Dahlia continued, pointing that pen of hers in the direction of Decker's and Peter's moms, "has been formed to recruit that teacher." Decker, who rivaled Stanton with his gifts for disruption. Peter, whose mother seemed to be one giant ball of fear and concern no matter what the subject. No, siree, this was not looking good. Anyone care what I think?

Dahlia continued to look everywhere but at Essie. Evidently Essie was going to get whomever they chose for her without the slightest request for input. Care to try looking for two teachers, ladies? In about three hours I'm going to have a lot of nice reasons to walk away from all this. I don't see any of you jumping at the chance to lend a hand, now do I? Even though she'd expected this, Essie's dander shot up instantly. It didn't matter that she'd been asking for backup for months. Not even a co-teacher, just plain backup. Another set of hands. One other adult in the room.

Essie felt more defensive with each passing second. She wasn't the only adult in that room when those boys decided to gang up on a poor defenseless piece of scenery. She was actually the adult situated farthest away from them, and they were supposed to be under the supervision of the costume committee getting their fittings. It's not like they were the most cooperative bunch of children ever raised, either. She'd been doing pretty well given what she had to work with. Well enough for someone to care what she thought about the whole mess. Still, so far, while a constant stream of suggestions and concerns had flooded her way since that rehearsal, not a *single soul* had offered help or asked her what *she* thought ought to be done. Not one.

Why do I even bother?

Essie could barely wrestle her attention back to the remainder of the meeting. It was all she could do not to simply walk into Mark-o's office afterward and tell him this time she was quitting for real. Someone handed her the rehearsal schedule for the last two weeks before the production. It was intense. Sure, it's not like I have to raise my child or see my husband or anything. Don't you people have lives? Birthday parties to plan? Laundry?

By the time the meeting was over, Essie would have rather invited Attila the Hun over for coffee than Dahlia Mannington. Right now, there didn't seem to be a whole lot of difference between the two. *I'm not enjoying this one bit, Lord. Can I point that out?* Essie nearly dragged her feet across the carpet toward Dahlia, who seemed to be unmercifully lingering, probably waiting to give Essie a private dressing-down over the harm her son had endured.

Sure enough, Dahlia fished papers out of her notebook as Essie came over. Probably another memo or something.

"How is Stanton?" Essie asked in a sheer act of will, not really wanting to hear the answer.

"Bumped up, but okay. I had his massage therapist check him out just to make sure."

The number of professionals serving Stanton Manning-ton no longer surprised Essie. The boy had a bigger en-tourage than most diplomats.

"I'm sorry he got hurt." Another sheer act of will. She was sorry, truly, but it was the last thing Essie wanted to say to Dahlia at that moment.

"Yes…well…" She folded the papers in half and handed them to Essie. "For some reason Stanton's rather proud of his injuries. Boys will be boys, I suppose. In any case, Stan-ton had to write an essay in his sociology enrichment class last week. They had the children write about a woman they admired in their neighborhood or some such thing. Stan-ton chose to write his essay about you, and I thought you'd like to read it." She actually smiled. "It's a rather lovely lit-tle piece of writing." As an afterthought, or a matter of pride, she quickly added, "They weren't allowed to choose their mothers or grandmothers. A community awareness exercise, you know."

"I understand," Essie replied, because it seemed to be what Dahlia wanted to hear. It really was a nice thing to do, actually, to give her a copy of the essay.

As if hearing her thoughts, Dahlia flashed a warm smile at Essie. "This one's a keeper, if you ask me. I thought about having it framed for you, but I thought that'd be a bit much."

"I'll save it for this afternoon when I can give it my full attention. Thanks for letting me read it. I'm sure I'll love it. By the way, do you think you can spare an hour next week to have coffee with Vicki and I just one more time? I thought it would be nice to have a quiet spot before all the chaos hits. You know, now that Vicki seems to be out and about more. Can we do Thursday?"

Dahlia started to shake her head, then stopped herself and pulled out her leather-bound datebook. "I was going to say no, but now that I think about it, it would be nice to know I'll have one quiet hour next week." She flipped through the book's crammed pages. "If we make it ten-thirty, I can be there."

"Ten-thirty it is."

Dahlia raised an eyebrow. "A box from Carmen, perhaps?"

Essie actually managed a small laugh. "Oh, I never turn down a box from Carmen. That'd be fine. Tell Stanton I said hello, and to stay on the ground from now on in, okay?"

Dahlia narrowed her eyes. "If I thought it would work...." Again, Essie couldn't tell if it was a joke or a jab. Knowing Dahlia, it was probably both.

Essie decided to forgo getting any further details from Mark-o, who was conveniently absent from this meeting. It was a lovely, sunny day, so she and Josh headed for a favorite window-filled coffee bar for lunch while she geared up for the interview. The respite would also provide her with a chance to read Stanton's essay.

Settling into a sunny booth, Essie gave Josh his midday meal of cereal and then opened the papers. It was typed. Somehow she hadn't expected that, but knowing the kind of enrichment programs in which Stanton was likely to participate, she mused that he probably had his own private secretary. The huge assortment of typographical and grammatical errors, however, quickly put that thought to rest.

It was an adorable little piece, one that brought Essie near tears by the end of it.

Mrs. Walker
By Stanton Mannington

Mrs. Walker is my Sundy Skool Techr. She is a mom. She is strong for a girl. She gets mad wen we mess up in class. Most of the time she is fun. She told us she was Queen once. We lafed but she *ment* it. She has rules we hav to follow so we can hav fun and not distroy each othr. God seems to like her lots. She seems to like him back. Church usd to be boring bifore her. Now it is fun. She told us she was a champiun at track stuff wich is cool. She is the first girl hero I ever know so now I think God maks girl heros too. She knows lots about Jesus (a boy hero you know) and has fun ways to teech us. She is more fun than lots of my other techrs. She culd beat my fensing teacher in two sekunds! Mom sais God sent her to us and I think Mom is right. Who thinks God sends girls??? She sees my talunts. She makes me think hard. She must like boys becus she is a mom of a baby boy named Josh. Josh is luky I think. I am glad she came to Bayside and to us. I hope she stays a loooooooong time becus I hear next year is even *hardr.* That is why Mrs. Walker (or she said Queen Esther!) is my hero.

The End

Essie read it three times, often laughing between tearful sniffs. "My mom says God sent her to us." That was the last thing Essie expected to read. How often had she felt as if Dahlia Mannington was simply tolerating her? It seemed such a far cry from the critical eye she felt from Dahlia. A swell of satisfaction surged in Essie's chest. Dahlia was absolutely right: this one was a keeper. It wouldn't have been too much at all if Dahlia had framed it—Essie thought she might frame it herself.

Essie Walker, Girl Hero. It didn't get much better than that.

Compared to such accolades, what did the frustrations of one silly church drama mean? Okay, they were big frustrations and it was the most grandiose church drama ever mounted, but still the sting of this morning's meeting melted away under Stanton's words.

I think I see, Essie prayed silently as she felt the sun warm her face. *I'm starting to see what matters most. To see with Your eyes, Lord.*

Essie thought about Cece, and how easily she bore the hysteria of the Celebration. Suddenly she could view the obsession from Cece's perspective. See why it was a good thing if Bible heroes rivaled baseball heroes. Even if it meant things got a bit out of proportion.

Okay, maybe a lot out of proportion.

Wasn't that the whole point of grace?

Grace.

She needed grace. Needed to get it. To give it. Grace to see beyond the stereotypes. Grace to smooth over the rough edges. Grace to go an extra mile, to see what Mark-o had called "the invisible things." Essie knew all about fairness and courage and strength, but she knew precious little about grace. She'd spent all her time choking down a long list of the "don't"s: don't judge, don't jump to conclusions, don't back down when it gets sticky, don't get discouraged. A long list of negatives.

Not once, before this moment, had she seen the "do" side of this lesson. Do reach for grace. Give grace. Recognize grace. Receive grace. See grace. Grace was the real red of the Golden Gate Bridge. That thing she had thought she'd been seeing, but now saw clearly for the first time. She craned her head for a moment, thinking surely she must be able to see the bridge from here, but the windows offered no view of the bay.

I don't have to see it, Essie thought to herself. I know it's red.

When she was competing, her coach would always say, "Don't think about the distance. Just see the target and reach for it."

How had she gone all these months without seeing the target of grace? Essie Walker was here to learn grace. Not to teach boys or tend parents or even to raise children. All those things were ways grace came *into* her life.

Grace. A single syllable that shifted a lifetime of thinking.

What now?

Essie knew it was no accident this essay found its way into her hands on this day. God had meant her to see this, to come to this understanding, *right now*. Before walking into the Bay Area Community College Athletic Department.

But what did it mean? Where was the grace in this situation?

What's a hero to do? Take the job and leave Sunday school? Decline the job and keep Sunday school? Do the seemingly impossible of doing both job and Sunday school? She had no idea.

Essie Walker, plan-maker, goal-setter, mild control-freak, was going to have to wing it.

After all, she thought to herself as she packed up her things and walked toward the bus stop, it's what any Grace-Filled-Queen-Girl-Hero would do.

It was, without a doubt, one of the oddest job interviews Essie could ever remember having. She was highly nervous and yet enjoyed an eerie sense of calm. How those two emotions could co-exist in one body at one time, she couldn't even hope to explain. All her planning with Doug suddenly seemed irrelevant. There was no more Plan A. As a matter of fact, there was no more Plan B. There was no plan period, and only God knew how things would unfold from here.

As part of the interview, Coach Jemmings had arranged for Josh to spend the afternoon in the child-care center— a trial run of sorts for everyone to see how such an arrangement might work out. It was the first time Essie left Josh with a complete stranger—somehow the Bayside nursery didn't fall into the stranger category. She thought it would be awful, that she'd spend every minute wondering if Josh was choking or crying or whatever.

She didn't. The center was clean and wonderful, and after a ten-minute "getting to know you" session, Josh practically leapt into the arms of the young girl assigned to care for him. Yes, she was pretty, and yes, she was holding Josh's favorite toy brought just for such a moment, but the ease of the transition still caught Essie by surprise. The pang of guilt as she walked through the center door wasn't nearly as bad as she expected. Which only fed the concept that nothing about this afternoon would go as expected. Essie had an odd sensation of falling as she walked down the hall with Coach Jemmings to his office.

If one were viewing the interview by ordinary standards, it could be called a good one. She toured through the facility again, talking with teachers, meeting staff and students. What made it far from ordinary was her unnerving sense of familiarity. She knew this place. Knew what they were looking for and how to get it. Essie "fit in" with an uncanny sense of ease.

But not completely. Something jarred in her. Something that defied the facts before her.

It was as if she were watching herself in a movie. Not just any movie, but one of those DVD extra features where the commentaries of actors and directors played overtop the actual dialogue. Essie felt like she was having two conversations at once: one with Coach Jemmings, but another one entirely in her head as she analyzed and evaluated the situation.

Everything was exactly right—but still felt a bit out of place.

This program would suit her—almost.

Something seemed to be just out of view. It was like looking at the Golden Gate Bridge all over again: she was seeing purples and blues, but somehow knew the reds were there behind the optical illusion. Essie asked every question on the list she and Doug had crafted, but still something remained unsettled in the back of her brain.

By the end, Essie was beginning to think she'd botched the interview. There was such a tumble of ideas crowding her brain she was sure she wasn't forming complete sentences anymore. To her surprise, Coach opened his top desk drawer and pulled out a large envelope.

"Essie, you'll find I'm not a man who deliberates for a long time. When I see what I need, I get it. I think you're what we need here. I've already made a few phone calls to the references on your resume, and I know you're the right person for this job. I'd like to offer you the position of Assistant Coach for Women's Athletics. These papers outline all the personnel details—vacations, salary progression, benefits—all those types of things you'll want to know. We run a good program here. I think you won't regret coming on board. If you want it, the job is yours."

She should have said yes, shook his hand, and been thrilled. She was thrilled, in a way, but there was something else going on here Essie could neither identify nor explain. Something not quite right. She hoped it didn't show.

But really, what in this world is perfect? What woman on the planet wouldn't feel a bit of trepidation at returning to the working world after becoming a mother? This was perfectly normal, right? At the end, all she could do was thank Coach for his time, take the set of papers he'd handed her, and shake his hand with all the confidence she could muster.

"I'll need an answer before the end of the month, Essie."

You and me both, Coach. "Give me a week."

"I'll expect to hear from you next Friday, then. Do you need me to walk you back to the child-care center?"

"No, I think I know my way."

Essie collected Josh's things and thanked the workers, her head again collecting all the factual perfection of the job. There were a million things right about this. So what was nagging at her? Where was the fog of doubt coming from?

Essie prayed the entire bus ride home. She thanked God for sending this seemingly perfect job. She asked Him to settle her spirit. She prayed for wisdom and courage. For her and Doug to know the right thing to do. For the ability to see what was just new job jitters and what was this indefinable something that tugged at the edge of her thoughts. She was so deep in heavenward pleas that she almost missed her stop.

As she scrambled off the bus, the answer hit her. With such a shock of clarity that it seemed downright stupid she'd not realized it before this moment.

She liked being a coach, but she liked being a mother, too. And her world wasn't going to stop making queen-sized demands on her anytime soon.

Essie didn't want to work full-time.

Here she'd been thinking in terms of full-time employment or full-time motherhood, completely forgetting there was something in-between. Essie Walker was so used to thinking in terms of one hundred percent from her athletic nature, she'd completely ignored the possibility of compromise.

Compromise. Why had she never considered it? In a heartbeat, she knew the answer: because champions weren't supposed to compromise. Champions were all about everything or nothing; win or lose. Black or white. Option one or option two.

The Queen Esthers of the world, though, knew the wisdom of option three. Just as the biblical Queen Esther knew to craft her own solution to the problem before her, San Francisco's Queen Esther was learning that new options presented themselves if she looked hard enough. Essie could control the chaos in her world. She possessed the strength and courage to make her own terms on the world. She'd learned it with her parents, hadn't she? To take the demands they'd made on her, and the demands of her own family, and find the solution that blended the two?

Why couldn't she do it here? BACC wanted her to work full-time. Her family—all of it, both old and young—needed her time as well. With determination and creativity, she could blend the two.

A quote from the sermon she'd heard in Nevada—one she'd brushed off before this moment—suddenly resonated in her head. "The path of peace, the path of grace, the real solutions to life's problems, often lies in the third. Not in the first person's view, or the other person's, but a third point of view with a new solution."

Essie had that new solution. She didn't want the entire coach's job, with the entire women's program coaching hours. She wanted part-time, mostly focused on track and field.

What Essie really wanted was to work part-time.

Could she convince the college to offer her part of the job? Now that was the tough question. Ah, but Essie knew where to turn for sales and negotiation help. She snagged her cell phone out of her purse and punched in a number as she started up the street.

"Victoria Hinton-Faber."

"Vicki, it's Essie. How are you feeling today?"

"Like a badly toasted bagel, but okay."

"Dahlia said yes to Thursday if we can do it at ten-thirty."

"Great. Nice going, Es."

"Yeah, but Vicki, I need to see you before that. Like tomorrow. I need your brain. I need to write the proposal of a lifetime, and I need your help to do it."

There was a long pause on the other end of the phone. "Well, I was wondering how I'd get the chance to repay you. My brain is all yours."

Chapter 26

Life's Major Moments

Doug read Stanton's essay, planting a long kiss on his wife when he was done. "Josh is a lucky guy, you know. Wow, Es, this is incredible. Is this the same Stanton Mannington who's been terrorizing your class for months? He doesn't have a twin hiding somewhere, does he?"

Essie burst out laughing. "Twin Stantons? Oh, the world's not ready for that."

"Speaking of not ready, your mother called again. Twice. Stuff you need to do for dinner tomorrow."

Essie rolled her eyes. "Why do they do this? They invite us over for dinner, and we end up bringing most of it ourselves. One of these days I'm just going to pick up the phone and have a pizza brought over there. It'd be less work for everybody."

Doug's smirk told Essie he rather liked the idea. It generally didn't take much coercion to get Doug to agree to pizza for any occasion. "I don't think they make low-fat low-cholesterol low-sodium pizza."

Essie ran her thumbs along the waistline of her pants. "I'd sure be nice."

"Well, whatever you eat, you'll be doing it without me."

"No," Essie said. "Oh, Doug, really?"

"I've got to work. I really can't get out of this one. But, it should be the only night this week—workwise. I should be home all next week when you have dress rehearsals. Except for…"

Essie put her hands on her hips. "Except for what?"

Doug imitated her. "Except for a couple of hours Saturday morning where a bunch of us have to get together and rebuild a certain tree."

"Yes, well…" She winced. "I suppose I should have seen that one coming."

"Hey, let's not talk about this anymore." Doug put his hands on her waist and pulled her close. Josh began crawling across the floor toward the coffee table. "Tell me about the interview, Coach Walker."

"Assistant Coach Walker, and maybe not even that."

Doug looked puzzled. "They can't demote you before they even hire you."

"No, it's something completely different. I'm not going to take the job they've offered me. At least that's what I want to do—not take the job. I mean, we need to talk it over, first."

"You don't want to work there now?"

"No, that's not it at all. I want to work there, now more than ever. But only part-time."

"You never said anything about part-time before. I got the distinct impression you wanted full-time if you were going back at all."

"I did. That's what I thought. Until…I don't know. I suppose I'd classified part-time as not worth it, as second-best. That none of the jobs worth having would be part-time." Doug raised an eyebrow at her, confused. "Look," she continued, confused herself, "I know that sounds stupid because it all seems so obvious now, but that's how I thought. I felt like I'd be less of a person—less of a coach—if I was part-time. Like no one would take me seriously. Part-time was compromise, and I don't like compromise."

"I've noticed. What changed? I mean, what changed your thinking?"

Essie scrunched up her nose. She wasn't sure she could explain this. Still, she owed Doug a decent explanation. "I think I never realized that I didn't have to accept what they offered. I didn't have to accept things the way they were. I suppose I always thought my only options were 'yes' or 'no.' Yesterday, I realized I can make an offer of my own."

"Well, of course you can. You always could."

Essie adopted a "Thanks, Einstein!" glare. "I know that. *Now.* I'm trying to relate a major life realization here, be nice."

Doug's eyes flew wide open. "Speaking of major life moments…"

"What are…?"

"Don't!" Doug looked stunned. He held up his finger to her face as if to quiet her.

"Wha—" Doug planted his finger over her mouth.

"Don't talk," he whispered, looking over her shoulder with a look of complete amazement on his face. "Just turn around…slowly."

There, with a look of smug satisfaction, was Josh. With only a finger or two of one hand touching the coffee table, the other hand stretched out toward them. With a garbled collection of syllables, he teetered away from the table and took a step.

A step.

Then another one. And, after a wobbly pause, another one.

Josh was *walking*.

Three more steps, each more certain than the last. Suddenly, he was walking as if he'd been doing it for years, not seconds.

At a rather alarming speed.

"Oh, we're in trouble now," Essie said, amused and afraid and very near tears. Josh was walking!

"Look at how fast he's going!" whispered Doug, squatting down to hold out his hands to Josh. "Look at you, sport! Walking! Way to go!"

"Of course," sniffed Essie, "he is a Walker."

"You sure are."

He was almost to Doug when *thud!* Gravity caught up with him.

Essie leapt toward Josh, who was now kicking his feet on the floor with an angry wail. "Oh, come here, honey. Let mama kiss that."

"A walker—ha!" Doug finally laughed, the joke just dawning on him as he sprinted off to find the video camera.

The next night, Mom and Pop went wild over their grandson's newest trick. "Look at that boy go!" Pop cried with a big dose of pride. Everyone sat around the living room watching Josh toddle from relative to relative. By dinner Josh had toddled himself into fatigue, simply slumping over onto the corner of his quilt and dropping off into a dead slumber. He sucked his thumb with an occasional great big sigh, obviously proud of his new abilities. Essie could only smile. This was a turning point of sorts for her. Josh was no longer an infant, no longer a baby, he was a toddler. Before she knew it he'd be in preschool. It astounded her.

Josh slept right through dinner, which turned out to be a blessing, for halfway through the salad—which Essie, of course, had to bring—Mark-o cleared his throat and said, "So, Pop, what did you think of Bay Harbor?" Mom and Pop exchanged glances.

"What's Bay Harbor" asked Essie, staring straight at Mark-o.

"Mark thinks that we should move into a nursing home," said Pop.

"Mark-o suggested you move into a nursing home? When did Mark-o decide you needed a nursing home?"

Mark-o's face took on a "come on, you know you were thinking it, too" expression and he shrugged his shoulders. "I didn't say that, I was just paying a pastoral visit to someone over at Bay Harbor and saw how nice it was. And it's not a nursing home, it's an assisted living residence. I picked up a few brochures and gave them to Mom and Pop. That's all."

"What do I think of a place that'll take all my money so I can be an old coot too sissy to change his own underpants?" Pop snarled. "It'll be a cold day in Fiji before I let you turn me into one of those."

The table erupted into arguments, as "now dears" and "wait a minute"s and "settle down"s flew across the place settings.

"Pop—" Mark-o's voice rose above the clamor "—I didn't

mean you needed to move in tomorrow. Do you have any idea how long it takes to get into one of these places? The nice ones? You need to plan ahead."

Pop banged a fork down on the table. "Plan for my own empty bank account? Settle in to a life of shuffleboard and board games? Pureed spinach and oatmeal? I'm not going anyplace with an 'activities director,' you hear me?"

"Bob…" her mother started in, "he didn't mean…"

"He didn't mean that, did he? Well, what in the world did you think he meant then, Dot? I saw what Eddie Mackenzie's kids did to him. All nice and suggestive they were. Stuffing shiny brochures in his face until he gave in. Oh, no, you don't."

"It is very expensive, Mark." Mom was trying desperately to keep the peace. Or, by the look on her face, trying very hard not to believe what Pop was saying.

"Come on, Pop, it was one brochure…."

"That's how it starts!" said Pop. "That's how it always starts."

"Well," said Mom in a hurt voice, "if that's what you and Essie are thinking, then…"

"No." Essie cut her off more sharply than she would have liked. "Mark-o did not discuss this with me." She turned to Pop. "Your children are not ganging up to stick you in a home, Pop. Calm down. One good heart attack, though, and you'll give yourself no choice. Let's all just hang on, and pipe down before we wake Josh up and start an argument nobody wants to have."

She felt her Queen Esther persona rising up, ready to take control of the chaos.

"Now, Pop, I won't say I haven't thought about how much longer you and Mom can live on your own. I'm wor-

ried about you. And I'm tired of making last-minute grocery runs for you every few days."

"You said she offered!" Pop turned on Mom. "You told
me…." Mom had obviously been sugarcoating all her calls
for assistance. Why did that woman measure love in how
willing you were to fetch things?

"I'm offering!" Essie said over his growling. "But that's
not the point." Pop started to argue with her but she bar-
reled right on through. "We were discussing why no one's
going to ship you off to Bay Harbor without your con-
sent…."

"You bet no one's…" he started.

"Unless—" she continued, giving her best Queen Esther
stare "—you do something stupid and leave us no choice. I
know you want to stay right here, but you *are* going to have
to do some things to make that happen. I'm thinking about
going back to work…."

"You're *what?*" said Mom.

"Will you let me finish?" Essie calmed herself. "I'm thinking about going back to work part-time so I won't be able
to run over here every other day just because you ran out
of pickle relish. We'll just need to work something out. You
know, pick two days of the week, keep a list, and I'll take
you to the store."

"I can go to the store just fine," Pop cut in.

"We'll get to you in a minute." Essie couldn't believe the
level of authority she was putting into her voice. "It would
be better for everyone if you would just realize that you
need a little more help than you used to. Not nursing home
confinement, just a little help. A little compromise. No one
wants to turn you into Eddie Mackenzie, Pop. But it's going
to take a little cooperation on your part." Essie turned to

Mark-o. "On everyone's part. It's going to take a little creativity, a little adjustment, but the next step for you isn't the nursing home, Pop. At least not now. How about we just take the year one month at a time, okay?"

Sometimes, all you have is what's in front of you. Essie looked around the table at the faces of her family. This was the balancing act that would be her life from here on in.

Mark-o might never have enough time to hold up his end, but he could be urged to do more. Pop would never be reasonable about his health, but she could get better at persuading him. Mom would never stop trying to gloss over things and would always need something, but Essie could find ways to keep the neediness in check. But no matter what the details, it really boiled down to a matter of love. Loving them here, now, despite the things that drove her absolutely crazy.

Extending grace.

"You know," she said finally, "we could just start by trying to get through dinner without anybody hitting anybody."

"No more brochures," mumbled Pop.

"Can we get though dinner without anybody hitting anybody?" Now which room was the Doom Room? I wonder if Queen Esther's Commandments work on grown-ups.

After a long pause, Peggy said quietly, "Can someone pass me the potatoes?"

A week later, Essie once again found herself hosting Vicki and Dahlia in her living room for coffee.

"Honestly," gasped Dahlia, genuinely baffled at Vicki's suggestion to take the secret society public, "do you *really* think it's necessary to be so public about this?" Vicki had made a powerful case for it—paperwork and all, in true Dahlia fashion. Essie was ready to sign up and they wouldn't even let her join.

"Yes, I do," Vicki retorted. "You have no idea what it's like to feel absolutely alone facing this. It so happened that you knew two other women who'd been through it. I knew no one except my family, and they weren't the kind of help I needed. And Jack…"

Dahlia held up a hand to stop. "Yes…well, we can't expect husbands to be very comfortable with this sort of thing, can we? Most of us can't even get our husbands in for a physical, much less get them to hold our hands through chemo. Still—" she put her hand on her chest and grimaced "—I don't like the idea of just hanging out a shingle for the whole world to see. It's a very private matter."

"It's a lonely, scary matter if you've got no one to turn to. Women do dumb things when they panic." Vicki looked right at Essie. "They turn people away who are right there to help them. They hide it from the people who most need to know. Really, Dahlia, if I'd have known how many people at Bayside have been through this—have survived this—I'd have been so much better off."

"Well, yes, of course, but we found you, didn't we?"

Vicki paused a long moment. She stared straight into Dahlia's eyes, with every deal-closing instinct, every sharp business skill she had, now trained to achieving this one goal. "What about all the women we didn't find? What about them? Do you think God wants them to go through this scared and lonely just because they don't show up in anyone's address book? Is that the kind of place Bayside is supposed to be?"

It was the first time Essie had ever heard Vicki talk about

God. *What a powerful force this woman will be for You, Lord. What a fierce fighter to have on Your side. Oh, Jesus, please let her survive this cancer. She can do so much for You.*

Dahlia fiddled with her pen. She was turning the idea over in her mind, exploring it, considering it. Vicki watched her closely with an expression that told Essie this woman wasn't going to back down for one moment.

"Think of it this way," Vicki offered, "nothing would really be different. The group would still work in the same way—rallying around someone quietly to take care of them without a lot of fanfare. You'd still be unseen, no one would really know who was involved until they got sick. All it would mean is that someone could find us if they needed to. We wouldn't rely on word of mouth."

Dahlia's furrowed expression was one of carefully hidden distaste. For better or worse, Essie could see what she was thinking. Such a setup would mean just anyone could ask for help. Not the exclusive social realm of Bayside's inner circle. That could mean it just might get messy. Dahlia didn't like messy.

"I know that means you might end up helping people you don't know well," Essie said softly. "But look at Vicki and I—I hardly knew her at all when I discovered she'd been diagnosed. I think…I think that's what God wanted. And," Essie quickly added, "I know I'm not really part of this, but in a way, I am. I want to know that if I got a bad mammogram, that there'd be someone who cared enough to walk me through it." Essie hesitated before continuing. Say it, go ahead and say it. "I'd be scared to call you on my own, Dahlia. Everyone at Bayside seems so put-together and in control. But there's loads of hurting people here. Someone needs to give them permission to reach out for help. I can't think of a single good reason not to do this. Not one."

Dahlia was quiet a long time. Vicki, ever the negotiator, knew enough to let the silence hang, gently pressing this issue. Finally, Dahlia crossed her arms and sighed. "You'd have to have unanimous agreement from everyone."

"I agree."

"And we'd have to let anyone out who wanted out."

"Certainly."

"And no names. Ever."

Vicki pointed at the proposal. "It's all right there. Complete confidentiality. Just a dedicated phone line in the church office, with only one person authorized to pick up the messages."

"And that's…"

"And that's me. Except that I'll need a backup if I'm… um…too sick to check on things."

Dahlia frowned. "And I suppose you want that to be me?"

Vicki smiled. "You're in the church office more than anyone else I know. Plus, I'll rig it so you don't even have to go in. There are voice-mail programs that will let you do this from any location."

"Who's going to pay for this phone? This voice mail?"

Essie raised her own eyebrows. She hadn't even thought about costs. Who would pay for it?

"Victoria Hinton Designs will pick up the first two years. As a corporate donation. After that, well, I think we have a few people who will want to keep things going."

Essie could hardly contain her excitement. "If you say yes, they'll all say yes, Dahlia. You know that. You can't turn this down, you just can't."

A small chuckle escaped Dahlia's lips. "Why do I get the feeling I'm not going to be allowed to leave this room until I do?"

Vicki grinned. "I didn't become one of the city's busiest design firms by taking no for an answer."

Dahlia closed her eyes, as if jumping off the high dive into a very cold pool. "Well, all right then. Do it."

"Fabulous!"

Dahlia opened her eyes, sending a concerned glance toward Essie. "Not one word, Essie. I don't know why you've stumbled into this, but evidently God had something in mind. But not one word. This stays between the women involved, is that understood?"

"I'll sign an affidavit if you want. Sign in blood. You name it."

They were getting their coats on to go when Dahlia stopped and turned to Vicki. "You do know what we call ourselves, don't you? I mean, we'll need some sort of name for this."

Name? It needs a name? Well, of course, Dahlia would think it needs a name. It can't very well be the Ninja Ladies now, can it? Essie thought to herself.

"You know, I hadn't thought of that," Vicki said, even though Essie knew better.

"Azaleas."

"Pardon?"

"The Azaleas. One of the first things we did was take turns tending Jul…*someone's*…azaleas while she was in the hospital. So we became the Azaleas."

Essie could tell Vicki had the same reaction she was having. Being one of The Azaleas didn't sound appealing. Like some sort of Southern women's tea club or an old ladies' quilting society in England. It needed a bit of updating.

"Well, then The Azalea Network it is." Wow, that woman was good. Just the necessary adjustment to make it fit perfectly. Even Dahlia seemed pleased.

"I think that will do fine." Dahlia pulled her coat on the rest of the way. "Now, if I don't get myself over to Bayside to see to things, the Celebration isn't going to get finished." With her usual flourish, Dahlia whooshed out the door. Vicki and Essie stared at each other as they listened to the fast-paced *clip-clip* of Dahlia's heels trotting down the hallway toward the elevator.

It was then that Victoria Hinton-Faber turned into a little girl. With a whoop and a silly little victory dance, she jumped in the air and high-fived Essie.

Essie laughed and high-fived her right back.

Who knew that out of the dregs of the Doom Room would spring forth The Azalea Network? With a little unlikely help from Queen Esther.

Well, God did, of course.

After a few more minutes of victorious silliness, Vicki and Essie sat down to go over Essie's part-time counter offer to BACC one last time.

It was perfect. Thanks to the baffling-yet-growing-more-enjoyable-by-the-moment pairing of Essie Walker and Vicki Faber. Somehow, Essie knew these two projects wouldn't be the last they'd tackle. Cece Covington had become a mentor to Essie here in San Francisco, but Vicki was turning into a true-blue friend.

And that made the Left Coast feel like home. Which felt wonderful.

Chapter 27

The Celebration of Bible Heroes

On Friday, January 31, Coach Jemmings called to accept Essie's proposal. Her victory dance had been a simple *"Yes!"* heavenward and a great big kiss on Josh's forehead.

Now it was Saturday evening, the opening night of The Celebration of Bible Heroes. The boys had run through their lines in the hallway while they waited to go on. Everyone knew their part, even if Justin Baker looked as though he might bolt for the bathroom at any moment.

She and Doug had hired a sitter rather than put Josh in the church nursery for the evening, especially since he'd been whiny and running a slight fever. Evidently, as if on cue, another ear infection was about to make its debut. Doug was on one side of the church's massive stage, serving on the backstage crew. Essie was standing in the wings on the other side, ready to cue her boys for their entrance. Mom and Pop joined Mark-o and Peggy in the front row.

Act One had gone well. The big tense moment—the separation of the huge Egyptian pyramid to let giant puppet representations of the plagues come forth—had a few minor hitches. Well, more than minor. Evidently some of the left-over twigs from the Garden of Eden jammed the rails on which the sides of the enormous pyramid were to slide. As it turned out, the pyramid sort of burped open, hopping over the jammed rails rather than sliding majestically, and making a distinctly belchlike sound as the wood groaned over the stage floor. This, of course, sent the Doom Room boys—and a large segment of the audience—into gasping hysterics. Who knew the only thing cooler than burping apostles was a two-story Egyptian pyramid belching puppets worthy of *The Lion King?*

Essie tried not to feel justified two scenes later as several parent volunteers wrestled sand out of the hands of the fourth-grade boys' class. Joseph's eleven brothers had delivered their lines of evil conspiracy perfectly on stage, but had fallen into a nasty sand fight the minute they'd walked off-stage. Two kids had already been hauled off to the first-aid room for sand in their eyes. Really, did no one else see that coming? Three parents muttered to themselves as they tried to quietly shovel and sweep the piles of sand now strewn backstage.

The first act finale—a choral reading of Isaiah passages by the fifth-grade girls' class—had been beautiful, even if Emily Mondale had hiccuped through the entire piece. After two or three minutes, a teacher had come onstage and gently maneuvered Emily away from her place directly in front of the microphone so that her hiccups now no longer echoed through the hall. That should have been fine, but evidently Emily felt slighted by the move, and was quietly sobbing into her choir robe by the end of the reading. She had seen Emily's mother comforting the poor child during intermission, stroking her hair and repeating that, "Surely Dr. Farnsworth will have a way to help you get past this. We'll tell him *all about it* in therapy next week."

Only two or three of the preschoolers who opened Act Two had wandered offstage during their song about baby Jesus. The second act was going rather smoothly. Essie hoped her boys wouldn't buck that particular trend.

"Okay, everybody, we're up next. Alex, your sash is coming undone. Justin, just remember to speak up and you'll be just fine. Stanton, get away from those swords and stay over here!" Essie found herself barking out commands in a loud whisper while she tried to keep the boys lined up in the wings. "Now, Decker," Essie chided as she helped Decker up the platform to his place—harnessed and all—in the rebuilt tree, "just remember what to do and hang on when we move the set out. Don't you forget to speak up, too."

The lights dimmed, and applause rose for the previous scene. The dancing lepers filed offstage past her boys, while some of the temple scenery slid off to the other side to make room for the tree. Five big men grabbed the scenery and began to haul it onstage in the darkness, along glow-in-the-dark taped lines that had been placed all over the stage floor. Essie helped Justin switch on his wireless microphone. He poked her in the eye as he turned back around, and Essie heard her "ouch" echo through the audience even louder than Emily Mondale's hiccups, followed by Justin's laughing. She hoped—only because it made her feel better—that she had done Justin a service by breaking the ice.

The lights came up. Both boys who had the opening lines remembered them, and Justin walked through the crowd as if he was teaching, just as they'd rehearsed. Essie watched a small scuffle erupt on stage left, though, as Stanton continually vied for his place at the dead-center-front of the crowd. David Covington kept trying to pull him back into the crowd, but Stanton insisted on making "notice me" poses out front. Finally, just as Justin said his first line, David grabbed Stanton's sleeve and proceeded to yank him back into the crowd, which left Stanton still standing out front, but David holding Stanton's now-torn sleeve dangling in his hand.

Justin stared, frozen. He had the next line. Peter, who happened to be standing next to him, elbowed Justin. Justin remained frozen, staring at the whispered fight now taking place between David and Stanton. No one seemed to know what to do—except Peter, who simply kept poking Justin in an effort to shake him out of it.

Finally, as Essie was ready to rush out onto the stage, Decker yelled, "Hey, Jesus!"

Definitely not in the script. Essie was sure there was no verse anywhere in the gospel that read "Hey, Jesus!"

Decker yelled again. "Hey, Jesus, look at me!" Improvisation, but at least it was within the plot, sort of.

Justin blinked.

Finally, Peter took Justin's face in his hand and turned it toward the tree, his robe brushing loudly against Justin's microphone in the process. "Hey, Jesus, look at that guy!" he said, far too loudly for his proximity to Justin's microphone. It boomed across the auditorium.

Justin looked. Decker waved. Decker waved again.

Essie held her breath.

By some fluke, Justin snapped out of it. Hand extended, his tiny voice exuding all the authority he could muster,

Justin proclaimed, "Zacchaeus, come down immediately. I must stay at your house today!" Essie found herself clutching her script, mouthing the words along with Justin.

Decker made a "who, me?" gesture, then mimed absolute joy just as he had been instructed. He turned to discreetly unsnap the harness and make his way out of the tree.

And he tugged. And tugged. He turned and looked off-stage to Essie, mouthing, "It's stuck!"

"Try again!" she whispered back as quietly as she could.

Justin seemed to have found his confidence. "Zacchaeus! I said come down immediately!"

For lack of a better solution, Decker shouted, "I'm trying!" Then added, as if he'd just thought about it, "Mr. Jesus, sir." The audience laughed.

Another fifteen agonizing seconds dragged by. It felt like an hour. Essie waved to Doug, as if to say "get out there and help that kid!" Doug was just putting down his clipboard when Essie heard Stanton's voice.

"I'll help you!"

Stanton practically strutted across the stage. "Here, let me help you. I know all about trees."

Essie rolled her eyes, but held her breath on the slim hope Stanton could actually free Decker. He was getting close.

Peter, who seemed to feel that improvised dialogue was the way out of any crisis, suddenly remembered that Alex had the next line. He elbowed Alex, who said, "He has gone to be the guest of a sinner!"

"Not yet," replied Justin.

"But you're going to," improvised Peter.

Justin, confused, blurted out, "Well, yeah, soon."

With a loud thud, Decker hit the floor, managing somehow to land on his feet. Which was amazing seeing as Stanton had practically shoved him off the platform.

"He has gone to be the guest of a sinner," Peter repeated, evidently feeling the need to get the scene back on track.

"Look, Lord," said Decker, his voice a bit shaky, "here and now I give half of all my possessions to the poor, and if I have—" he paused for a minute, forgetting the rest of his line until Peter, of course, whispered it to him "—cheated anybody out of anything, I will pay back four times the amount."

The crowd oohed as instructed. Stanton, naturally, oohed the loudest and most dramatically.

Justin took a deep breath, readying himself for his big final line. "Today," he began, "salvation has come to this house, because this man—" he gestured stiffly to Decker "—too, is a son of Abraham. For the Son of Man came to seek and save what was lost." With the tiniest bit of a flourish and something close to confidence, Justin made a "let us walk this way" gesture to the crowd of boys.

They followed him, miming congratulations to Decker, who added an unbiblical but enthusiastic victory sign to this exit.

Essie exhaled, letting her head drop softly on the script in her hands.

After the finale, and subsequent coffee, punch and cookies, Essie made her way back through the congratulatory crowd to close up her classroom. Her boys had done it. Yes, there were a few bumps along the road, but they had a whole year to gear up for a better performance next year.

That's right, Queen Esther had decided to stick around. Just this morning, Essie slipped a note into Mark-o's mailbox saying she would teach the Doom Room for the remainder of the year.

And next year.

And maybe even the year after that, if life didn't get in the way.

Essie walked into the classroom to find costumes strewn everywhere. She could only laugh. The boys were so thrilled with their scene she couldn't muster the ability to be mad at them for forgetting to hang up costumes.

She'd just picked up Stanton's torn robe when a scribble on the chalkboard caught her eye.

"Queen Esther Rules!" was written in sprawling second-grade handwriting across the board.

Smiling, Essie took the palm of her hand and rubbed through the Queen Esther.

She picked up the chalk and wrote "God" in its place.

But, she thought as she switched off the light, Queen Esther Rocks!

DISCUSSION QUESTIONS

1. Do you have a Cece in your life—a woman who's shared her experience with you and offered much-needed support? What are some of the valuable things she's taught you? If you don't know a woman like that, where might you look for one?

2. If you've been a mother, what challenged you most in that first year? Think about your trials as a new mother and how they compare with Esther's. Share a funny or encouraging story with someone who could use a boost.

3. Do you have an odd stress reliever like Esther's grapefruit-throwing? Why does something silly like that help so much? What keeps us from seeing those solutions and using them when the tension sets in?

4. Think about the times a friend (or even just an acquaintance) has pushed help away, the way Vicki did. What did you do? Did it work or blow up in your face? Would you change how you handled it? How?

5. What was it about your parents that drove you crazy once you were an adult? How did you deal with it? What insights did you take from Esther's experiences?

6. Think about some of the children in your life—either your own, nieces or nephews, students or neighborhood children. Did you see any of them in the Doom Room boys? What did those children bring to your life? Did they teach you anything?

7. Sometimes it's the near-strangers who end up offering us the best comfort. Did Lenora at the pharmacy remind you of someone in your life—a grocery clerk, highway worker or nurse who said just the right thing at the right time? How did it help? Can you thank that person if you didn't then?

8. Is there a time when you were quick to judge someone, as Esther initially judged Dahlia? What changed those judgments? How did your relationship with that person change? What did you learn from that experience?

9. Consider Esther's handling of Thanksgiving. What was good about it? Where did she go wrong? What would you have done in her shoes?

10. Have you ever been part of something that became overblown like the Spring Celebration? What was the worst thing about your experience? What was the best thing about it? Did you change your mind during or after your participation? What makes it worth the effort? What could you have done without it?

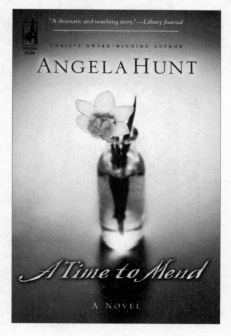